Nudges from a Wet Nose

Dog Stories in Assorted Genres

Nudges from a Wet Nose

Dog Stories in Assorted Genres

H. A. Byrd

Bibliogoblin

Nudges from a Wet Nose by Harriet Arden Byrd

Bibliogoblin Publications

habyrd.com

© 2023 Harriet Arden Byrd

Cover by Catherine Wesley

Photos by the author unless otherwise noted

Interior design by Keziah Wesley

ISBN: 978-1-7342084-3-6

This is a work of fiction. Unless otherwise indicated, all the names, characters, businesses, events and incidents in this book are either the product of the author's imagination or used by permission. Any who follow advice or example from these pages must keep in mind that the author is a dog walker.

Contents

The Maltese Figurine

The following story involves a dog named Larry.

His owner Michelle says that he is a
Corgi/Chiweenie mix.

"It says 'Walk In,'" she said in a tiny voice.

Sam Silva looked up from his Tuesday edition of the San Francisco Chronicle and lifted his reading glasses to peer underneath them. He removed his feet from his desk.

A girl of only eighteen or twenty stood with her hand still on the door handle, poised like a scared deer, looking unsure whether to enter or bolt. She could have used a few inches in height; otherwise, her body met the sinuous ideals of femininity which set the current fashion. She wore a crepe blouse with a long flowery scarf tied into a lopsided bow at her throat. Wrist-length gloves concealed her narrow hands. A cap of dusty pink complemented her softly-waved blonde hair and the lavender shades of her high-heeled shoes.

"How do you do, Mr. Silva," she said in a voice only slightly deeper than her first effort. "My name is Loretta Fontaine."

Sam's little sausage-shaped dog Larry rose sleepily from his bed by the door and reached to sniff the young woman's hem.

Sam rose and came around the desk, cleared some papers from a worn oaken chair, and pulled it closer for her. He bowed and gestured toward the seat with his thick fingers.

Miss Fontaine murmured, "Thank you," and perched herself on the edge of the chair's wooden seat.

He returned to his desk, taking a moment before he sat down and turned, squinting, to look her over. His pinched and angular features became more so. He had a swarthy complexion and receding hair. Dark, straight eyebrows set low above his deep brown eyes accentuated the naturally serious look of his face.

He settled into his squeaky swivel-chair and waited for her to speak. She watched the cobwebs on the ceiling fan go around.

Sam cleared his throat. She looked at him as if she had suddenly remembered why she had come.

"What can I do for you, Miss Fontaine?" he asked.

She swallowed. Her voice low, she said hurriedly, "I need you to follow someone for me."

When she didn't add to that, Sam replied, "Well, that's what I do, honey. If there's a reason."

"This man, Joe, double-crossed me and stole a valuable item of mine." Loretta peeked out from under her thick lashes.

The dog stood up, yawned, and shook himself. He looked at Sam.

"Cute dog," she said.

"Thanks."

"What kind is he?"

"His mother was part Dachshund and part Chihuahua. His daddy, well, he's not sure who his daddy is."

"He really is cute."

"He's talented."

"Is that so?" Miss Fontaine raised an eyebrow and gave the little brown dog a faint smile, her lips slightly pursed.

"Watch what he can do." Sam rose halfway to a stand and whistled softly. "Larry, come here."

The dog obeyed, and waited just in front of the desk. Sam winked at Larry who rolled his eyes as if he knew what was about to happen. Sam pulled his hand out of an imaginary holster and pointed his finger at Larry.

"Bang," he said.

Larry jumped and fell to his side. Then he rolled over a couple of times and ended up on his back, with his feet in the air. He stayed in that position until Miss Fontaine had finished laughing. Releasing her grip on her handbag a bit, Loretta emitted a tiny sigh. She looked at Sam.

"So tell me more about your problems with Joe," Sam said.

She opened the plum-colored leather clutch and pulled out a folded, dog-eared clipping. It was a several-year-old article from the New York Times, dated 1929. As she handed it to him, she explained that as a young girl she had received a ceramic statue of a dog as a gift from an aunt who had traveled overseas. She had always treasured that little dog. Then she sat quietly and allowed Sam to read the short article.

"This here describes a statue of a Maltese dog," he said.

"Yes."

"It was to be auctioned at Christie's in England."

"Yes. Mine is the missing twin it mentions," she said. "It's clearly old, and looks exactly like that one, from the photos. Exactly. It has that little collar with the sapphires in it."

"It says here," continued Silva, "the figure is one of a pair Napoleon gave Josephine when he conquered Malta."

"That's right."

"Hmm," said Sam.

"You can believe me or not, it makes no difference," Loretta said. "The thing is, when Joe saw this clipping, he nabbed my dog statue."

"And that's why you're here?"

"Yes."

"You'd rather not involve the police?"

"Correct. I can pay."

"Well," Sam sighed, looking at his broken blinds and ratty

office, "I could sure use the money." He offered a cigarette to the girl. She took it, and let him light it. Then he lit one for himself. He puffed and sat thinking.

"I heard you were a good detective," she said. "Pardon me for asking, but why aren't you in a better part of town?"

"Before the depression hit, I was over on Van Ness," he replied. "But now my name is against me."

"Silva?"

"Mmm-hmm." He frowned. "They think it's a Mexican or Filipino name. It's Italian, not that it should make any difference. But people show their true colors, so to speak, in times like these."

"It's horrible, the way they're chasing those people away."

"People are horrible."

"Well, the thing is, you'll have to come to Bellingham for this job," she said.

"Bellingham. That's north of Seattle!"

"Yes, but I'll pay you well. And I'll put you up in a nice hotel."

"All this for a ceramic dog?"

"I tell you, it's the missing figurine," Loretta said, fidgeting with the diamond necklace she wore. "I'm not a child, Mr. Silva. And I'm not a fool."

Sam tilted his head to scrutinize her face. "I half believe you," he said. "But, I'll tell you, in this neighborhood even glass can get you robbed these days. You should be more careful."

She smiled, her bright red lips showing off the gloss of white teeth. "Oh these sparklers are real, Mr. Silva." She let go of the necklace, uncrossed her thin legs, and stood up slowly, leaning forward over his desk to look him in the eye. "So what do you say about it? Are you going to take my case?"

"Sounds risky," he said. "I'll need one hundred dollars to start."

She fished for some bills in her plum-colored purse and tossed them onto his desk.

"Two hundred dollars," he said. "Well, I guess we have a deal then."

"You understand, Mr. Silva, that the people Joe is involved with are dangerous. He runs with a bad crowd."

After Loretta Fontaine left the office, Sam turned to his assistant. "So, Larry, what is the most predictable moniker a dame would choose for herself? Right. A movie star's name. And a French surname to go with it. And that helpless act sure didn't last long. But, as 'Loretta' pointed out so eloquently, we could use the money."

The following week, Sam Silva put Larry's goggles on him and placed him in his special basket which rode over the saddlebags of Sam's Indian motorcycle. It was summer, and the two took several days to make the trip, driving the coast highway as far as Otis, Oregon, and then heading up 99. When they arrived in Bellingham, Sam checked in at the Hotel Laube, where they gave him the key to a small room already registered in his name. It wasn't the nice hotel he'd been promised, but it would do.

He set to work immediately. He smoked a couple of cigarettes while making phone calls from the ugly Deco desk in the lobby. After that, he followed up on a tip that Loretta had given him by choosing the Horseshoe Cafe for his late supper.

Larry waited patiently outside the door while Sam went in and seated himself in the booth behind a tall man with a tousle of red hair. Joe sat with a companion, but it wasn't Loretta. A cloud of cigar smoke hovered over their booth. Sam ordered chicken with a waffle, and some coffee.

The conversation remained uninteresting for most of Sam's meal, apart from when Joe's friend Frankie brought up the subject of Longacres. The two discussed the logistics of how Frankie would arrive at the Longacres stables before a certain race. Joe and Frankie flirted heavily. Snuffing his cigarette, Sam got his check and pulled out his wallet. But then Joe mentioned the dog figurine. It came up as the couple21 discussed their plans.

"So when are you going to dump her and take me back to Greenwich Village like you said?" came Frankie's soft, deep voice.

Joe answered so quietly that Sam had to strain to hear, "You know I've got that business coming up next month. That big package to drop. I need her for that. I've got to keep her on the hook with that little statue at least until that deal pays out."

"I never should have shown you that old paper," Frankie muttered.

"Are you kidding? Helen completely believes that puppy dog is the same one. She expects us to retire on it. You know she hates the business."

"You shouldn't treat her so mean, Joe. Don't you care enough about me to tell her about us?" As the two spoke, a spoon clinked in a coffee cup for an unwarranted amount of time and lingered briefly before it clattered on the saucer.

"Just let that little dog do its job, Sunshine. When that deal is done, I'll take you to New York."

The next day Sam met his client outside Matt and Millie's corner cafe. This place was farther down Holly Street, and not far from the bay. She stepped off the trolley in pumps that matched her expensive-looking mauve and seafoam dress perfectly.

Larry lay against Sam's well-worn oxfords while the two sat and sipped their coffee. Sam reported on his findings so far. Her man Joe had been a young bootlegger down in Louisiana, he'd spent some time in prison in east Texas. In jail other inmates had brutalized him, and since then he'd been an angry man, and out for blood. "He's seeing someone," Sam said. "A certain Frankie, who lives in a room in an old house in Fairhaven."

"I told you he double-crossed me. He's my husband."

"He's your husband."

"Yes."

"I see." Sam finished his cigarette and snuffed it. She tapped hers on the clear glass ashtray. Ashes had almost covered the rose design in the bottom.

"You'll need to be straight with me or this investigation will cost a lot of time," Sam said. Loretta adjusted a bobby pin in her hair and looked out toward the water.

Sam tipped back in his chair, frowning. "Why are there no marriage records?"

She tightened her lips together, flicking a glance at him in passing as she diverted her gaze from the bay to scan the upstreet sidewalk.

"Peachy," he said. "It's your money."

Loretta leaned forward, speaking in a low voice, "I think Joe's friend Frankie is planning to poison a horse at Longacres." She dabbed at her lips, smudging the paper napkin with cherry red. "I heard them talking," she added.

"You want me to look into that?"

"Please."

"OK, why don't you take this to the police?

Her left eyelid twitched, and her fingers went to her temple. "I'm more comfortable hiring you," she said. She fixed her eyes on Larry, who happened to be staring up at her. "I want that vermin Frankie to go down. But I don't want Joe to be implicated. He's not giving poison to any horses. Joe is a scoundrel, but he's my scoundrel."

"OK," Sam said. "Do you happen to know when they plan to commit this offense?"

"Before the sixth race on Wednesday."

"This coming Wednesday?"

"Yes, this Wednesday."

Sam asked for more details about what she knew, and then they discussed the Maltese figurine investigation for a while. Finally, he drained his cup, patted Larry, and stood up.

"One more question. Why Loretta?"

She looked at him strangely, her tongue between her pearly teeth. She took a moment to answer. "Helen's such a boring name," she said.

It took Sam less than thirty seconds to pick the lock and open the door to Joe and Helen's apartment. He closed it quietly behind himself and Larry. Sam peeked from the foyer into the living room. Furnished in leather and bronze, the room had a fireplace and, in one corner, a cocktail bar. Clothes were strewn everywhere. Empty bottles and full ashtrays littered the place. It stank.

Larry stepped into the bedroom, and Sam followed. The bedroom was a mess, too. Heavy drapes covered the windows, so Sam used his flashlight. The unmade bed had a dark headboard with an inlaid border of ivory. A huge closet held enough men's and women's clothes and shoes to start a small shop. Larry sniffed at the dressing table, on which all sorts of cosmetics sprawled in front of an engraved, fan-shaped mirror. Sam noticed apparatus for heroin use on a nightstand and also on the carpet.

Helen had left several stylish handbags on top of the bureau. Sam searched inside these. Her surname was Harris. He found a scribbled note about meeting an airplane at Graham's Field by Squalicum Creek. They were to bring six cans of salmon. Odd. A pink beaded purse contained silver dollars, another bag had several hundred in bills. Sam clucked his tongue and held up the wad of twenties for Larry to see. He paused to wipe his brow. Next, he found a receipt from a pawn shop. A receipt for a dog statuette.

Over the telephone that evening, Helen admitted to Sam that Joe wasn't her husband. He was her boyfriend, but they had plans for marriage. She said she'd been given the dog statue as a wedding present.

"From your aunt?"

She paused. "Oh, yes, from my aunt Mable."

Her aunt gave it as a wedding gift when Helen got married at sixteen. But not to Joe. She left that boy. He spent most of his time in jail, though technically she's still married, she guessed.

Sam said to her that he knew some things about the Maltese figure. He'd made some phone calls when he arrived in town, and now he shared some of the details about what he'd learned. That statue of hers had a high chance of being the real thing.

13

After he hung up the phone he said to Larry, "Don't look at me like that, pal. I'm just playing along with her game. It will keep the dog food coming in."

On Wednesday, Frankie drove Joe's Pontiac to the racetrack. Sam's binoculars were trained on the car as it pulled into the parking area. Frankie spent some time fumbling around with something while still in the car, but eventually slammed the door and sauntered off toward the backstretch. Sam and Larry looked at one another. Sam went straight to the car, Larry at his heels.

Much like the apartment, Joe's car held a jumble of belongings. Sam took pictures. On the front passenger seat, he found beetles. Mostly they were pieces of crushed beetle, but there were a couple of whole ones. Some kind of striped beetle. Blackstrap molasses, leaking from a half-empty can, made everything sticky. Using a cardboard film canister, Sam collected some samples of the beetles.

"We'd better get over to the barns, Larry. This doesn't look good," he said.

Larry was busy investigating something in the back seat. Something very interesting back there had his full attention. It smelled like fish. Like salmon.

"What are you looking at, Larry?" asked Sam through lips that were gripping his cigarette. He pocketed the film container.

Larry dug at a box of something. Oddly, it contained hundreds of labels for cans from a salmon cannery on Bellingham Bay. "Well, what do we have here?" Sam muttered, as, along with the labels, he found a set of scales and several glassine envelopes. The envelopes were empty. Or almost. They had some whitish residue inside. It might have been heroin. That was likely. Then, under a blanket, Sam found a sawed-off shotgun. "Beyond a doubt, Larry," Sam said, "that's heroin."

They exited the car and Sam brushed off his pants. They headed to the stables. Sam walked so fast that Larry's normal trot wouldn't do. He had to run to keep pace with his boss.

The bad news was that Sam didn't have a barn number. The worse news was that there were over thirty barns at Longacres. The good news was that Frankie had stopped to flirt with a groom just outside the entrance to one of them.

Sam and Larry simply circled out of sight behind that barn and entered the shedrow from the far side. Larry stayed in the big doorless entrance and sat panting, waiting for a signal from Sam. Eight sets of Dutch doors opened onto the covered walkway from the stalls, and most of these were wide open, with only chains across as barriers. People worked currying or cleaning inside a couple of the stalls, but no one else came around. Sam ducked into an alcove in the outer wall just as Frankie started walking from the far end of the barn. Horses leaned out of almost every stall, looking toward Frankie.

Sam pressed his back against the wall and a board creaked. Frankie looked in Sam's direction. Larry barked and turned in a circle. The distraction allowed Sam to go unnoticed. With some soft words, Frankie approached one of the horses and patted her neck. The horse searched for a treat. Frankie looked around suspiciously, but then appeared to have second thoughts, stroking the velvet nose and turning to leave. But when Sam looked up from removing his lens cap, he saw the horse licking something out of Frankie's palm.

Sam snapped a picture, and shouted, "No!"

Frankie looked up, eyes blazing with guilty indignance, before vanishing down the shedrow and around the corner.

Sam and Larry hurried to the stall door, and several stable workers came to see what the commotion was about. One of them identified himself as the horse's groom. Sam flipped open his wallet and showed his badge, explaining what had just happened. The horse had been poisoned.

One of the men told Sam, "You must be mistaken, Sir."

"Frankie's been coming to the barn every Wednesday since the track opened!" said the groom. "Frankie would never hurt one of the horses."

Still, they sent for the veterinarian. The vet found some swelling in the filly's throat, which certainly indicated poisoning by blister beetles, as Sam had suspected. They went right to work on the animal, tubing her, dosing her with a charcoal slurry, and then Epsom salts. They probably saved her life. But she didn't race that day. The trainer and the groom couldn't stop shaking their heads about Frankie. "You think you know someone . . ."

Within the hour, while Sam still talked with the police, another filly registered for the same race suddenly became colicky in the receiving barn, her mouth foaming. She died in a matter of hours. The vets examined her. Frankie had visited another horse. Larry rode in his basket back to Bellingham. It had been a tough day, but they had done their job.

Helen had herself let into Sam's hotel room that Friday evening. Without turning on the light, she pulled a pistol out of her bag and turned the wobbly wooden chair to face the door. She sat, waiting. Someone walked up the hallway. She heard a man's voice, two men. Helen raised the gun and pointed it at the door.

The men passed by and then a key could be heard turning in a lock down the hall. Helen lowered the pistol. She sat on the edge of the chair, but with her back straight, her breath slow and even. Behind her, on the other side of the bed, Sam sat on the floor. He had his gun out too. Larry was hiding under the bed. If Helen had listened closely, she might have heard Larry's panicked breathing.

Sam sat considering how he might make Helen aware of his presence without getting shot by startling her. Larry solved the problem by whining ever so quietly. Helen turned to look and forgot about the gun for a second, rather than readying it as she turned, as an experienced shooter would have done. Sam took his opportunity.

"You may wish to take into account that I have a .38 Detective Special pointed right at your nose," he said quietly. "Slowly put down the gun and then raise your hands."

In the dim light, the quality of Helen's movements suggested a scowl on her face. She put the gun on the floor obediently, but then she crossed her arms like a spoiled child.

Sam stood up and retrieved her revolver. He unloaded the bullets and tossed the gun on the bed. Keeping his own gun on Helen, he turned on the light. Under the bare bulb, her skin looked yellow and her green dress lost its color.

"A real lady removes her gloves before she kills someone," he said.

She didn't miss a beat: 'What? And get my hands dirty?"

Sam holstered his gun. He rotated the chair back around, with Helen in it, to align it with the bed again. He sat down on the edge of the bed. Larry remained safely underneath, silent as a mouse.

17

"Well," Sam said, "Helen, I thought we were friends. I didn't expect you to be waiting in my apartment with a gun."

"Apparently you did."

"And why would you want to kill me? Was this a part of the plan all along?"

"No, not at all, Sam. Unless you snooped into the wrong part of my life. Which, I have heard, is just what you've done."

"And how would you know this?"

Helen smiled.

"So, you were thinking you'd just bump me off at the first sign of trouble?"

"That's why I hired a guy with only a dog for an assistant. So I wouldn't have to shoot two people."

"You wouldn't hurt Larry!"

"No, of course not. Why would I? Larry's adorable."

"I'm not?"

"No, not really. But mainly it's a matter of how big your mouth is."

"I'm not obligated to tell the police about your involvement with the horse."

Helen fidgeted with her necklace and tilted her head forward slightly. "Are you referring to the one at the racetrack?"

"You're not involved with that, are you?"

"No, I'm not. And you did a great job, thank you. Frankie's going away for a while."

"It's none of my business, but clearly your Joe put Frankie up to the whole thing." Sam lit a cigarette and handed it to Helen. Then he lit one for himself. "Probably wouldn't have done that to an animal, otherwise."

"Frankie can go to hell," is all Helen had to say. She blew some smoke and rested the cigarette in the ashtray that sat on the bedspread.

Sam nodded as he sat there thinking. "No," he said finally, "The horse I'm talking about is the white one."

Helen spoke in a guarded tone, "You'll keep quiet about that?"

"What I'm wondering is how you got your hands on the unused labels."

She flapped her hands in his direction, her bracelets jingling. "Simple," she said. "Frankie had a job at the cannery."

Sam peered at her through the lower part of his glasses. "So you were packing heroin in those cans and passing it off as salmon? Probably driving it right through customs. Or somebody was."

"With a pound of homemade play-dough in each one to give it some weight."

"You seem proud. Was that your idea?"

"Oh, you *are* good," Helen said, hiding her face as if she were blushing.

"So, if I let you walk, you promise not to kill me?"

"I don't make promises," she replied.

"It's in your best interest."

"I'll try not to. How's that?"

"Good enough, I guess, as long as you pay me the money you owe me."

Helen pulled her compact out of her handbag and opened it. She held it up so she could use the mirror while she refreshed her lipstick. "No problem," she said. She smacked her lips together, snapped the compact shut, and looked at Sam.

Larry crept out from under the bed.

Sam winked at him and addressed Helen: "You still want help retrieving that figurine?"

"Of course."

The following evening Sam had just returned from supper and was reading a paper in the lobby before heading up to his room, when who should happen along but Helen. She stepped out of the elevator followed by an adolescent porter pushing a luggage cart with just one wooden crate on it. Sam held the paper up to shield his face from view. Helen stopped by the reception desk and handed the fellow a folded note. He saluted her, and she directed the porter out the door.

Sam went right to the desk. The clerk held up the note and said, "Oh, Mr. Silva! This is for you."

He thanked the man and handed him a tip. Unfolding the paper, he read:

Hello Friend,

Your assistant decided to accompany me on a trip. Just until things settle down without any monkey business.

Then I'll let you know where he is. And bring some food because he'll be real hungry by that time.

I'll pay what I owe then, too.

Sincerely,
Loretta

Near the signature, she'd left a kiss mark of bright red lipstick.

Sam growled audibly, grabbed his coat and hat from the chair, and ran out the door. Down the block, he found the porter straightening straps on the empty cart.

"Which way did she go?" Sam shouted.

The boy stood dumb, staring.

In record time, Sam's motorcycle was speeding up the street in the direction of Helen and Joe's apartment building. He caught every red light, and they stayed red for way too long. Fuming, Sam didn't dare cross while the lights showed red—he wasn't acquainted with any cops in this town. He couldn't risk being detained. When he arrived, he saw Joe's car just leaving. He could see Helen in the passenger seat.

He followed the Pontiac from the greatest distance he could. Few cars traveled at that late hour. Without traffic to hide among, Sam turned off his headlight. The car headed northwest out of town, toward the airstrip on Smith Road. They'd left the city streetlights behind, and at the speed they were going Sam strained to see the road, let alone what might be off in the fields. The flying field was not the destination. They continued on to meet Highway 99. Then they went north.

Riding with the taillights of the car barely in sight ahead of him, Sam had gone six or eight miles when a gray wall of fur flew in front of his face, right across his handlebars, and something sharp struck his shoulder, knocking him off balance. His motorcycle veered in a serpentine path. Sam gripped the gas tank tight between his knees and used his hips to counteract the g-force. He pulled gently on the outside handlebar to realign the front wheel with the back one. He managed to recover his balance and his steering, heading straight down the road again. It all seemed to happen in an instant.

A deer had jumped right over the front wheel of his motorcycle, grazing him with a rear hoof. As Sam took a quick look behind him, two more bucks with full antlers bounded across the road. Anyone would have been shaken after such an experience. It would have made sense to stop and check for damage. Or at least drive slower, as deer were obviously active in the area. But the word "Larry" came from Sam's lips, and he sped to make up for the delay which had cost him visibility of those taillights.

He followed those red lights for about three more miles up the highway, and then several miles east along a narrow road. He saw them turn left up a driveway, or maybe a farm lane. Then they disappeared. They must have turned the car off. Sam approached carefully. He saw the lights moving among trees. They'd driven into a thick woods.

He pursued them along the narrow forest track. The loose and stony dirt made driving difficult. Exposed roots and other obstacles, even ferns, showed up at the last second. At the speed Sam went, he had a high chance of cracking his skull on a tree. Several times he got too far behind to see the lights through the forest. Other times he got too close, where they might hear him. But finally they emerged from the trees at a crossroads. Darkness obscured the name on the street sign.

Joe's car continued in the direction they'd been going. The road went straight, a well-maintained highway, running through farmland and orchards. Sam followed at a good distance. They traveled on this same road for about half an hour, eventually passing the lights of a small town just off the road. Not long after, the car turned up a short driveway and parked. Sam turned off his motorcycle and stood next to it, just up the street, watching. Dobermans rushed to the Pontiac, barking and jumping.

The car had parked in front of a fine Victorian house. The lights were on upstairs. Situated at the crest of a low hill, and with a tower, the place must have had a view of the surrounding area. The car doors opened. Helen and Joe were arguing about something. Joe removed the familiar crate from the rear seat and set it on the ground. He yelled at the dogs to back off, and then he removed something from the crate, presumably Larry. It was too dusky to tell, with only the lights from the windows. Their voices carried across the street, but Sam could only catch bits of the dialogue, "I told you," in Joe's voice, "poor doggie," and "Whatever for?" in Helen's.

The couple took Larry indoors but left the Dobermans outside. With those dogs guarding, there was no approaching the house. Sam turned his motorcycle around and walked with it down the road before he started it up. He rode back toward the town he'd seen. He passed a co-op feed mill and then turned up a street with a row of businesses. Beyond a hotel and a dry goods, he found a ratty old place with a fading sign which read Paddy's Pub.

Dark inside, the place looked mostly empty. Two men with overalls tucked into rubber boots sat at the bar. Dairymen. On the green wall behind them hung a large photo of King George. Sam sat down, ordered a pint of beer, and chatted with these old fellows. Their conversation confirmed he'd entered Canada. Apparently he'd passed the border illegally through the woods. His new friends, who had been drinking for a while already, happily told him all about the house on the hill over in Port Kells. They knew it as "the Castle" locally, because of the tower.

Bill and Burt didn't know anything about the folks living there now, but the man who built the tower was a young German baron named von Mackensen. He and his friends used to ride the countryside, leaping the fences with their horses.

"The Baron threw tremendous parties; my brother went to his Christmas party one year," Bill said. "Gifts for everyone. Plenty of food and liquor."

"When the war came, though, he was interned up at Vernon," Burt noted.

"That's right," Bill said, "he got in a pile of trouble over flying a German flag from his bell tower, eh?"

"Yep, he did. Old Fred Kells was going to shoot the flag down."

"Oh yeah, him and Moody, they were absolutely furious. The Baron finally took it down. But that's what got him arrested, I believe. But, yeah, I don't know. They deported him, eventually." Bill sounded wistful. Or perhaps sleepy.

Burt stared at Sam like a puffy red-faced owl, "You know, there's a tunnel from that house down to the river. They say the Baron used to sneak Germans across the border. They say he was a spy."

"Aww, they said he had a radio in the tower, too, eh? I don't believe it." Bill blew his nose with his big red handkerchief.

"But the tunnel is real. I've seen it," Burt said.

"Is that so?" asked Sam, putting down the cigarette he was about to light.

"No way!" cried Bill.

Burt nodded. "Yes, sir! My dog was digging around near the

riverbank north of that house and she uncovered the entrance. My boy Danny explored up inside there a bit, but a few hundred feet along it didn't look safe."

"Now hold on just a minute, Burt," Bill said. "That house is nearly half a mile from the river. Don't know what you found, probably some old mine, eh?"

"I tell you, it's the tunnel up to the Castle. I'm sure of it."

"Why didn't you tell anyone, then, Burt?"

"Danny wanted to wait, eh? He wants to go back up there and explore." Burt drained his glass. "Hasn't got back to it, though, so far as I know."

"Say, I'd love to take a look," Sam said.

"Well, let's go have a look right now!" Burt spurted. He looked at Bill.

Bill stood up and put his jacket on. Minutes later they were all headed north on the road that went past the Castle. Sam followed Burt's farm truck, using his headlight this time. Bill's arm pointed out the window at the house as they went by. Before they reached the end of the road, Bill turned off into a gravelly area and parked. Bill and Burt teetered over to Sam with their flashlights in hand.

"The river is just down there." Burt may have thought he was whispering. He took Bill and Sam a short way into the night, his spot of light leading the way. Among the scraggly bushes and saplings lay a sheet of plywood. It took him a while to find it. "Danny set this here," Burt explained. He lifted the wood off to reveal a hole in the ground. It didn't look like much.

Handing Sam his flashlight, Burt gestured toward the hole. Sam got down on his knees and peered into the opening. It looked like a hole. Maybe two feet deep.

"Look behind that rock, though," Burt said.

Sam got on his stomach and reached down to shine the light farther into the hole. "Well, what do you know!" he said.

Bill had a look, too. Out of sight to a casual observer, behind a boulder half-buried in the hole, an opening led to a square tunnel braced with timbers. The opening proved barely big enough to squeeze through, although the tunnel was bigger and looked passible.

"Danny went up there a short ways," Burt said. "But, as I say, it's not lookin' too good farther up."

The men stood up and brushed off their clothes. They laughed and joked, but the old men had gone through a long day and a lot to drink and were soon ready to find their way home. Perhaps since Sam had paid for all their beers, Burt graciously agreed to let Sam have his flashlight. After the truck pulled away, Sam wasted no time before investigating the hole further.

He crawled headfirst through the opening, squeezing behind the big rock. It wasn't easy. Once into the actual tunnel he had some room to move, but a great deal of debris had fallen. He had to shift some rocks to get by. After a few more feet a downward shaft appeared, and Sam could see that the real tunnel took off from the bottom about seven or eight feet below. A ladder had been built into the shaft wall. As Sam started down, he said softly, "OK, Larry, hang tight. I'm coming."

Shored up and braced with wooden posts and planks, the tunnel ran a couple of feet wide and high enough to move through reasonably well, hunched over. Straight as a rod, it allowed Sam to see quite away along the passage. Rails ran along the floor and ventilation pipes came down through the ceiling. Someone had put a great deal of work into this project.

There were a few places where the walls of the tunnel had lost a stone or two. At one of these points, Sam surprised a rat. A huge wharf rat, it screeched and bared its teeth. The thing was fully the size of a cat. It came at Sam's face. He clubbed it with the long metal flashlight, sending it flying up the tunnel. It scampered off in the direction Sam traveled.

After catching his breath, Sam continued on his way. The strain on his back from walking in a stooped position made him grunt and puff. After going on and on for ages on the flat, the tunnel began to ascend. It climbed gently for about two hundred feet until he came to the end: another shaft, going up. A shorter height, but this one had no ladder. A soft light came from above.

Sam shoved the flashlight in his belt and put his back and forearms flat against the smooth rock wall. He placed the soles of his feet on the wall across from him and strained hard with each movement to shinny up the shaft. He had to stop and rest every few minutes. When at last he arrived at the top, he found it opened to the floor of a basement dimly lit by moonlight through a window. Sam crawled up out of the hole, looking very much like a rat himself, at this point.

Before he had time to look around, he heard a noise behind the door at the top of the long wooden staircase. There was a scratching sound. Then the muffled voice of a woman. It sounded like Helen. There was the sound of a latch opening, then the door itself opened.

"Fine, Larry," she said, "go ahead down there. Maybe you can catch some of those rats."

The sound of Larry's paws, and then, the most welcome sight in the world, Larry appeared on the stairs. He looked right at Sam, but he didn't bark or whine. The door closed again but didn't lock.

Sam sat on the cement floor of the basement with his back against a brick wall, rubbing Larry's belly, and waiting. The rescue was a success, but now they had work to do. The Dobermans remained unaware of Sam's presence, but he didn't know how many people might be involved in Joe and Helen's gang. He didn't know what they might have in the way of firearms. He'd have to operate on guts and luck.

When he'd heard no sounds coming from above for quite a while, Sam crept up the stairs, Larry at his heels. They emerged into the central hall, and Sam paused for a moment to look. They'd entered a splendid room, with a grand staircase wrapping around and leading to the balcony hallway above. Through doors at the far end, Sam could see drapes and a fireplace. Larry wasn't impressed. He trotted to the stairs. After ascending a few, he stopped and stared at Sam. Suppressing a chuckle, Sam drew his gun and followed Larry up the stairs.

No floorboards squeaked as the pair slipped along the hall. Larry led Sam into the bathroom straight at the end. A deep, old-style bathtub stood on four lion's-paw legs. In response, perhaps, to Sam's puzzled look, Larry sniffed at a door in the bathroom wall, just to the left of the basin.

Sam opened the door silently, his free hand at the ready by his shoulder holster. The door led into a corner bedroom, a secret room with no entrance to the hallway. Larry stepped in. A window in each outside wall let in the moonlight, and a fringed table lamp had a soft glow. No bed inhabited the room, it appeared to be a study used for storage. An upholstered high-backed chair spun slowly around, and in it sat Helen in a red dress, smiling from a daze of heroin. Sam could see an eye dropper, a spoon, and other articles from her joint on the table beside her.

"Oh, hello, it's you," she said quietly.

Sam answered just as softly, "You took my dog, Helen."

"Just for safekeeping," she replied.

"His?" Sam reached down to pet Larry.

"Mine," admitted Helen. Her eyes rolled, and she looked about to pass out. "Just until I get to . . . well, it doesn't matter."

She saw Sam's gaze fall on the Maltese figurine, sitting on the table among the drug paraphernalia. She laughed.

"Here, want this?" she said as she picked up the dog. She threw it at Sam, hard. It fell short, and although he tried to grab it, the statue hit the bare floor and smashed to pieces. Nobody came running. The other residents of the place were either in a stupor themselves or were used to such noises.

The joy of seeing Sam's expression seemed to wake her up a bit. "It's just a piece of junk anyway," Helen said. "It doesn't even look like the one in the paper. It's worthless crap I got at a pawn shop." She peeked down the front of her blouse for some reason, and then returned her gaze to Sam. "I just needed a reason to engage your services, that's all. I didn't want to tell you about the racehorse thing until I knew you better. I don't trust cops." She looked at her bright red fingernails.

"I'm not a cop," he said.

"Looks like you are to me," she replied.

"No, a cop couldn't have broken into your house."

"Ha, good point."

Sam gestured toward a large stained-glass window, leaning in its frame against the wall. It depicted a military man. "Who's that?" he asked. "Do you know?"

"It belonged to the baron who lived here. It's Kaiser Wilhelm."

"You don't say!"

Sam held the top of the frame to look more closely. "He sounds like quite a man."

"Wilhelm?"

"No, the baron," Sam said. "I heard he was a spy, but that tunnel I just came up was made by bootleggers."

"How do you know?"

"The rails. Meant for transporting goods, not for smuggling people." Sam looked back at Helen. She had fallen asleep, but he went ahead and finished his thought. "I suppose bootleggers could have improved on a tunnel which was already there . . ." He crossed the room to whisper in her ear, "You took my dog. I'm turning you in, you know."

"Mmm-hmm," came Helen's distant moan.

After the Mounties had taken over the case, and Sam had been back in San Francisco for a few weeks, Hugh, the street corner cop, came into Sam's office with some news. In his bright Irish brogue he told Sam, "I wanted to give you the heads up, Silva, before it hits the papers. That wee statue you photographed up in Bellingham? The lads on the force up there had the pictures examined by some fellow back east." He paused and wiped his brow. "Turns out there's a mighty high chance that little dog statue was priceless. Belonged to Napoleon himself, or so they say. Ain't that the dickens?"

Larry rolled over twice and put his feet in the air.

Showdown at Gravelly Gulch

The next tale features

Chance, a ninety-pound Black Labrador pup,
and Shamus, a Cavalier King Charles Spaniel,

both owned by Christy and Dennis.

Big Orange Tom lay in ambush under the rusty bumper of a gray Silverado. A couple of trash bins hindered our view, and Tom lurked there in the shadows behind one of them rear wheels, but Mrs. Walker spotted him, even so. We tried walkin' a little ways further. Tom narrowed his eyes at me and spat. I growled and bared my teeth, and I looked daggers at him, but Ol' Mrs. Walker turned tail like she always has done, and Shamus and I had no choice but to accompany her. I stopped and swung around, though, and looked at Tom in a real mean way again, and pulled out my pistols, gave them a fine twirl, and slid them back into their holsters. He knew. He knew I meant business and I wasn't afraid of no big ugly alley cat desperado.

Ol' Mrs. Walker, now, this ain't her first rodeo, if you know what I mean. She figures she can keep me out of trouble but she don't understand that I'm a hardened trail-wise cowpoke. She takes these daily walks, and I've never asked her why, figurin' it's none of my business. Why any lone woman of her years would cross that dangerous chaparral, full of snakes both reptilian and otherwise, I can't begin to imagine. I'm sure it ain't just for her health. So Shamus and me, why, we go along just to make sure she's all right.

Seems like every time we ride up that narrow canyon back of the ranch, Big Orange Tom is there. Bills offering a reward are posted all over town. We see his picture plastered to every telegraph pole and fence, but we already know about Orange Tom and his gang. Yes, he is lost. Don't need to tell us that. He's a lost soul if ever there was one. He and them dirty cutthroats have a hideaway around here somewhere, and I aim to find it.

Anyhow, after we made our way back out of the canyon, we passed near our ranch. We had to ride past that neighbor's place where every time I go by their dog calls out to me, "Bart! Bart! Bart! Bart!" If I told him once I told that dog a thousand times. My name's not Bart. It's Chance. Thunderation! Say it slow, dog: "Chay-ance."

We turned east, to head on up past the crossroads—that's where the wide open prairie begins. In our effort to track down Big Orange Tom's band, we decided to make for a certain mesa beyond the schoolhouse off in the distance. They call that school the middle school. I don't know, I can't read the sign, that's just what I heard 'em say. Sure don't know what it's in the middle of, way out there. Nowhere, I guess.

As we crossed the prairie to approach the school a tremendous noise fell upon us. All sorts of hollerin' and a-yellin' and the sound of mooing, too. A cattle drive! Out of the dust came a great herd of critters in gym shorts, runnin' along to beat all. They streamed across the plain, each naturally followin' the ones ahead, the way they do, with only a shout from a cowboy now and then to keep them on in the right direction.

We stood and watched the magnificent herd pass. The words "cute doggies!" made it to our ears, but I'm sure it was the call of the cowpokes, "get along little dogies!" as they ushered the cattle on. Oh! How I longed to join them as they drove those animals off to market. Weeks of riding, and sleeping under the stars. But I had my responsibilities here at the ranch.

When the dust settled enough that we could see ahead, I turned to the others and told them I was burnin' to find that bandit hideout. We headed across the flatland under the blazing sun. Prairie dog mounds scattered the plain. I had the urge to dig one of them creatures up for dinner, but I guessed we didn't have the time. A red-tail hawk followed us for a spell, soaring overhead in lazy circles. We had barely enough water, only what Mrs. Walker had brought in a little flask.

We crossed miles of prairie that day, and then we climbed the mesa. We didn't find any hideaway up on top. There was just some shacks and some chickens, and a couple of plum trees under the tall pines.

But then I spied something. Years of experience had taught me to keep my eyes peeled. An old signpost stood near the top of a draw which led back down the hill, roughly in the direction we had come, but not quite. The sign, whatever it had said, was long gone. Just a lone post standing there doin' nothing. Or maybe that's how it seemed.

Something was at the very base of that post. Marks. Little marks were there. Now, like I said, I can't read letters, but I knew what those drawings meant. Rovers of the plains, fugitives, they often scratch those marks onto posts and trees and fire hydrants to let others of their kind know where they've been or maybe some information about the place they're at. These scratches, barely noticeable to the untrained eye, are easy to read if you look close. And these markings told me we were on the right trail to that hideout belonging to Big Orange Tom and his gang.

We needed to go down that gully. I could just smell those bandits, their hideout was that close. I was sure of it. My pardner Shamus agreed: that was the way to go. It took some convincin' of Ol' Mrs. Walker, but I was sure she could do it. I told her she was a tough ol' biddy. She laughed, but then she set out to prove I was right. I know how to handle a woman.

The gully was rocky, and rough goin'. We had to keep an eagle eye out for bears and cougars. And rattlesnakes could be sunnin' themselves anywhere amongst those boulders. Sure enough, about halfway down the hill we heard the telltale sound of a rattler. I reached for my rope.

Shamus looked at me like I was plumb crazy. "What you gonna do, lasso it?"

"Naw," I said, "Just you watch and see!"

I tied a heavy knot in the end of my rope and then I swung it hard at that snake. I hope that ol' boy said his prayers, because I sent him straight on to the next world.

I intended to bring that snake along for dinner, but Mrs. Walker wasn't havin' any of that. So we left it to lay there and continued down the wash. I truly had my nose to the ground at that point. We tracked those outlaws to a little creek at a place where it goes under the road. Beneath the overhang we spied a culvert. We'd found the tunnel entrance to their hideout!

It was a great day for a shootout. Black scruffy birds sat on the telegraph wire, makin' a ruckus with their "Caw! Caw! Caw!" Obviously they were buzzards, waiting around for a fresh kill. Those ghouls can always sense a standoff. Shamus and I were all set to face down the bandits right then, to go in shootin' and take no prisoners. But the shadows were growin' long, and the hours of daylight short. We had to head back to the ranch. Anyway, we had Mrs. Walker to take care of. We'd have to be patient. We'd get those rascals next time, now we knew where they were hid.

We figured if we struck out due north we'd find the ranch. Back we were in the chaparral. It wasn't too hard to pick our way through, and soon we found some wagon tracks leading into a narrow canyon. Judgin' by my compass readin's, that canyon led right in the direction the ranch lay. We had a good time makin' our way along that canyon, whistlin' and countin' the miles. Then I saw a row of pine trees ahead. I pulled up sharp. I knew those trees.

Yup, yup. There was the hollow black stump and the ol' busted-up wasp nest, too. We were in the canyon just back of the ranch. We'd not come up it from the other end before. I figured Old Tom would be off someplace else by now. He couldn't still be settin' under that same Silverado, waitin' all this time. But there he was. And his head turned as he heard us comin'.

Shamus was all up for fightin' him with me, but I knew the honorable thing to do was face Big Orange Tom alone. I told Shamus if I didn't make it to tell my Maw and Paw I done my best. I told him he could have my fine boots and my squeakin' squirrel, too. Then I called out Big Tom.

Tom come out from under that rusty wagon and he just stared at me. He looked much bigger, somehow, than I'd expected, and he was full of spit and cusses. Surprisin', he didn't have no gun on him, but he came at me with Bowie knives in both hands. I quick handed my holster to Shamus and stood in front of an old oak tree, with only my huntin' knife. It seemed like Tom was all claws.

I pretty much thought I was gonna bite the dust. I looked at Shamus. I looked at Mrs. Walker. Maybe this was goodbye. But Shamus thought fast. He grabbed a big hickory stick and tossed it to me. It fell a few feet from my toe. Now I had a problem. That stick gave me a hope in this fight. I could use it as a club and I could fend off Tom's attack. But when I reached for it, Tom could get me.

I swallowed hard and reached for that stick. I guess Tom figured he'd set on me while I was distracted. He lunged at the exact moment I bent to grab that club. Tom went shootin' over my head like a cat on fire and rammed smack into that oak. His fancy knives stuck well into the trunk of that tree, and Tom scrambled upward to get out of my reach. I took a stab at his rear end but missed; he was up that tree real fast.

Shamus and I had a few things to say to Ol' Tom while he lounged in those branches, but Mrs. Walker reminded us we were expected back at the ranch. So we threw him a couple more insults and left Tom to his business.

On our way home we walked by that dog again. He just won't let off calling me Bart.

Mrs. Walker opened the ranch gate, and I did a very good sit, too, while she did so. She opened the front door and we went inside the house, and she took off the leashes and checked our water. We had plenty. It was a day of adventure for sure, and another walk is coming tomorrow. In the meantime, I'll go back to being a half-grown Labrador pup. Maybe tomorrow my Spaniel buddy Shamus and I can be Don Quixote and Sancho Panza.

Yep, we faced all kindsa danger, but the folks in the community will never forget the day young Chance the cow dog and his trusty pal Shamus treed Big Orange Tom. Leastways, that's how I see it.

Gus and His Country Charm

This story includes wisdom from
Gus, the English Cream type Golden Retriever

dearly loved by Robin and Dave.

THIS MAP depicts existing geography against a representation of roads in the north of Arlington, WA, around the time the barn was built in 1936; the approximate year that Sally Fingarson and her brother ended up in the river.

In those days, the river's edge ran along Eagle Creek (shown), with the modern-day cottonwood forest area under water. A road descended the end of the bluff and circled the bottomlands, presumably lost due to recurrent flooding.

The barn location is shown, along with the approximate location of the pioneer store, slightly to the north. The barn was constructed by Jens Jensen with hardwood lumber from the old Lincoln school. Gorgeous inside, it had a banistered stairway up to the loft.

If allowed to choose his path while on leash, Gus will head north to the river, either to the boat ramp or a quarter mile upstream to the site of the old Country Charm Dairy.

A big guy, Gus has a thick coat of long white hair with a soft and fuzzy undercoat. On warm days we often stop by a certain neighborhood park. Technically, Gus isn't allowed in the fountain pool, but don't try to tell him that. There's a sign that says No Wading. I challenge anyone with a heart to walk Gus past that fountain without letting him take a quick dip, though. The cement pool with tile mural has become known to his humans as Gus's Roman Baths.

From the Baths to the dairy land it's a flat walk through a tidy old neighborhood of cute houses. The people are friendly along that street, and barky dogs are kept away from the road, indoors or in backyards. As a walker, I know where the obnoxious or potentially dangerous dogs live around town. I generally avoid those blocks.

A few years ago, when I started walking Gus, a metal sign still read Dairy of Merit. The old barn stood near the road, looking sharp in a coat of red paint and with its brickwork and decorative white balcony. Built in a Gothic arch style, the smooth curve of roof extended down to the lowest story on either side of the building. Topped with a shiny pair of steel cupolas, the roof had a beautiful crows-beak extension to shield the hayloft doors. An antique store occupied the barn by that time, a friendly shop stuffed with rooms full of treasures.

Gus takes an interest in human activities, but old dairy buildings and even the panoramic vistas from the bluff fail to attract his attention. I could stand for ages, gazing out at the view framed by curtains of cedar boughs, but it wouldn't be fair. We have only an hour for his walk. We'll hurry past the barn and he will eagerly lead me along the short trail down the wooded hillside to the bottomlands, where cattle grazed on the lush pasture years ago.

A horseshoe bend of the river surrounds the lowlands of the former dairy. Beyond the river are forest and mountains. The dairy land has been cleared for a hundred years and is still farmed, but most of the open area has a cover crop and invites a stroll. Alder and cottonwoods fill the eastern portion, where much of the land sits in the meander belt of the river. Paths through these woods cross a creek and lead to the pebbly beaches. Several generations of townspeople and their dogs have gone down to the river at this spot to swim, fish, hunt for bullfrogs, or otherwise enjoy the wild, constantly changing beauty.

On a sunny spring day in the mid-1930s a boy stood on the beach here, whistling. He and his eight year old sister Sally had wandered north along the river's edge, reaching what was, in those days, the Sill farm. Several fawn-colored Guernsey cows meandered out onto the sand and gravel as Sally played a few yards away. They stood looking. Perhaps they wondered what was making that sound.

One of the cows glared at the kids, and turned broadside. The boy realized this wasn't a cow. It was a bull. The boy's eyes grew huge. Sally stopped trying to skip stones and looked at her brother. The bull tossed his head and began to breathe a deep growly sound, "Rrrrruuumph! Rrrruummph!" The animal eyed Sally and put his head down.

Sally froze. Her brother screamed, and shouted at the bull in a shrill voice, "GO ON, NOW! GO! YOU! BEAT IT!"

The huge, muscular creature pawed the ground, sending gravel flying over its own back and onto the other cattle behind. "The RIVER!" squeaked Sally's brother.

The bull charged at Sally but stopped short, blowing hard and glaring, head down. Holding their breath, Sally and her brother backed slowly, a step at a time, toward the water. Then they scrambled into the ice-cold river. Anything to get away from that bull! They struggled through water rushing past their knees, but braving the spring current paid off. Luckily, the bull wasn't ticked off enough to tolerate a wetting that day, and Sally lived to tell the story. She shared this with me just recently.

The lowlands of the farming area hold a lot of memories for the community. For Gus, they hold a lot of interesting smells and small adventures. To run through the field, maybe dig a hole somewhere, to splash in the water, what could make a big dog happier?

Silvers were early this year. Unlike some runs recently, this was a good one. Yesterday the river was quite low, and shiny salmon popped out of the water, here, there, and there! What a primal thrill to see a big fish jump! With no fishermen in sight along the river, it could have been a scene from somewhere in the wilds of Alaska.

The decaying remains of a fish lay on the gravel, looking like something only a dog could be interested in. And Gus was. Our interactions went something like this:

"So. Sorry. Boy." I grunted, overruling his pull on the leash. "You can't eat that fish. Raw salmon can give you a deadly parasite."

Gus kept straining toward the fish.

("I'd like access to that fish.")

"Gus!" I said.

He stopped pulling and looked at me imploringly.

("I don't want to eat the fish. I simply wish to roll on it.")

"Come, Gus!" I gave a quick tug on the leash when he didn't respond. "Look, if you roll on that fish you'll stink. You'll stink horribly."

("Yes, dear. That's the idea.") Gus looked at me, and lay down. ("I REALLY would like to roll on that fish.")

"Are you serious, Gus? You're going to lie down? C'mon, buddy! Let's go!"

Gus stood up but wouldn't budge.

"Okay," I said. I led him a couple of steps in the general direction of the fish. Then we took a short zigzag course to travel in my desired direction. Gus caught on right away, but it didn't matter. Pretty much any mammal will keep moving if you can get them going. Even husbands!

We continued down the shoreline. Our strolls along these beaches have taught me how dramatically a river can change from season to season and even day to day. Each rise and fall of the water level can alter the river's contours and may affect the location of rapids or the giant gnarled tangles of fallen trees. Sandbars disappear and pop up in other locations. Never made up of the same water, the river changes form but always remains the river.

Since the days when the ice sheets retreated many thousands of years ago, Indian kids have played here in the swimming holes and picked berries while their fathers and uncles fished for salmon. Before Europeans arrived, the People of the River numbered in the thousands. A well-known village stood here, where the waters of the forks combine before running west to the sea. As the lifeblood of the region, the river provided plenty of fish and allowed transportation through the thick forest.

As Gus and I walked along the riverside, I let him wade in the water. He splashed around happily. I marveled at the beauty of our surroundings, imagining what this spot must have looked like just over a century ago. Those tall conifers along the river would have been huge old-growth trees with thick forest undergrowth, and the river would have been jammed with fish. Otherwise, not much would look different. I took a deep breath. What a joy to absorb the beauty of this place on the river. Gus had a good, hard shake.

After a while, we crossed the broad rocky shore and headed back through the cottonwoods. I let Gus root around under some trees for a moment, and then he returned to my side, looking quite pleased with himself. Or did I imagine his gleefulness? Anyway, they call the creeping plant sticky willy, or sticky weed, or catchweed, among other things. I call it a nightmare. Gus had tiny round burs covering his front half and most of his underbelly. A few waved at me from his tail, just for a laugh. "Oh, no Gus," I whined, "What have you done?"

I sat Gus down and started frantically picking. Of course it would be easier to comb the burs out using a dog conditioner or cooking spray, maybe some coconut oil. But I had to pick out the burs one by one, sliding them along the long white hair with gentle fingers but with desperate speed because I can't return a bur-covered dog to his family. Dog walking is more of an art than one might think.

Gus sat patiently and indulged me while I fussed with his coat. "Oh, Gussy. Thank you," I said. "You're such a good boy."

As I handled Gus's beautiful white fur, it reminded me of something. For all those centuries, the native people lived well in this land of abundance. Their world became rich in art and ceremony as part of highly structured and deeply spiritual traditions. Winter ceremonies took place in the longhouse, and for them the women wove especially beautiful blankets from mountain goat wool. They also used a fiber which might be surprising: dog hair.

As in other communities along the sound, the people raised a special breed of little white "woolly dogs," which they kept in herds like sheep. These dogs looked like a Spitz type, resembling the long-haired Shiba Inu and the American Eskimo Dogs with fox-like faces, pointed furry ears, and curled tails. However, they were of a distinct breed propagated at least several thousand years before Golden Retrievers appeared in the nineteenth century. Gus's cream color coat resembles theirs with his fleecy undercoat and long outer hairs, but their hair was denser, fluffier and ideal for weaving. The hair of the Salish Wool Dogs produced a high-quality yarn, finer than the mountain goat wool.

In the traditional native viewpoint of this locality, everything is alive in spirit. These blankets embodied the essence of the animals and plants they came from, and this essence merged with those who created or wore the blanket. Because it was important work, women of status owned and cared for the woolly dogs, pampering them and feeding a rich diet to maintain the luxuriousness of their coats. To keep the breed pure, these special dogs were raised on islands or were penned up, often in caves. It's said that the woolly dogs didn't bark, although they did howl.

I picked the last few burs out of Gus's coat, still thinking about the woolly dogs. How sad it is that they are gone. The horrific decimation of the local tribes, primarily due to the smallpox epidemics, left few people to care for the dogs in the traditional way. Inexpensive blankets manufactured from sheep wool replaced the more precious textiles: goat's wool, dog's wool, and the soft and comfortable woven cedar bark. Woolly dogs were left to interbreed with other dogs. As a result, the breed has been extinct for over a hundred years.

"Come on, Gus," I said. "Let's get you home."

We decided to trot through the forest. It was my choice because we were running a bit late, but Gus merrily complied, offering to break into a canter. I was fine with trotting. We slowed to a walk to go up the hill and past the barn and farmhouses, then we cut through a few alleys of the neighborhood and got Gus home right on time. I closed the gate and peeked over it to say goodbye. Gus stood and watched me leave before heading off for a nice roll in his favorite spot. And so another wonderful day of dog walks came to a close, and I headed home after a beautiful trip with Gus down to Country Charm.

On the walk back to my house, I thought about how Gus had been sniffing and marking along these trails long before I moved to town. I'm one of the many newcomers to this area. I could be considered an intruder. I arrived only a half dozen years ago to put down my roots, while dairy and logging families have lived in this little town for several generations. Even so, the many hours spent exploring have given me a sense of belonging. On our walks together, Gus and I have made many friends in the neighborhood and left our footprints on every nearby road and trail. I suppose there's a fine line between a sense of belonging and a feeling of ownership. Perhaps I crossed that line.

It seems to me that Gus and I had been visiting the old farm for about a year before a great crack began to appear in my happy little world. One afternoon I stopped by the bluff's edge and had him pose for a photo with the foggy farmland below and the blue mountains as a backdrop. As part of my dog walk business, I find a suitable background and give the command, "Sit for a picture!" The dogs are familiar with my habit of playing peekaboo from behind the flat shiny thing I carry in my pocket. They sit patiently for a moment but usually are just as happy when we move on. Not Gus. He strikes an attractive pose and holds it until I've taken the picture. Then he'll offer another angle, another look. He loves to give me his profile, head held high, gazing into the distance, not moving a whisker. I tell him these photos are for his owners, and I know he'd do anything for them. And it's hilarious how he hams it up. But how could he possibly understand photos? Why does he pose like this? I don't know.

And so, to take a photo, we stood at the spot with the prettiest overlook. An Eagle Scout had installed a bench there, made of thick fir planks from a local tree. He also put in a rose garden. Another Eagle Scout constructed a kiosk which is used to display a map of the conservation area. I decided that Gus could wait, just this once, while I read the details on the map. He wouldn't mind, as apparently, cottontails had left their scent in the long grass nearby.

I looked at the map. I knew that the farmer had given the town a heck of a deal on the land so it could be preserved and be used as a park. "Well, Gus," I said, "this looks pretty good. Community gardens. Fishing pond. Wait—sports fields? What?" This came as a bit of a blow. I was not too fond of the open grassland turning to turf and stripes and maybe chain-link fencing. Sports fields. Blast!

We continued down the old farm road that ran along the top of the bluff. Heavy equipment by the old house on the far end made both Gus and me curious. The family had moved out of the house not long before. By our next visit, the house would be a pile of rubble. *Hmmm*, I thought, *the place doesn't look like it's in such bad shape. Maybe they had mildew problems or something.*

"Geez, that's too bad, huh, Gus?" I said.

Gus looked at me with his big brown eyes and his Golden Retriever smile. I rubbed his head. This was one of his favorite places to walk. We had plenty of time to continue along the gravel road down the end of the bluff to the lowlands to have some fun. And so we did.

When we got to the bottom I stopped momentarily and looked out across that peaceful scene. I watched a heron stand hunting in the ryegrass and clover. He reached out slowly, so slowly, with his long neck until he was at such an angle that I thought he would fall. Then he struck at some unfortunate thing in the grass with his long swordlike beak—a quick end for the lizard or mouse. An eagle swooped overhead to land in the crown of a hemlock. Why couldn't those people just leave this place alone?

"On the map it says it's a conservation area. Sports fields," I muttered. "What does that mean?" I felt for the farmer and his legacy. They'd spoil his beautiful meadow. I looked down at Gus.

He returned my gaze expectantly. I went back to staring into the distance, annoyed at the world. After a while, Gus came to me and gave my hand a quick nudge. Using his weight against the leash, he steered me to the edge of the field. I didn't particularly notice. Eventually I snapped out of my daze. Gus was right. *Forget about it*, I thought; *Let's go to the river.*

We were both disappointed to find the path to the river impassible after the recent heavy rains. For humans, anyway. At least for humans who hadn't thought to wear their boots. So we continued along the creek which borders the woods until we came to a place where rows of conifers had been planted. Someone had put a lot of work into creating campsites, each bounded on three sides by hedges of spruce trees. As we passed the farthest site, Gus turned his head to look behind us. A man had emerged from behind one of the rows of trees. He waved when he saw us look at him.

I wasn't sure what Gus thought, but this fellow looked questionable to me. He was a big hefty man dressed in grubby brown overalls. The sleeves of his red flannel shirt had been torn off. He had short messy hair and a full beard. I figured he was either a friendly backwoods guy or an insane killer like in all those movies and I couldn't tell which. The worrisome thing was the pitchfork he carried. It had long narrow tines. Very sharp. I waved back to him and kept going to make a loop around the field. But when Gus and I arrived at the trail which goes up the bluff, the man was standing there.

As we were obviously about to head up the trail it would have been awkward to turn around, so I continued. Instinctively, I held Gus on a shorter leash. As we approached the man to pass him, I tried not to glance at his pitchfork. I couldn't think of any sane reason to walk around with such a thing. And then, of course, just as we passed, I said, "Hi, again!" and stumbled over a root, nearly falling.

"Oh, my! Are you okay?" asked the man.

"Yeah, thanks, I'm fine," I replied, doubly embarrassed. "It's so muddy today!"

"Great time to catch bullfrogs, though!" He smiled and held up a big bucket I hadn't noticed.

Oh. Bullfrog hunting. I felt so stupid.

His name was Otis. Without any hesitation, Gus offered himself for Otis to pet. Our new friend told me what a beautiful dog Gus was, and we fell into conversation. I learned from him that bullfrogs here are an invasive species which cause harm to a wide range of native species populations, disrupting the wetlands ecosystem. He also told me a bit about the history of Country Charm.

This is how I found out about the first store in the area. A couple of enterprising Scandinavian pioneers from Minnesota set up their shop in a tiny log shack.

"It was right here, above us on the bluff," Otis told me. "Yeah, located under speculation that this would be the site of the town. I've always assumed this trail we're on right here is the one that came up from the landing spot on the river.

"The woods were thick and lush in those early days, impassable. The river was the only road. Only the Native Americans could navigate the wild river, so they charged the settlers a healthy amount to transport them and their belongings up here by canoe. One family brought a full-sized organ upriver, I guess."

"By canoe?"

"Yeah, can you imagine?"

"Successfully?"

"Yeah, I guess so!"

"Wow." I enjoyed hearing about these adventurous people. "So, was the store here for a long time?"

"No, it wasn't. Folks started to build downriver by the forks. You know, where the boat launch is. So when they went to build a bigger store, they set up shop down there instead. But that town site didn't pan out either, and eventually those boys put their whole building up on rollers and moved it a quarter mile up to what now is the town. Ended up being quite successful."

"Wow, that's crazy!" I said.

I looked down at Gus, who waited patiently. "Oh, sorry Gussy!" I said. "I'd better get going, I'm supposed to be walking Gus. So nice to meet you, Otis. Enjoy your frog legs!"

"Oh, I will, thanks! Have you ever had them?"

"No, but I hear they taste like chicken," I said.

He laughed. "Yeah. Yeah, they do. If you deep-fry them."

Gus and I headed up the trail, and then the street toward home. We went by the spot where the full three-ring circus set up on the old farmstead back in the sixties. That must have been something.

My next walk down to those fields with Gus was a rough one. First, we passed the barn, then the big old loafing shed, and started down the trail. Though I tried to suppress my emotions, I knew Gus would feel them. I'm paid to walk dogs, not to depress them. I couldn't help it, though. I started to sob.

Gus stopped his sniffing around and looked at me. I took some deep breaths and gave him a smile. He rolled on his back and then jumped up, brushing against my leg.

"They're going to fill the bluff with condos, buddy. I just found out." My voice croaked, "But this is a conservation area! Protected! It shows it on the map! I don't understand." I kicked a rock off of the path and down into the ditch water below. I heard it splash. "It's supposed to be safeguarded! Ticky tacky townhouses? What's going on? And sports fields? What the hell, man!"

Gus stared at me.

"Sorry, Gussy, I'm just so sad about what they're going to do to this place." I coughed and sighed.

The handsome white dog nudged my thigh, and then sat in front of me, with his head back, looking expectant. He stared at me as if to say, "C'mon, you've got this whole playland of interesting smells and splashy water, and you're going to sit here worrying about some stupid thing?"

With that nudge, all the steam of my built-up frustration disintegrated, *pfft!*

Gus wagged his tail.

"You don't care about townhouses." My smile came back. "All you want is to be with someone you love, having fun. Live in the moment! Yep. Be present! Enjoy the journey!" I pulled a tissue from my jeans pocket and wiped my nose. "Yeah, okay, boy. Let's go enjoy the beauty while it's still here." And so we did.

It was, in fact, the TARDIS that explained things to me. Gus and I continued our walks at Country Charm and other places. A regular stop when I walk dogs on the hill above town is one of those little free libraries. This particular one is blue, made to look like a TARDIS, the time-traveling ship from Dr Who, which disguises itself as an old British police call box. Girl Scouts made this one, and they made it well; an excellent carpentry job, beautifully done. After years of use, the door fits tightly and still opens and closes just fine. It truly is bigger on the inside, because the books it contains can take us anywhere. On one of my walks with Gus that spring, I found a bunch of old local newspapers in the TARDIS.

From those papers, I learned some things about the dairy farm. This got me thinking, and affected my discussions with folks as I walked around the community. In this way, I found out that my idyllic conception of a dairy had been outdated for a hundred years. Of course I know that farms are large-scale and milking is mechanized, but I didn't understand how industrialized the business has become since the economics changed in the mid-twentieth century. Certainly, dairy families care about their cows, but there have always been elements of the occupation which aren't pretty, and this is even more the case with modern dairying.

Dairies had to go big to survive. A farm has to have many cows, and keep them in barns throughout their short but high-producing lives. Apparently the Country Charm Dairy was no exception. Eight hundred Holsteins resided there during the peak years. They lived in relative comfort, with stalls where they could lie down on sawdust on the concrete floors. It was a clean, well-run dairy. But it wasn't a place where cows frolicked in sunny, daisy-filled pastures, at least not in the later years.

While this knowledge helped me calm down a bit about the loss of the dairy uplands to development, I realized that the red barn held an even more precious place in history. Built before artificial insemination of cattle, before growth hormones and other unnatural advancements, back when most cows were milked by hand, the barn really is a symbol of simpler times, the passing of which is lamented by just about everyone.

What the locals miss most about Country Charm, though, is the ice cream. The Graafstra family, owners of the dairy, made a lasting impression throughout the county with their ultra-fresh dairy products. When Hank Graafstra got his hands on some used equipment, he started bottling and distributing his own milk, cutting out the middleman. Nobody did that! In the 1970s the family turned the old red barn into a store, selling their direct-from-the-cow milk and rich ice cream. Huckleberry, wild blackberry and butter brickle! Lemon custard! Swiss chocolate cherry! Black licorice! Everyone had their favorite flavor. Neighborhood kids would head down to the Country Charm barn after school.

The Graafstra kids grew up riding horses and fishing, enjoying the beauty of nature, and living the small-town lifestyle. They worked hard on the farm and as they grew they worked to remodel the red barn into the milk processing plant and store. Then, as the dairy industry struggled more and more through increased costs and lower demand for milk, small-town communities along the coast watched their farms disappear, replaced by urban sprawl. These changes increasingly affected the business.

After forty years of running a successful farm, there came the point when the family's circumstances changed. The old processing equipment blew apart one day, and brought production to a halt. In his late seventies, Hank was already living with a cancer diagnosis. The weight of it all felt overwhelming. The heartbreaking reality was that it was time to sell off the cows and close the dairy.

But dogs aren't concerned about these things. I felt so thankful that Gus was with me on that rainy day when I saw the backhoe demolishing the barn.

"No!" I whimpered, "No, you bastards! No!"

I couldn't bear to look anymore. They'd already taken down the family home and were swinging away at the barn. The vroom of the excavator filled my ears, along with the bang and crunch of old-growth lumber.

I felt panic. I ran past the scene with Gus and down the bluff-side trail. Skidding on a slimy patch of wet leaves, I shrieked

as I teetered backward, flailing my arms like a cartoon character. *Flump!* I landed flat on my back. At least I didn't let go of
the leash. Then, with a groan, I forced myself to a sitting position. And there I sat, my teeth clenched and brows knit, feeling
helpless. Powerless. Feeling sorry for myself. For the loss of
something I couldn't control. History was being chipped away,
swallowed up by greed. Tears formed and ran down my cheeks.

Gus stood looking at me. I started to get up, slipped again,
and fell right back down, soaking my side in addition to my back.
I looked at the sky through the branches above me. Before I had
time to laugh or bawl or whatever I would do, Gus came over to
sniff me. He set his big, grimy paw in the center of my chest and
began to lick my tears away. I covered my face with my arm and
leaned on him to help myself up.

"I'm okay, Gus," I said as I stood. "You're such a good boy," I
added. His show of concern touched me.

He stared at me. He nudged me hard, almost knocking me
off balance again.

I'm truly thankful for that nudge. My big furry dog friend
opened up my heart at the right time. Instead of spiraling down
into a well of depression, I caught myself. I'd had my moan and
cry, and now it was time to stop. I wanted to enjoy my time in
the park without getting worked up whenever I went there. I
was on a pleasant walk with Gus. The world was not mine to
carry on my shoulders. No point in taking life so seriously. Why
do we torture ourselves? Silly humans.

To my credit, I do make an effort to take care of myself and
reduce anxiety. One way is to teach the dogs I walk a few special
commands which make my life easier. "Fix your leash!" is an
example. Gus is perfectly capable of raising his front leg over the

leash to remove it from behind his leg. He'd rather I did it. He'll stop and look at me. So, it all depends on my mood. Some days, I'll say "Gus, really. Fix your leash." If I'm in a mooshier mood I'll sigh and fix his leash for him. Because I'm a wuss, and he owns me. But if you met Gus, you'd understand. He and I sometimes play these little cat games, but we are there for each other. Like the day he helped me catch Stella Chapelle.

It was around the time they constructed that first batch of townhouses along the far end of the bluff down at Country Charm. Gus and I had set out for somewhere; I don't remember our destination that day. We'd gone only a few blocks from his house when the horrifying screech of brakes came from the intersection just downhill. A squirrel had darted right in front of a little white car, but it managed not to get run over and now it was headed up Fourth Street. There were two squirrels. No, the one giving chase was a dog. A tiny little dog!

Wow. As a walker of other people's dogs, I usually avoid the off-leash ones. In this case, though, there wasn't much of a threat.

"Gus, that's a tiny little guy!" I said. "He'll get hit by a car. Come on, let's go!"

That next block has some big maples, so I thought the squirrel might scurry up one of those. Then maybe I could catch the dog. Unfortunately, that car had driven off, so it looked like it was up to Gus and me. We could hear the "yap yap yap" of the excited dog. When we arrived at Fourth and turned the corner, we could see him barking into the tangle of shrubs.

"I think, whatever that is," I told Gus, "it must be a puppy. But I've never seen a dog that small! What the heck is it?" Gus held his snout up high and started working his nostrils. He must have been wondering the same thing. The dog looked at us and took off again across the street and into the alley behind the church. He trotted into the yard of the kind lady who grows gorgeous dahlias in her flower garden. Good. Maybe the dog belonged to her. But, no, there it went down the alley again toward a road with much heavier traffic. Gus and I followed at a distance while I snapped a picture to share on lost dog sites.

The dog turned up the next street, but Gus and I cut through the church property and headed it off. It stopped when it saw us. Panting and holding my side, I managed to loop Gus's leash around a tree where he couldn't reach the road. I hoped this dog wasn't frightened of big dogs. Gus helped out immensely by standing calmly, his mouth hanging open in a lovely smile. His tail made soft congenial swishes, signaling to the little dog that he had no plans to hurt him or even rush at him excitedly.

I felt that calling this dog would probably scare him away. These things happen so fast, but my instincts kicked in, and I didn't have to think about it. I stepped closer to the little guy and squatted, facing sideways and sneaking glances at him out of the corner of my eye. I didn't want to be a threat.

I pulled some imaginary treats out of my pocket and noisily pretended to eat them, (yum yum!), seeming to ignore him. I could see I'd caught the interest of the little shoe button eyes. Oops. I dropped a piece. Oops, I have dropped another. He started sniffing the ground in front of himself. This would be easy. I gently held out my hand, palm down. Momentarily the tiny dog was in my arms, nervous but friendly, and licking me. Oh, and he was a she.

I tucked her into my hoodie pocket and supported her with one hand while retrieving Gus. He gave her a quick sniff, and we were on our way. But where? What should I do now? Then I saw the woman in pink trotting and puffing up the block. She had a leash in her hand with no dog attached.

"Excuse me," she said as she crossed the street, "Have you seen—"

An excited yap from the furry little head peeking out of my pocket interrupted the lady.

"Oh! You found her!" Tears started down the lady's cheeks. When she reached me I placed the dog in her hands. "Oh, Estelle!" she scolded, "Don't you ever do that again!" She held Estelle up to her face and cried into her as if she were a handkerchief.

I waited respectfully and then asked, "Is that a Yorkie? She's so tiny!"

The lady wiped her eyes (not with Estelle), and then she laughed. She held the dog at eye level with both hands around its chest, letting its body dangle, as one might with a kitten. Still unable to take her eyes off the pup, she said, "She's a Snorkie." Then she looked at me and said, "Thank you so much for catching her! I heard brakes squeal somewhere. I was terrified. Thank you so much."

"A what?"

"She's a Snorkie. A mix of Mini Schnauzer and Yorkie." She laughed. "Yeah, I know!"

"She's so little!" I said again as if it were necessary.

"Her name is Stella Chapelle. She's still a pup. And she's the runt of the litter, too."

"Well, she certainly has a large presence! She's not even afraid of Gus here."

"I know, she's completely size-blind! She's hilarious!" the woman said. "What a beautiful dog you have!"

This led to introductions and the inevitable explanation about my being a dog walker. The woman's name was Amy.

We talked for a few minutes, and then Amy said she and Stella might as well continue on down to Country Charm. Would Gus and I like to come along? Of course, and that's how we made a new pair of friends. As we neared the old dairy property, our conversation focused on the changes taking place.

We walked past the devastation of the barn area, all graded off now, with a forest of construction stakes. Ends of various colors of tubing stuck up here and there, waiting to connect to water heaters and broadband one day.

"It breaks my heart," Amy said.

I groaned. "Mine, too. I can't imagine what it must feel like for those who grew up here. Are you from this town originally?"

"No," she replied, "but I come here a lot, to the park. I was one of the volunteers who planted trees down on the floodplain, back in the day."

"Oh, I saw something about that in the paper. Native trees, right?"

"Fifteen hundred trees! Through various projects, we helped the land recover from a hundred years of farming. We improved the river's health. Our work lowered the temperature of the water in order to help save the salmon."

"Wow."

"It was amazing to see the community come together like that."

We passed a series of signs put up by the developers to inspire sales. One showed an attractive young couple standing smiling by the river, wearing serious, multi-day backpacks.

"That cracks me up!" I said.

"I know," Amy said. "These places have no yards at all! The people who this development attracts aren't going to be people who care about the outdoors. They are never going to be wandering down to the river!"

I laughed. "Certainly not with backpacks!"

Farther along the freshly paved road, we passed between the blocky, intrusive multiplexes, some still under construction, some already sold, with cars in the driveways. When we came to the park gate, Amy set Stella down so she could walk. Gus and Stella sniffed noses. I took a picture. We went down the road at the end of the bluff. At the bottom, Amy picked her dog up again because a pair of eagles circled overhead.

"I can't believe it's going to be sports fields," I moaned.

That was when I found out that it had been the farmer's dream to have sports fields. "Yeah," Amy told me, "Hank loved to encourage youth sports. He and Betty wanted the community kids to have a ball field and to be able to play by the river. To have room to run and play."

"Wow. Somehow that makes me feel better about it," I said. How narrow my perspective had been! "Knowing that the farmer favored the sports fields makes a difference."

"Why wouldn't he?"

"Well, it will spoil the beauty of the place."

"Oh, I don't know," Amy said. "I think it could help the whole area remain a park."

As we passed near the bridge over the creek, Amy stuck Stella inside her jacket because a young woman was returning from the beach with her German Shepherd. We talked with her for a few minutes. She was a resident in one of the new townhouses. Her dog was handsome, with a thick, dark coat. A four-month-old male.

". . . yes," she mentioned, "I'm training him for hiking. I go out to the mountains every weekend."

"Oh. Hiking," Amy said. We exchanged sheepish glances.

The big Shepherd pup sniffed Gus, who bowed low, ready to play. The Shepherd thought that was an excellent idea, and then both the owner and I had jump-around dogs who needed to face the sad truth that they were on leash. She made kissy noises and called her dog to her. I moved between them and told Gus to sit. Both dogs made us proud. Perhaps we'd see each other down there again.

Amy and I followed Gus and Stella through the grass. Before heading back up the bluff, we wandered near the off-leash area, all fenced and obviously at one time cared for, but now overgrown.

"This would have been such a great place to let Gus loose to play. What happened? Why is everything going back to brambles down here after all that work?"

"The town used to employ a conservationist," Amy explained, "a guy named Bill. He grew up in the neighborhood. Bill told me that his youth spent here at Country Charm led him to become a biologist. That man was the driving force behind the whole project here. He brought together the service clubs and the scouts, and he worked with Hank (the dairy owner) and his wife Betty, and the tribe. It's amazing what one person can accomplish by inspiring people to come together."

"But what happened?"

"Well, things change. There are all kinds of people with all kinds of priorities. That's the beauty and the tragedy of this world."

Gus plopped down in front of us and rolled his eyes. We both laughed.

Amy petted him. "He is terrifically expressive! So cute, he's telling us to move on and enjoy our day."

"Yes. He is, isn't he!"

We laughed again.

"He tells me that a lot," I added.

"He gives good advice," Amy said.

I patted Gus. "Okay, Gus. Sorry, boy. Off we go!" We resumed our walk. "He's so right, though. There's no point in going around and around about whatever has recently pushed my buttons."

Amy nodded. "It's action that makes a difference."

"That's so true."

Passing back through the townhouses, I stopped to pick up after Gus.

While Amy stood waiting, holding her Stella, I turned to her and said, "You know, one thing I really do appreciate is these dog waste stations they have along here now. I used to have to carry the black bags all the way home."

"Yeah, you know what, change can be tough but it's not always so bad. I remember something that Bill told me a friend of his had said. 'You can't stop progress, but you can help steer it.' Hank and Betty wanted to preserve the character of Country Charm for generations to come. And in a lot of ways, that's happening. For many years this was private property, now it's preserved and we have access to it as a park."

We said goodbye at the corner where Stella had nearly been hit. She was fast asleep inside Amy's jacket.

"Thank you again for rescuing my Stella!" Amy said.

"Thank you for bringing a Snorkie into my life!" I replied.

We both laughed.

Gus picked up his pace on the way uphill and toward home. As always, he was eager to see his family.

After a few more blocks, I stopped and gave a huge sigh. "Gus," I told him, "I've made so many assumptions about Country Charm. And they were mostly wrong."

He looked up at me. He sat. Maybe it was the tone of my voice. I squatted to pet him.

"Why do I do this, Gus? Why do I grasp onto things and overthink everything? My mind clenches onto speculations and stressful thoughts like an obsessed Terrier hanging on to a ball."

Gus smiled his golden smile.

As a favor, I removed the leash from behind his front leg as I stood up.

I took a deep breath and looked at my pal.

"Well, buddy," I said, "You're right. Drop it. That's what I need to do."

But, dammit, they never should have taken down the barn.

How Am I Still Alive?

The following story concerns dogs owned by Lynnett and Greg:

Emma, an Aussiedor,
and her "sister" Abby, a Chihuahua/Miniature Pinscher mix.

Emma draws back, straining against the leash and twisting to test her collar. Do I not see them? Hideous creatures headed right for us! What are we going to do? They've got young. This makes them even more dangerous! With her blue eyes wide she glances at me, then stares again at those invaders coming up the trail.

Gentle-hearted Emma is an Aussie mix. Her eyes are the color of a hazy morning sky. They are centered with stunning coronas of faded indigo. The effect is expressive, penetrating, and just slightly unsettling.

The trail I'm walking along today with Emma and her sister dog Abby follows an old railroad grade a good thirty miles through woods and farmland, crossing creeks and rivers on sturdy old bridges. Wide and paved, the path is used by two-legged monsters in T-shirts, and even scarier pedal-monsters who zip by, their sole purpose in life to frighten Emma.

With tactful movement, I switch Emma's leash to the other hand before it can wrap around my leg. Emma ducks and tries to bolt. "It's all right, Emma." I speak in the closest thing to a soft baritone I can manage, "Easy, girl. Take it easy."

The monsters pass by. They somehow neglect to eat Emma, and soon have traveled a good way down the trail. All is well. I sit the girls in front of a cheerful yellow bloom of yarrow and squat to capture their portrait. Emma moves out of the view. I draw a long breath to stay relaxed and then guide her back to where I want her. "Sit," I say, "Sweet girl. Sit for a picture!"

A tri-color blue merle, Emma looks pretty as she strikes an elegant pose for me. Her chest and face have a lot of white, and it's the snowiest white I've ever seen on a dog. She's always been great about sitting for a photo. Abby has too, although she's seemed hesitant about scrubby areas since that day I accidently had her sit on a stinging nettle. Abby is Emma's beloved companion, a dear, happy-go-lucky cream-colored little girl. Her cheery business-like demeanor comforts Emma as they trot along, her waggly tail curled over her back as she pauses to investigate the more interesting smells.

On this particular day, though, Emma's fears turn out to be valid.

The funny thing is, I am in the middle of a conversation when the deer appears. I often have a dialogue with myself in my mind while the three of us walk along. Sometimes I mumble. It's how I chew through ideas and get my thoughts ready to write down.

This time I prattle on about how well Emma mirrors my own disposition. She overthinks things. And, as she and I both know, overthinking translates to worry. Active imaginations require tactful handling. How easily I can see the pointlessness of all Emma's concerns. I only wish she could. "Your day," I tell her, "would be more enjoyable if you'd just calm down. Simple, really." *Says the pot to the kettle!*

While I coo to Emma about what to focus on in life, a doe slips out of the bushes and walks alongside the trail just ahead of us. I should realize that something's up. Why would she come out onto the trail in the middle of the day, choosing to keep company with me and a couple of dogs? But I don't think about it aside from what fun it is to walk along with a deer.

She looks well-fed and healthy. I back us off a little, not wanting to spook her out toward the highway. She dawdles and nibbles a leaf or two. The dogs don't care about the deer. They apparently don't want to know about a big animal like that one.

We tag along behind her, passing through a tunnel of shade

where thick old maples with mossy limbs curve in lofty grandeur over the pathway. The doe's rump flashes in front of us, her tail held high. The path opens out onto a sunny stretch, and still she strolls just ahead. Abby pauses to investigate a smell in the fresh-mown grass on the shoulder of the trail. The dogs still seem oblivious of the deer who stays right with us for almost a quarter mile. Eventually she bounds off across the overgrown pasture of someone's family farm. We enter the wetlands area. On impulse, I decide to see if we can access the lake.

About the size of a soccer field, the lake lies only several hundred feet from the paved trail. However, the narrow path gets muddy, impassibly sloppy after a rain (especially if you need to keep your dogs clean), and cuts through dense grass which grows taller close to the water. On this late summer day, the grass and shrubs rise quite a bit higher than my head, causing a nerve-racking lack of visibility. By this time of year, though, the mud has solidified enough to walk on without worrying about dirty paws. The girls go cheerfully before me in single file, pulling gently on their leashes. It smells rich and boggy. A red-winged blackbird trills.

Wetlands encircle the lake. Beyond, a swash of deciduous trees edges the dark conifer forest. One lone house is visible far to the north. In addition to the grasses, the lake is rimmed by a labyrinth of leafy hardhack thickets with long oxblood spikes of dried flowers. Sometimes, a guy in boots or waders will drag a small boat across the paved trail from the roadway and out to the water, but when we arrive on the mud shore we see no one fishing on this day. Besides the rush of an occasional passing car out on the road or the drone of a logging truck, the air is still. Strangely still.

Here among the thick, tall shrubs, my mind starts in on me, imagining that some creep might be crouched nearby. I feel like an ass for allowing this fear, yet as a woman, sadly, these thoughts will come to mind. I gaze out over the part of the lake that I can see. Clusters of yellow lilies float, here and there, on the murky water. The dogs nose a clump of reeds and sniff a thin log that extends into the water. But I feel uneasy. An eerie electric feeling prickles my skin. The tiny hairs at the base of my scalp stand on end.

Busy with their half-submerged log, at first the dogs don't feel my tug on their leashes when I call, hush-voiced, "Let's go, girls!" As we turn to leave, a flutter of thirty or forty yellow butter-flies bursts from behind a clump of grass at our feet, swarming into the air. I nearly fall backward but as the spooked dogs lunge, they pull me back to my feet. A leash snaps and flops to the ground. Abby's curled tail disappears into the hardhack shrubs. Somehow, the clasp has opened. "Abby!," I cry, "Abby! Come, Abby!" I grab up the empty leash and stare after her. I can see only the shaking of the bushes. That, and her owners' teary faces. I use some rather bad language.

My chest still pounds from dodging the swallowtails, and now it burns with worry. I start off to bushwhack south around the lake in the direction I think that Abby went. Leading poor confused Emma, I call for Abby, forcing as much calmness into my voice as I can manage. I repeat her name, whistle, and re-mind her that I have some treats. As my mouth dries out it becomes more and more difficult to whistle. My heart keeps on pounding.

Emma and I forge our way through the vegetation. We follow what I hope is Abby's trail—I've never gone this far off the little path before. I barely notice the cold water sloshing in my shoes. Maybe we should go back to the paved trail. She'd likely head for home. I keep calling, "Abby! Abby!"

High ground. I should seek high ground and get a view of the area. I shade my eyes. Wetlands don't offer a lot of hills. There! I see an alder growing from some sort of little rise. Maybe I can shinny up that. We push through the cool damp shrubs, making our way toward the tree. I try not to think about spiders. Or leeches. Emma balks. She can sense I'm not comfortable.

We have no room for zigzag maneuvers here. "Come," I tell her, but Emma stands fast. Nothing is going to move this dog. Meanwhile, Abby could be getting far away. I continue to call her as I try to encourage Emma. I do my best, but my hand trembles. Squatting at leash end, facing sideways to her, I softly encourage, "Let's go! Let's go, Emma!" I walk in front of her, without looking back, until the leash stops me. Nothing. Emma isn't budging. I shout for Abby. It comes out in less of a gentle way than I intended. I try to apologize by petting Emma, although I know better. Emma recoils. I have to make her move. Why would she do this? I stand, flustered, looking at nothing in particular, trying to think. Emma puts her head down, and starts walking.

We arrive at the aspen tree. I tell myself I should have gone out to the trail. Fumbling, I unclip Emma's leash, pass the clip end around the tree trunk, and feed it through the leash handle. Then I clip it back to her collar.

I grab the tree as high as I can, wrap my shins around it, and hang on with my knees. When I planned to climb the tree, I'd forgotten how terrible I was in PE at school. I stretch for a higher spot on the trunk. Not as easy as it looks in movies. I inch-worm my way up a couple of feet, and have just paused to consider giving up, when a bone-chilling scream comes from somewhere nearby.

It isn't the sound of Abby—a woman cried out in terror. I cling to the tree, paralyzed. She shrieks again, her wail breaking off with a tone of dismay. I feel her shock and horror. I can't breathe. The world around me waits for another scream. It never comes. Through a vague awareness I know that down below me Emma digs desperately, trying to hide, but she can't quite reach good cover.

No more sound comes, not from the woman. My ears fill with the throbbing pressure that pumps through my body. I don't breathe. Only rapid pounding, throbbing. My chest. I gasp for some air, dizzy.

A car door slams, out by the road. Then an engine. Someone roars away. The murderer! How long have I been in the tree? They certainly saw me. *Call 911!* I pull my phone out of my pocket. I realize my vision has gone blurry. Fumbling, still perched in the tree, I shade the phone screen and strain to see. The phone slips through my numb fingers. Trying to grab it, I bat it instead, slamming it into the ground. I can't see anything from my perch. I descend the tree. Emma comes to me, trembling. I feel shaky too.

My phone has fallen into the hole dug by Emma. The hole had filled with water. With mechanical movement, I retrieve the phone, glance at it, and shove it in my pocket. I may have dropped to my knees, I don't know. Pounding, shaking, everything goes foggy.

Reality melts into a dreamscape, but I have to *think*. I can't see very far, but Emma could tell if someone waited there.

Couldn't she? She'd be no protection, though. How can Abby have gone and also this? What should I do? Getting out of here would be the best idea.

I see no choice. I struggle to remove Emma's pink leash from around the tree. I gather up Abby's leash; hang it around my neck. Cold with fear, I determine to search the bushes in the direction of the scream. A woman might lay bleeding, needing help. I don't want to think about what else I might find. Some strange force propels me onward through the shrubs. A disbelief, a need to know. Emma doesn't want to follow but she clings near my ankle, obediently escorting me through the grasses and leafy shrubs. It is a stupid thing to do, and I know it. But I can't help myself. That chilling scream consumes all my thoughts. A sickness grips my stomach, yet I feel an amazing rush of strength. As if from a distance, I watch myself take action.

I break a branch off a young willow for a weapon, a silly, thin stick. Pushing through the rough greenery that hides my path in damp shadow, I can't see where to step. Sometimes I can't see my feet at all. Hands could reach out and grab my ankles. *Anything* could grab me.

Emma and I approach the end of the lake. I hope Abby will come if she sees me. I don't dare call. Forcing my way to the water's edge I strain to see what I can. No bodies along the shore. I feel a thrill of fear along my spine. A morbid excitement. And so beautiful to see this view of the lake.

I know I should go. Head back, go see if Abby is up by the trail. Have someone call the police. First, I want to check this one area. Just a quick look. I feel detached, surprised at my own courage. But I have to see.

With Emma at my side, I make my way further into the high

grass. Each step a risk. It becomes almost too marshy to pass. My shoe plunges into ankle-deep water. Then the other, cold. I have to walk by feel, testing and stepping, sticky and cold. Then the ground firms up, and the shrubs grow further apart too. Grass flows between them like rivers, rippling in the slight breeze.

I see it before Emma does, staring at us through the grass. Oh, shit! Oh shit! The long skinny form gliding through the grass triggers visceral fear. Cougar! Instantly, my status becomes prey. I freeze. My daily life vanishes. I have to gasp for breath. I don't move. The cougar doesn't move. I know to keep eye contact. We stand, watching. It looks at me, pondering my fate. Now it makes sense. The scream. No murder, there was no murder. But it had sounded so human!

The creature watches. The long, thin cat observes me. In dread I stand, looking. I don't know what to do. I don't know what to *do*! Good kitty, please don't eat me. Slow movements, I know I must use slow movements. I stare. My breath comes hard. I show my palm. "Stay." Force of habit.

Emma growls and raises her hackles. Right, Emma. Look big. Bending as little as possible, I pull Emma up into my arms. I hoist her up to my shoulder, her front legs gripping my back. The cat stares. Emma growls. With my free hand I grab the hem of my coat and hold it out like a wing. "Hey! Go! Go home!" I shout, using the deepest voice I can muster. Emma doesn't whimper, or struggle to ditch me and run. She holds on tight and continues to growl.

The cat stares. It licks its lips. I take a step backward. I take another step, praying that I don't stumble. The cougar, still staring, continues a couple of paces in the direction it had been going, toward the lake. Out of sight for a moment, it reappears through the leaves. Then it stops. It twitches its tail. Just the end of its tail. I inch backward. The cat takes a step toward us. I shout again, and wave my arm. "Shooo! Get!" I yell, "Get out of here!"

Emma has stopped growling. Blood runs down my neck because of her claws. Only part of me notices. The cougar hisses. "No, no, no," I shout. "Just go back. Go away!"

I continue to back up, taking tiny steps. I wonder if cougars are attracted to the smell of blood. Some distance builds up between us. Maybe it will leave us alone. I pause. Those staring eyes. They have a worried, slightly indignant look. Or is it cold detachment, calculating the benefits of my demise? I can't read them. I withdraw further. The cat advances the same distance. Then it comes closer still.

What if I throw Emma at it? As I keep backing up, the animal follows, one great leap in distance. One leap away. No, I can't. Not Emma.

"Help! Help!" I cry, with eyes still on the cat. No one can help me. Not in time. "Please let me live!" I beg. Am I addressing God or the cougar? I don't think about it. Whichever will listen, I guess. "I'll be a good person! I won't waste my life! Please, I want to live!" Hearing my own words gives me strength. I keep walking backward through the shrubs, through the tall grass. I trip twice, carrying Emma, wobbling. Somehow, I don't fall.

The giant kitty keeps coming. The enormous, terrifying cat. A vole or mouse, something, scared up from under its feet, darts past my leg. I don't care. The cougar slowly advances. I slowly retreat. Dog over my shoulder, coat open wide, checking behind me for course correction. If I fall it could be death. Will it be death anyway? Here is my death, maybe. My heart races.

The cougar stops. It snarls—all those teeth! My god. My blood stops running. Breath comes so fast I can't think. I see the whole scene from the air above. Looking down, I see the tawny cat, I see myself, holding Emma on my shoulder. Emma growls, snapping me back into place. I shout at the cougar. Such a meek sound I made. No good. I yell again, "Go away!" I hope it will turn then, but it keeps coming. My anger flares. I shout cruel insults. The cat keeps coming. Why should it care? My blood pumps.

Emma shifts and struggles, almost knocking me down. I regain my balance. Every time I peek behind me to check my way, the cougar seems it might pounce. I weave through the hardhack scrub with Emma heavy on my shoulder, clawing and moaning and panting hot damp air into my ear. But together we are big, or maybe confusing. I have to adjust our direction. I want to reach familiar ground.

Ears flattened, the cougar makes a couple of small leaps toward me, slapping the ground with its paws. I spit out my heart, and I think a lung or two. "Shit! No! That's it, pal! You go! Go Away!"

The thin, powerful cat turns sideways to me, looking. The long tail reaches to the ground, then curls upwards. Such a long tail. This cat knows. It knows we are supper, should it choose. I glance around for a rock to throw, anything. A sea of grass and mud surrounds us. And anyway, if I bend over the animal will surely attack. I keep up my slow retreat.

I feel in my pockets. Nothing there. Some treat crumbs. A

roll of dog waste bags. The cougar resumes its slow approach, keeping pace with my retreat. What else do I have? Maybe in my jacket? My phone. My waterlogged phone! I manage to extricate it from my jacket pocket with my one free hand. With a great shout—"raughhhhh!"—I throw the phone with all my might. It hits the mud a yard from my feet, standing on end like a lawn dart. The cougar slows its pace, but doesn't flinch.

I have to do something. I grab the silly roll of poop bags and shout as I throw it. It goes high into the air, right over the cougar. As it flies, the bags unfurl, streaming a waving trail of shiny fluttering plastic between us. Emma growls again, and barks aggressively. The cougar turns with a leap and vanishes from sight through the bushes, gone in an instant. I stare after it, and then I hug Emma. "I think it's gone," I say. I take a few steps to retrieve my phone.

I stand for a while, holding Emma in my arms, afraid to put her down. I can't see any activity through the shrubs, but that doesn't mean much. I look in the other direction. We've nearly reached that same alder that I tried to climb.

Afraid to turn around, I walk quickly but still mostly backward in case the cat's eyes are on us. I carry Emma. She's had enough of this whole thing and struggles to get down. She growls. Not at me. We are both in shock. And then, I trip over something in the grass and fall flat, tossing Emma in the process.

I push myself to my feet, covered in water from the mud. Emma strains on the leash. I don't make it quite all the way up. I fall again. But this time, Abby breaks my fall. Abby! I roll over and sit up. I've tripped over Abby. The dogs sniff each other. I grab Abby's collar, hook her to the leash, then pick her up and kiss her. Warm tears wet my cheeks. We've made it back to the little trail.

A siren approaches, then blue lights flash from the shoulder out on the road. The noise stops, the lights don't. Remaining vigilant about the cougar, I carry Abby, staggering back along the narrow path with Emma leading. I still have Abby under my arm when we near the paved trail. There, an officer, two cyclists, and an elderly man stand staring at us.

The female cyclist says, "Oh my god!"

The officer asks, "Are you all right? Was that you screaming, ma'am?" She steps down onto the narrow trail to meet me.

"Well, yes, but not as loud as the cougar, I don't think. I thought someone was being murdered!"

"Were you attacked?" she asks, eyeing the blood on my neck as she helps me up to the trail. "We've had several calls," she continues. "That pair of cougars was sighted just north of here."

"Pair?" I repeat.

"Yes, ma'am. Are you okay?"

"Yeah, I'm all right," I say. I wonder if the dogs and I will be late getting back. The world looks oddly bright. Abby wiggles. I set her gently on the pavement.

Two more police cars arrive. A door slams. "Everything okay here?"

I look at Emma. She stares back at me with those pale, blue, penetrating eyes. "Emma and I just defeated a cougar," I say with pride.

Good for the Gander

In this story,
human characters have personalities
based on several animals owned by Leslie and Elwood:

Maggie—a Mountain Cur
is the inspiration for "Maggie" Margaret Ida Griffin.

Waco—a Blue Heeler (Australian Cattle Dog)
is the inspiration for "Theo" Constable Theodore Wakefield.

Zeke—a Red Heeler (Australian Cattle Dog)
is the inspiration for "Zeke" Ezekiel Hammond.
With age, Zeke's coat has grown mostly white.

Francis—the family cat
is the inspiration for Maggie's adult son
Francis Mackerel Stripes.

Other characters:
Kitty is cat-like.
Lollie is German Shepherd-like.
Joseph Frye is Husky-like.

Maggie

Naco

ZEKE

Francis

Although Margaret Ida Griffin did not care for the rain, nothing in this world could keep her from her daily walk. She stood on the edge of the Quincy Street wharf, gazing across the inlet. Tiny drops pattered on the fabric of her big black umbrella, accompanied by the slosh of waves against the pilings and the cry of gulls overhead. Two bald eagles perched on the railing, lazy and full of fish.

The dark, threatening skies of that springtime afternoon were not typical. Maggie sniffed the salt air. And now, the hairs on the back of her neck prickled. Something felt wrong. Before she could fully register this impression, a piercing shriek made her jump. Behind her, near the landward end of the pier, a cluster of people had gathered. Maggie strained to see. Several men stood over something on the shore and a sobbing lady swooned, embraced by her husband.

"Oh dear!" Maggie exclaimed, lifting her fine wool skirts to rush along the uneven hardwood. Had someone drowned? Her umbrella dragged in the wind like a sail, so she took a moment to close it and button the strap. Panting, she reached the end of the pier and looked down into the shadows at the foot. Oh no! It was a woman's form they'd gathered around. Half in, half out of the water, her feet poked out of the puff of a red dress that floated in the lapping tide. A saloon girl? Maggie strained to see more. Theo had arrived, along with another constable.

A view opened between the shoulders of two of the men in the huddle. Maggie glimpsed the face. Covered in bruises, mostly at the throat. Stomach-turning. Maggie gasped. "Kitty!" Now it was Maggie who wanted to swoon. Constable Theodore

Wakefield, down below, noticed her for the first time. He leapt up onto the deck, showing the vigor of a much younger and less portly man, and grabbed her by an arm to keep her steady.

"Don't look, Maggie!" He barked the words, not meaning to, and did his best to hustle her off the dock and away from the scene. In shock, she craned to see as he guided her toward the street, but the shadows and her aging vision made it impossible to see anything more.

"Stay right here, Maggie. Wait, will you?" the constable said as they reached Water Street. "I'll return shortly to walk you home." Beneath an awning, he set an apple box on its end and gestured as if it were a velvet armchair. Maggie nodded but simply stood. Theo glanced at her and then trotted, puffing, back down to the crime scene. Maggie stood for a long time, staring into the distance, shaking her head now and then. Eventually, when Theo returned with his white-haired pal Zeke, they found her seated on the apple box.

"Maggie," Zeke said apprehensively, raising his hat.

"Ezekiel," Maggie said.

The front of Constable Theo's uniform was drenched with salt water. His coat sleeves dripped onto the sidewalk. Maggie looked sideways at him. She sighed. "Even now, Theo," she said. "You couldn't resist splashing in the water, could you." Theo eyed the curb, and then his eyes traced an arc across the underside of the awning as he pretended not to hear. He offered his sodden arm to Maggie and she rose and walked with him, letting him hold her umbrella. Zeke wisely positioned himself on the other side of Theo. Although "the fellows" were her friends, Maggie had never forgiven Zeke for a past offense.

The three of them climbed the hill a block to Maggie's street and then walked for a dozen more to reach her home near the end of the bluff. Along the way, they spoke very little and ignored the sweeping misty ocean views and the glimpses of the downtown area at the base of the cliff below. As they neared her house, Maggie dabbed her eyes and asked Theo what was to be done about catching the murderer.

"You can be sure, Maggie, that the force will make every effort to apprehend the assailant and bring him straight to justice," he replied.

"But what is it that will be done?" she demanded.

"Well, you know, the police departments as far away as Seattle will be contacted by telephone. There will be a report in the paper; perhaps someone witnessed something."

"Will there be an investigation?"

Theo looked uncomfortable.

"An investigation, Theo?"

"Yes, of course an investigation! But you must realize that our hands are full. And your friend, she—" he took a breath, "she had a risky occupation. We can't spread our nets too thin! We have legal citizens to protect."

"White people, you mean to say," Maggie muttered. "Caucasian citizens. What's happened to you, old boy?"

"She was illegal."

Maggie kept silent. She adjusted her hat, looking off toward the water with a frown.

Theo continued, "It was kind, Maggie, your attempt to help her. You tutored her in English, isn't that right?"

"And with reading." Maggie sniffed and wiped her eyes again. Then she added, "Kitty planned to become a dressmaker, to live in San Francisco."

"That was her dream?" Theo asked.

"Yes, after her husband disappeared."

"And you say he was one of the Chinamen dumped overboard by Pig Iron Kelly."

"Apparently. That's what she said to me."

Looking at the ground, Theo shook his head. "With a half pig of iron bound to him, probably. He was on his way here from Canada to join her, correct?"

"I believe so."

"Oh yes, Kelly dumped that load of Celestials straight in the path of an oncoming revenue boat," Theo said. "Dreadful."

"That's what they say. One of a number of groups cast overboard by the smugglers, sadly," Zeke said. "We all know it."

Maggie sighed. "And now, this," she said. "Try to find her murderer, Theo. Please try."

They'd reached her house. Maggie said goodbye to Theo. She looked at Zeke. The thought occurred to her that, as the town undertaker, he'd be the one to prepare Kitty for the next world. The idea made her lip curl slightly. She guessed they'd already be delivering Kitty to his parlor. "Good day, Ezekiel," she said, and went indoors to seek solace in a cup of tea.

The next day found Maggie standing before her husband's grave, speaking out loud to him as she often did when she felt at a loss about a situation. The headstone read:

JOHN RUSSELL AIREDALE

B 1833

D 1894

Maggie had brought a few small branches of dogwood flowers from the back garden to lay on the mound. "I don't know what the world is coming to, my dear Jack," she said softly. "There's so much unpleasantness, so much hostility. Now Kitty's gone, in a terrible way. It's just awful."

Bird song and sunlight filled the cemetery that day. The rhododendrons bloomed in pink and lavender and white. A doe and two fawns busily trimmed the grass a few plots away. Lovely and tranquil landscaping surrounded her, but Maggie felt too riled up to care. After several minutes of silence, she added, "You know, Jack, I don't believe the police will make much of an effort to find the murderer. I've decided to look into the matter myself."

And Maggie didn't waste any time. On her way home, she made a right turn to walk along the road that bordered the south end of town, where the estuary lay. She'd usually see herons there, fishing among the grasses and pickleweed, and sometimes a river otter or two down by the water. More importantly, a certain man lived in a shack just back from that road.

Joseph Frye had been mentioned by Kitty several times. Maggie couldn't remember exactly, but she knew the man had harassed her. This same Joseph had tried to steal Maggie's son's dogs during the gold rush, back when every worthless scoundrel stole dogs to sell. *Stupid man*, thought Maggie. *Francis and Cathryn had only the two Dachshunds at the time. Imagine using Dachshunds as sled dogs in Alaska!*

It was the only lead Maggie had, and she planned to follow it. Joseph's shack stood among other outbuildings off of Lawrence, just on the edge of town. She turned uphill on that street and picked her way along the muddy path to his door.

No one answered her knock. She didn't hear anyone snoring. She cracked the door open and found the smelly little room unoccupied. Not a surprise, really. The man surely spent all his time downtown, drinking and carousing like others of his kind. Maggie stepped in, breathing through her handkerchief, to nose around for clues. She had no idea what she was searching for but the shack had nothing in it, anyway. Only a makeshift bed and some soiled clothes on the floor.

Not one to give up easily, Maggie went out back to poke around in the other sheds. She found the landowner's smokehouse. She peeked through the doorway. The empty shed had no clues to offer but certainly smelled good. As Maggie stepped inside to inhale the aroma, she remembered that she ought to put in an order soon for some jarred salmon. But someone shoved her from behind! Forced a few steps forward, she nearly fell. The door slammed shut! Maggie turned to push the door open but heard a stick rammed through the hasp.

"Hey!" she shouted. "Let me out! What are you doing? Let me out!"

She stood, her body tense, listening for any reply. She couldn't hear anything.

"Let me out!" she howled.

Someone banged on the wall of the shed several times. Then a man made a growling noise. A choked, husky voice said, "It's your fault, old woman. You made the bitch think she was something."

Maggie bared her teeth and snarled, "Let me out of here, you sarding and scurvy mare-buggering son of a blaggard!"

After a moment of shocked silence, the husky growl came again. "Shut up, bitch, or I'll give you something to wail about!"

The sound of a man spitting some distance off, followed by the absence of his nasty odor, let Maggie know that despite her further protests and demands to be released, he had gone away. As she stood holding up her skirts to keep them clear of the greasy soot, stripes of light from between vertical boards fell on the flower design of the fabric of her dress. She looked at the shed walls. They were too sturdy to kick her way out. She listened for signs of anyone in the area. Several times she heard a wagon on the road, or voices somewhere, and she called out repeatedly. And between times, she waited.

Late that same afternoon, Maggie's son Francis escorted her over to the courthouse. They entered Theo's stuffy office. After he invited them to sit, Theo shook his finger at Maggie. "You might have been in that shed for days had those children not heard you howling!" he said. "What were you thinking, Maggie! That fellow Frye is a dangerous man. He's in and out of jail. All the time."

"That's why I went to see him," Maggie replied.

Theo adjusted his monocle, peering at Maggie through it. He sighed. He stroked the close-cropped white beard on his pointy chin. His brown eyes showed kindness but they had a piercing look too, especially at that moment. "Drop this, Maggie! You'll need to nip this whole idea in the bud. It's preposterous! You're not a detective. For goodness sake, leave crime-solving to the police!" He turned to Francis. "Sonny, it's imperative that you keep an eye on your mother. You know she has her own mind. It's not right for a lady, especially someone of mature age, to put herself in danger this way! She ought to stay out of the downtown area entirely. No more of these walks along the shore! And poking through the belongings of a miscreant—my word!"

"Yes, sir," Francis said. He glanced at Maggie and then stared out the window.

"But what have you learned about the culprit so far?" asked Maggie.

Theo sat up in his chair. "Great Scott, Maggie, it's only been a day!"

"Well, keep in mind what that man Joseph said to me."

"We will, Maggie. But it doesn't prove anything, one way or the other."

Maggie leaned forward. "Not what he said, no. It's a clue, however."

"How's that?"

"It's a clue because it shows he knew I tutored Kitty. It shows he has . . . had . . . an interest."

"All right, that's a good point. It is." Theo stood. "Now, let it all rest. Go home!" He waved the two of them away. "My word, Maggie," he said. He came around his desk to show them to the door.

Maggie licked her lips. "One more thing, Theo. Who's taking care of the funeral arrangements?"

"Kitty's . . . er . . . landlady is handling that."

"What's her name?"

"I don't know."

"Yes, you do."

"Lollie. Lollie Schafer."

Theo had supplied the information Maggie needed. The following afternoon she paid a call at the establishment where she felt fairly certain Kitty had been employed. She found a young woman loitering on the front walkway and told her that she wished to speak to Lollie.

The girl grinned, and said, "Of course, dear." She told Maggie to wait, that she would return in a moment. Maggie stood uncomfortably at the corner of the building for quite some time. She began to think that the young woman wouldn't come back. At last a door on the side of the building opened and the same woman peeked out, giggling. She gestured for Maggie to enter there, and led her down a narrow hallway to a small room. It had a red Persian carpet and was furnished with a few chairs, a cabinet, and a writing desk. An ornate plant stand held a delightful Art Nouveau lamp. Again, Maggie had a long wait. Music came from down the hall, and the sound of laughter. Besides the odor of cigar smoke, it smelled good in the room; not the scent of perfume but the smell of herbs. Behind the glass of the cabinet door she saw several pots and tinctures with Chinese writing on the labels.

Eventually, a lady made her entrance. Adorned in pearls and European finery, she whisked in and seated herself in one of the chairs, spreading her purple and scarlet dress so it wouldn't wrinkle. "Sit, von't you?" she said, motioning toward the other beautifully upholstered armchair.

Maggie sat.

Lollie must have been slightly younger than Maggie, though it was difficult to be certain of her age. She wore makeup and had eyebrows painted on. But she did have attractive features.

She sat facing Maggie. "I'm a busy voman," she said. "But I must admit, I'm curious. Who are you and vhy did you come to see me?"

At that moment, a Toy Poodle with a pink bow trotted into the room. It went straight to Maggie and licked her fingers. "Trinket!" Maggie said. It occurred to her that she hadn't seen Kitty's dog at the pier the other day. Kitty always brought her dog with her when she went for her stroll.

"Ah, you're Maggie," Lollie said.

"Yes, I'm Maggie. Did Kitty mention me?"

"Von or two times, rest her soul."

"I took care of little Trinket sometimes for her," Maggie said, lifting the dog to her lap. "She'd say 'Take care of my little dog for me, will you Maggie?' and I'd end up with Trinket for several days. I didn't mind."

Trinket jumped down and started tugging at Maggie's hem.

"Leave off!" Lollie swatted at the dog to make it stop.

"Oh, it doesn't bother me, really."

"It's a small yapping rat."

"Kitty loved her."

"Vhy did you come here?" Lollie asked. "You vant the dog, take it." She started to stand.

"I thought you might know something about what happened to Kitty," Maggie said.

Lollie sat down again. She leaned forward to look at Maggie. "You the police? You don't look like the police. Vhy do you care? She's dead. You can't undo that."

"The police aren't going to find her murderer. I thought you might have an idea who it was. I want justice for Kitty."

"Justice? Never there will be justice. Anyway, I don't know anything."

"There was no one tormenting her, or causing concern?"

"Ve have a bouncer here, Elmer. He takes care of those types. Don't vorry. Now, be smart. Go home."

"You don't know anything that might help me find out who did it?"

Lollie dabbed her eyes with a silk napkin. She sniffed and sighed, then she wailed, "I can't bear to talk about vhat happened to Kitty! So sad. I'm back to my business now. Lizzie vill show you out. Take that dog if you vant."

Maggie ended up with Kitty's Toy Poodle, but no more answers than she'd started with. That evening she let Trinket play in her backyard while Francis did some repairs on her gazebo.

Surrounded by a high cedar fence, and set well back from the cliff's edge, the yard offered privacy but no view of the strait. The house itself had, over the treetops, views of the water, the islands, and the mountains beyond. Low hedges trimmed the perfect lawn of the front yard, where neat roses grew up a trellis, shading the marble birdbath. But behind the house, only the efforts of a pair of goats and several ducks held back the jungle.

They sat while Francis took a rest and gazed out over the scene, sipping coffee. "Your goats do enjoy the mounds, though," he commented.

Jack R. Airedale, mining engineer, had borne an obsession with digging. High mounds and small pits filled the yard, along with a few garden beds, a root cellar, and a rather large pond. Trinket thought the whole place wonderful, except for the goats.

"Mother . . ." Francis sighed, petting the dog, "I'm sorry, Mother, but you simply shouldn't have kept up your acquaintance with someone from that profession. You've invested a great deal since our arrival here to build a genteel reputation. Kitty was a sweet girl, but this whole thing was bound to happen. I'm sad to see you in such grief."

"She was an easy target for that woman Lollie after her husband died. What should I have done? She needed help. She had dreams, Sonny. She had dreams of a better life."

"You've a heart of gold. You do. And I probably shouldn't mention this, but can't help myself: This afternoon I saw old Zeke walking arm and arm with that Joseph Frye. They both looked three sheets to the wind, and lacking ballast too, for all that!"

"What? Are you certain? Joseph Frye? But where, Francis?"

"They were attempting to climb the steps at Zeke's, I didn't wait to see if they made it in the door."

"But he lives above the funeral parlor!"

"I know. It was all quite odd."

"That Ezekiel. Why am I surprised?"

"Now, Mother. He's not a bad fellow. You need to let go. It's been a quarter century since the article. It's old news."

Maggie lifted her eyebrows and tilted her head, "Has it? That many years?" She shook herself. "Those were biting words, though. We were new in town. He shamed me for my heritage. For my childhood in the mountains."

"You should try to forgive him. It was only a gossip column. He was a drunk in those days, mourning the loss of his Indian wife, remember? He's told me the story several times. He went after any newcomer. He had his hackles up because it was immigrants that carried the diphtheria that killed his Minnie."

"Yes, well, lashing out is a poor way to heal pain."

"Well, wouldn't forgiveness be a good way?" Francis didn't

dare look his mother in the eye after saying that, but stood up and set to work again on the gazebo. A few minutes later he called, "Shall I go ahead and build a new floor in this thing? The old one has some rot."

"No!" replied Maggie. "Leave the floor alone today, Sonny. My only concern is the trim."

It was nearly a month later that Maggie treed her prey. She'd been out with Trinket for his evening stroll, and as they reached her front walk she saw a man peeking in the window of her library. A shabby, shaggy man. She knew him. Joseph Frye!

He noticed her and bolted, heading down the block toward town. Maggie trotted after him along the sidewalk, carrying her dog and waving her umbrella like a baton. Joseph ran into the park and climbed a tree, attempting to hide in the darkness. He certainly didn't expect the old lady to follow him.

Maggie stood at the base of the maple, brandishing her umbrella. Trinket yapped full steam with glee. "You, there!" Maggie called to a passing boy. Then while he stood with big eyes and mouth open, she instructed him to fetch Francis, who lived only a few houses away. When Francis arrived he told Maggie he'd sent the boy to fetch the police. They waited under the tree, with the man swearing at them.

Theo was on duty, and it didn't take him long to appear from the direction of the courthouse. He rushed at the tree, grabbing its trunk and glowering up into the branches. "Oh, it's you. Just come on down, Tom. We'll have no more of this!"

The man stared at Maggie as if he wondered whether the cop could protect him. Then he began to ease his way down the tree.

"Tom?" Maggie asked. "I thought this was Joseph."

"No, this is Squirrely Tom. What was he doing that you ran him up a tree, you two?"

"I caught him peeping in the window of my house!" Maggie replied.

"He didn't open the window or anything?"

"No. He may have been about to do so."

Theo turned to the man and waved his finger at him. "You go on, now, Thomas! You go on home. But if I hear of you pulling this kind of thing again, I'll drag you straight to jail! You understand?"

Tom nodded meekly, and then scurried off. They watched him until he'd crossed the park. Theo said softly, "That man won't bother you again. He's a half-wit. Nervous fellow. Never done anyone any real harm." But then he addressed Maggie specifically, "You thought he was Joseph Frye?"

"Well, yes. He looks much like the man."

"I don't know about that, but you needn't keep worrying about Joseph. He has disappeared. No one's seen him for weeks." He paused. "I have to say, Maggie. I was hoping not to see you in a professional capacity again quite so soon!"

"He's escaped? Got away with murder?"

"Easy, now, Maggie. We don't know that he killed Kitty. I must say, though, you were right about him! He was a former client of hers. Obsessed! Wouldn't leave her alone! Followed her around town. He beat her a couple of times. No one has seen him lately, though. I imagine he's moved on. He's no danger to anyone around here anymore."

"He went somewhere, Theo. What about justice?" Francis

said this before Maggie could get her mouth open. But it did no good. What could the police do? If the man had gone, he was free to roam.

When Maggie walked into the funeral parlor a few days later, Zeke had his back to her, unpacking jars from a carton labeled *Hill Mortuary Supply*. She watched him for a moment, and then coughed.

He turned. "My dear lady, what are you doing here?" he said softly. After shoving the bottles into a mahogany cabinet, he hurried over to greet Maggie, wiping his hands with a cloth and licking his lips. He pulled out a chair for her at a table. "Please, sit."

"Thank you," she said.

"Maggie, what brings you to my parlor?" he asked, drawing up a chair for himself. "I don't believe you've ever been here, outside of a funeral. Jack's was a beautiful ceremony, wasn't it. Oh! But I'm forgetting my manners!" He stood up. "Would you like some coffee? A molasses cookie?" His eyes bulged, the whites showed like big crescent moons.

Maggie chuckled. "I'm not going to bite you, Ezekiel." "Although I probably should," she added in a less friendly tone. "I'm fine. I've just had a cup, and a muffin."

Silence fell upon the two.

Zeke mentioned that she had a particularly nice hat.

More silence.

Finally, Maggie spoke again, "A short while ago, Francis saw you carousing with Joseph Frye. The word uptown is that you'd stopped drinking years back. I guess not."

Zeke twiddled his thumbs and avoided her eye.

"Ezekiel, are you drinking?"

"No!" he squeaked, "No, only that once. Or maybe a few times. But, yes. I did tip back a few with Frye."

"Did you poison him?"

"What's that?"

"Did you poison the man?"

"Maggie! What? What are you talking about?"

"You might as well be straight with me. I'm not a fool. I know that you and Theo detested that feist nearly as much as I did." She sniffed. "Tell me the truth, I'll not go anywhere with it. I only want to know."

Zeke peered at her and then mentioned that he required a glass of lemonade. Was she sure she wouldn't like one? All right, she'd have a glass.

Some clinking and clanking happened in the other room, and the bang of an icebox door. Zeke reappeared with two lemonades, looking ruffled. Then he sat and quietly told Maggie the story.

"No, it's not what you're probably thinking. I figured what's good for the goose is good for the gander, that's all. I nipped into that saloon a few blocks down on the corner, for a quick drink. Only to wet my whiskers. Frye came in, he was a regular there. The guy was drinking himself into a stupor. I decided to help him along. Got him very drunk and then I invited him to have one last look at Kitty. We walked up here. I left the guy in this very room, went down to the basement to tap a keg, and returned with a flask in my pocket. Embalming fluid, mixed into some whiskey."

Maggie gasped. "You killed him!"

"Now, just listen please, Maggie. When I returned, the guy had gone into the back room and he'd opened her coffin, for

Christ's sake. I grabbed his hand, just as he reached to touch her, and offered him another drink. Frye looked at Kitty, so beautiful lying there, and began to sob, the lout. He accepted the drink.

"The next morning I just carted him right down to the docks. Who's going to question an undertaker with a motionless body in a pine box? I sold him to the first ship's mate I saw. More than likely he woke up at sea, and he's now living his life as a deck swab. That's right, I simply helped him to be crimped. Not so unusual in this town, is it, after all?

"So, you see, you're safe," Zeke said, finding the courage to rest his eyes on Maggie for more than a glance. "The man won't be back. And if it helps you to know, I've used the money to order a nice monument for Kitty at County Cemetery."

Zeke's story got Maggie thinking. The very next day she and Trinket went over to Francis's house for a visit with the family. She had an enormous number of grandchildren, and adored each one. When the time came to leave, she asked if Francis would mind going to fetch the pony and trap. Within an hour, the two had searched County Cemetery. The Chinese section had no fresh graves. Only a new sailor in the Soldiers and Sailors area. Francis suggested that Kitty might have been buried at Laurel Grove, or elsewhere.

"Theo specifically said County Cemetery. He'd know," Maggie said. "Would you drive me to town, Sonny?"

Along the way, she shared the story Zeke had told her. "It was his 'good for the goose' comment that struck me. Why would he say that? Do you know what, I don't think Kitty is dead."

"Whoa!" Francis cried, pulling up the horse. He turned to stare at Maggie. "You don't think Kitty's dead? What are you talking about?"

"Well, Ezekiel subdued Joseph and snuck him out of town by placing him in a stupor."

"Umm, yes?"

"And he said, 'Good for the goose.' You see, I think an herb was used to paralyze Kitty so she'd appear dead. Not the embalming fluid that Zeke used, but something that would make her truly seem dead. As in Romeo and Juliet."

"But why? What would be the point of that? She wasn't a prisoner at the brothel. She'd no need to sneak out of town."

"Ah, but that Joseph was at her heels all the time. And there were others like him. She'd saved up some money, she told me so. But, I gather she couldn't leave town without that Joseph following. She would have always had to worry about those men looking her up. Likely Joseph would be blamed for her death, or at least this would put an end to his infatuation with her."

Francis sat for a moment. "You could be right," he said, finally. "But, Mother, she was covered in bruises."

"Yes, but Ezekiel is an expert with makeup. And so is Lollie. The one who had control over the funeral arrangements. Do you know what else? I noticed, when I went to see Lollie—"

"You what?"

"I went to see her. How did you think I ended up with Trinket?"

"Well, I assumed someone delivered the dog to you!"

"No, no, I went to visit Lollie to enquire about suspects. And," she peered at Francis, squinting an eye, "while I was there I noticed herbs and tinctures. A large collection of them. Lollie is, apparently, an herbalist."

"And, that's where we are going right now."

"Yes, to pay a call on Lollie," Maggie grinned.

"I should be having my nap. Curled up on the sofa. Instead, here I am on the way to a bawdyhouse. Cathryn would not be happy about this."

"You should tell her, though. It's not wise to keep secrets from your wife." Maggie lifted her chin and folded her hands, adding, "And please don't use that sort of language!"

Francis laughed. He clucked to the horse and they started on their way again.

As they approached that same side door of the brothel, the one Maggie had used on her previous visit, she stopped to whisper something else to her son. "Do you know, not only did this woman and Zeke help Kitty leave town, I believe Theo assisted them."

Francis pursed his lips and nodded, looking up at the sky, thinking. It made sense that if Zeke had acted to protect Kitty, and then got rid of Joseph to protect Maggie, Theo might have been involved also, despite his vocation. Zeke and Theo had been chums for years.

Francis knocked on the door. A curtain parted slightly in a nearby window. Nothing else happened. It took several tries. Eventually the door opened, and they were shown to the same study where Lollie had received Maggie previously. On this occasion, Lollie neglected to appear until a generous sum was offered to reimburse her for taking up her valuable time.

She put up with Maggie's friendly but rather shocking interrogation, and managed to answer every question while providing absolutely no information. Finally, though, she gave an exasperated sigh and said, "Listen, Sunshine, I'm mindful of your efforts to help some of these Chinese. You treated Kitty so kindly. Therefore, I vill tell you this. But after, you leave the whole thing alone. Forget about it. Okay?"

Maggie spoke truthfully, "I only want to understand what happened. We won't bother you again after this, ma'am."

Lollie regarded them both for a moment. "You von't talk to the authorities?"

Francis spoke up to reassure her. "We won't repeat your words to anyone," he said.

Lollie paused again, apparently assessing the situation. "All right, sen," she said, "I'll explain to you. But I'm afraid it vill be unhappy news.

"The things you say—you're very smart—you've figured out much of vhat happened. I did give Kitty some medicinal powder to help her sleep, make her seem dead. So she could fool people and be free from that Frye und those other men also, diese Schweinehoden. I took care of the funeral arrangements und asked the mortician to help Kitty get to the boat. But he did not take my money. He refused to take money at all. He, along vith his police friend, they took care of everything."

Lollie paused. She glanced around the room as if she wanted to run and hide. "To help Kitty," she continued, "I gave her somesing from ze Chinese doctor across the street. Dried powder of hòh tyùhn. It means river suckling-pig. Zeir vord for pufferfish. Dried powder of pufferfish. To help her sleep.

"But Kitty, she took too much powder. Und she departed this life for real. I told her take one pinch. One small pinch. She took too much. Those men load her onto a boat. They didn't know she vas indeed deceased."

"No, that can't be!" Maggie whispered.

"She's dead, all right. I'm sorry to say. Such a shame. An uncommonly pretty girl. A nice girl. Gone for good. Now you go home, ma'am. Stay on The Hill. Stay out of trouble." Lollie nodded to both of them, got up and left the room.

Although it saddened Maggie to hear of what had truly happened to Kitty, she felt glad that at least she knew. She did stay home after visiting Lollie, not because of the woman's advice, but because mourning required it. Her sorrow about Kitty made her not want to go anywhere outside of her own grounds, other than to visit Francis and the grandchildren. But one day a package arrived for her and she took a walk downtown to retrieve it.

Maggie stood on the wooden sidewalk in front of Rothschild's on Water Street with a pouch marked "Wells, Fargo, & Co. Express." It had been shipped from San Francisco. Inside she found a beautifully embroidered square of yellow silk, with birds and flowers. A carefully penned note on perfumed paper said only these words: "Care for my little doggie, won't you?"

Just Before Woodstock

The next story involves the personalites of two dogs once
rescued by Theresa. At the time of writing these are quite
elderly dogs, but because of their buoyant and youthful spirits I
have chosen to present their human characters as teenagers.

Theresa's Maggie is a fox-red Golden Retriever mix.

Lucky is a Black Labrador Retriever/Flat-Coated Retriever/Pit
Bull mix.
In this story he is Luke.

Maggie leaned over the railing on the upper deck of the ferry *De-fiance*, ignoring the announcement to get set to disembark. The rumble of the engine slowing the old wooden boat, the churning water, the screech of gulls, it all felt like a personal welcome home to her. She peered through her granny glasses, searching for her friends on the dock.

"Lukie!" she cried. "Luuukie!" Maggie waved and shouted, "Hey, you guys! Hey!—Hey!" She beamed her big smile. Turning to enter the cabin, Maggie soon emerged downstairs on the car deck. A couple of minutes later she reappeared on the upper deck to grab her backpack. She flashed the peace sign at her friends and made for the stairs again.

Maggie had to wait for the cars before she could go. The ferry worker scowled at her, but she didn't notice. After charging across the ramp, she met her friends with outstretched arms for a hug. "How was Mexico?" they asked.

Maggie replied from inside the colorful, patchouli-scented group hug, "Oh, man, it was fantastic! Hey, where's my parents?" She poked her head out to look around.

"Did you tell them you were coming?" Alice asked in her smooth rabbit-like voice. Alice, with her long straight blonde hair and deep amber eyes, had known Maggie since first grade.

"Oh—I don't know," Maggie said. "Maybe not. But I made it in time for the moon landing!" she cried. "We gonna watch it at your place? Ha-HA!" She burst free from the group and tried to ruffle Luke's hair. He had a huge natural; he looked a lot like Jimi Hendrix. "Your hair's bigger!" she laughed.

"Let's go hang out by the water for a while," Luke suggested.

"Yeah! Old times!" Maggie said.

Soon they were sitting in the shade, passing a joint, and Maggie's head rested on the crossed leg of one of the girls. "Tell us about your journey!" said someone.

Maggie talked about her five months hitching and riding buses and cattle trucks down to Guatemala. She showed off her new Mayan *huipil* and her new crop of freckles, and how her silky auburn hair had bleached to a strawberry blonde at the top. Then she leaned her head on the boy next to her.

"Hey, Maggie," Luke said. "I saw a ghost at your house!"

"No way," Maggie replied.

"Yeah, I really did. I was helping Steve clean the gutters and it was getting dark. There was this guy, just standing, looking at us. Right out there by your gazebo. I could sort of see through him!"

"No WAY!" Maggie cried. "How cool is that! I wonder if he'll come back!" she said, sitting up. "I wanna see him!"

"What did he look like?" asked Kat, a girl in a peace sign T-shirt. She wore a narrow beaded headband.

"Well, he had, like, old-fashioned clothes on. Like, from the eighteen hundreds."

Kat gulped and coughed, handing the joint along. "A ship's captain, maybe. Or a smuggler?"

"I think he was a farmer or something, a Chinese cat," Luke replied.

Brainzy Marc spoke up, "Well, that makes sense, man. A lot of Chinese folks suffered around here back in the day. You know, when the Exclusion stuff was happening."

"Shit."

"Yeah, I know," he said.

"How long did he stay there?" Maggie asked.

"I dunno, about, oh, ten minutes? Five. Well, maybe just a few minutes, I guess. He appeared and then he went away," Luke said.

"Where'd he go?" Marc asked.

"He just faded, dummy. He's a ghost," said Luke.

"You're just yanking our chain, aren't ya, Luke? You love to yank people's chains," Marc said.

"No, man, I saw him. And anyway I don't pull on the leash or yank people's chains, or whatever. I'm a really nice guy."

"Yep, that's true," Maggie declared. She laughed and reached to scratch him behind the ear. Luke tilted his head and leaned toward her. "Who's a good boy?" she said. "Such a good boy." She scooted forward, cradled his jaw with her fingers, and through puckered lips added, "Look at dat diddle sweet face!" She kissed his cheek. Luke nudged her with his nose before resting his head on her shoulder.

Alice agreed. "Yeah, Luke's a sweetheart. We love you, Luke." She patted him too.

He smiled a big smile. His puppy dog eyes looked droopy and happy and very puppy doggish indeed. "I do growl at burglars," he said.

Alice laughed. "Well, that's different."

When the sunlight had faded noticeably, Maggie thought she should get home. Luke went with her even though he lived downtown. He didn't feel ready to say goodnight. "I missed you, Maggie-Pie," he said.

"Come with me next time!" Maggie grabbed his hand and the two of them climbed the hill a block to Maggie's street, and then walked for a dozen more to reach her family's beautiful

Victorian near the end of the bluff. Along the way, they could peek between houses for sweeping ocean views and glimpses of the downtown area at the foot of the cliff below.

Port Townsend's disappointments a hundred years before had nearly left it a ghost town. Buildings abandoned and left standing became frozen in time, never facing remodel or replacement as they would have in a thriving community. These days, people had begun to seep back in, people who appreciated the many Victorian-era buildings and remarkable Northwest Coast scenery. Boards were coming off windows, artists were painting bright colors on walls. But the town didn't have enough going on to keep Maggie anchored. Not yet, anyway.

After a joyful supper with her parents and an evening of sharing stories and small treasures, Maggie sat in her room, cuddling her cat and staring up at her dusty collection of horse models. Before she got into bed, she stood by her window to absorb the ocean view. But what the heck! A light flashed just outside the old gazebo in her yard. It might have been Maggie's imagination. There! She saw it again. With a hard stare to see through the darkness, she wondered if it could be one of her friends pranking her with a lighter or something. She couldn't see anything down there. Tiredness had made her eyes flaky, that's all. She'd had a long trip home.

Maggie's crowd of friends decided to investigate this ghost. Early afternoon of the following day found them by the lily pad pond in Maggie's backyard, munching on potato chips and sipping from tall blue plastic glasses the same orange drink that the astronauts would bring to the moon. Most were sitting around smoking and talking about the ghost, but Luke and another guy were pawing through the ornamental grass between the broccoli bed and the little Victorian gazebo. "This is right about where he was," Luke said. "Hey Maggie, can you get me a shovel?"

"You can't dig up my parents' grass! What are you thinking, Lukie? Dad would have a fit!"

"Umm," Alice piped up, "wait." She'd been holding some chips, she crammed them into her mouth and said with her mouth full, "Uh, I think you should start over there." She pointed to a spot on the south side of the yard, by the weathered cedar fence. She got up and started in that direction. Turning, she saw everyone watching her, but no one moved or said anything. She reached her destination and looked around. "Guys, come here. There's something here."

Maggie arrived first. She took a gulp of juice and looked around. "What do you mean?" she asked.

"Man, I don't know! It's just . . . I got this strong feeling. It started just a minute ago. This is where we gotta look." Alice started scratching at the fence with a stick. "You know I'm about as psychic as a rock, Maggie, but this feeling is really strong."

"I imagine rocks are pretty psychic, Alice!" Luke said, as he and the rest of the friends stood looking at the fence. "Imagine being a rock; sitting around quietly since the Hadean Era. That's very Zen, you know." He looked up at the sky. "I had a feeling, too, that we should look for something hidden somewhere. Like that ghost wants to show us something."

"Me too!" Maggie whispered.

The youngest girl, Becca, decided to go home at this point. After a hug from Maggie, she left through the white picket gate. One of the guys borrowed a skinny iron walking-staff from a large garden gnome. He started tapping on things. As the other kids hunted for writing on the fence or anything strange in the tomato bed, Roger hit several places on the bare path with his tapping bar. One spot had a distinctly hollow sound. Everyone looked at one another.

Maggie fetched a couple of shovels from the shed. The group huddled around the hollow-sounding place while she and one of the boys turned the hard-packed earth over with gusto. About a foot down they hit something solid. "Do you think it's treasure?"

"What if it's a coffin?"

This thought made the kids silent for a moment. After all, the latter was the more likely of the two suggestions.

With the shovels they scraped away at the layer of dirt. Roger tapped again. Whatever they'd hit made the thunk of metal. Crowding around, the kids used their hands to brush away the remaining soil to reveal an old round manhole cover. About two feet across, it was a plate of cast iron with concentric braided rope designs and a waffle texture. It had to be very old.

"Wow, gorgeous!" Marc exclaimed. "I bet this is worth something!"

"Sewer cover?" Luke asked.

"I don't know," Maggie said, "but there's one way to find out!" She headed back to the shed for a crowbar.

Maggie strained to pry the lid up, but it must have weighed well over a hundred pounds. With the help of Luke and Roger and the gnome's walking stick, she managed to lift off the cover and slide it to the side. It had fit into a little ledge around what looked like the entrance to a pipe, although the diameter increased in size as it went down. Crowding like hungry pups around a food dish, everyone struggled to see down the hole. Maggie and Luke made a run for flashlights. They found several working ones in the house and garage.

Climbing head-first down the hole, Maggie made a bunch of muffled exclamations before backing out and handing her flashlight to Alice so she could look. "It doesn't look like a sewer," Maggie said. "It has a dirt and rock floor and big wooden support beams. It's some kind of tunnel."

As the other kids took turns looking, Maggie and Alice (who now had a smudge on her nose) agreed that the tunnel had caved-in about twenty feet to the south and filled with rubble, but in the direction of the gazebo, it looked clear and probably fairly stable. The air smelled very bad down there. But how utterly cool— a tunnel! Because they knew Maggie's mom and dad would never let them, the kids decided to explore the tunnel right away. Maggie loved her parents and tried to please them. But her passions had a great deal of influence on her, also. She had a T-shirt that read, *I Gotta Be Me!*

As always, Maggie went first. She thought she'd be fighting spiderwebs, but she didn't see any. The rest of the kids followed close behind her, breathing heavily, scraping up their hands and knees on the rough granite surface of the tunnel floor. They squealed a lot and joked about trolls and bats. The passage curved slightly to the left and back to the right again. Without warning, it opened into a good-sized chamber. "Whoa," said Kat, following Maggie. "No way!"

Shining their flashlights around, they saw a room the size of a small bedroom. Everyone made it inside without the whole thing collapsing on them and all but Roger had room to stand up. A couple of narrow old beds stood in one corner, one stacked on the other, with fragments of ancient bedding still on them. A plank table with benches on either side filled much of the space. The cavern smelled earthy and rich, but only a thin coat of dust lay on things. Only their voices pierced the absolute quiet.

"What is this place?" Luke asked.

Roger pointed to a collection of objects in the harsh shadows on the table. "Look," he said, "there's candles! Let's light them up."

"Wait." Alice held Roger around his skinny waist. "Lighting one won't cause some weird methane gas to explode everything, will it?"

Marc thought for a sec. "I don't think so," he said.

"Hope not," Roger said as he blew the dust off the wick of the half-used candle which still sat in a holder on the table. He flicked his lighter. With a bit of effort, he lit the wick.

"What is this place?" Kat asked.

Roger's face lit up. "Look! A peace pipe! This was an Indian hangout!"

Luke took a look. "You goofball, that's an opium pipe. They have some at the museum."

"Peace pipe? What a dumbshit, Roger!" Marc said. He grabbed and wiggled Roger's cheek.

"Hey! How the hell would I know?" Roger whined, pulling away to snatch Marc's hand. He licked the palm.

"Eew," Marc said, shaking the slobber off his hand.

Alice picked up the pipe. "Is there any opium in the bowl? I wonder if we could smoke it."

"It's probably full of spiders," Maggie said. "Jesus! Don't drop that! It's an antique!"

"Oh wow, look at this! There's all kinds of paraphernalia here!" Luke said. He lit another candle on the first one and held it over a cracked lacquer tray that held various small tools and containers. Beautifully made from brass and ceramic, covered with tiny designs, these items required examination by several of the kids. Luke laughed and said, "What the heck? Your ancestors must have been interesting people, Maggie."

"No joke!"

"Yup, I'd say so." Marc lifted the hinged lid of an old wooden box. "Holy cow, look over here!" he said. He held up a pair of old flintlock blunderbuss pistols. "Look at these guns!"

"Oh my god!" someone shrieked.

Maggie reached for one to examine. The grip end of the gun curved like the handle of a cane. The wide iron barrel flared out on the shooting end slightly, reminding her of a bell. Both the hardwood and metal were etched with intricate designs. Although instruments of death, these were strikingly beautiful.

"Look at that!" Alice whispered. "And there's another one here. Oh, no, this is a telescope. A brass one. Like a ship's mate would have!" She extended it and held it up to her eye.

Kat asked to try. She looked through it. "Can't see anything. It's cool, though."

Alice pointed out that they were in a cave. Then she asked, "Those designs on the gunmetal, are they Chinese?"

"No, definitely not." Maggie said, "They look Egyptian or something."

"They're pretty," Kat whispered.

"No, I think . . . East Indian?" Marc said.

"Well," Roger said, "whatever they are, those guns are super old. I'll bet they're worth something!"

Luke took one to examine. "Yeah, but I don't know, they're all corroded-looking."

Marc stood up, as much as the ceiling would allow him to, and looked around. "Man," he said, "this stuff is from a long time ago. Are there dates on any of these papers?"

A few yellowed, barely readable pieces of paper lay on a small table, and a crate on one of the benches had some more.

"Look at this!" Maggie said, "Old photos!" She set the crate on the table. Carefully, she lifted out some of the material and held it on her forearm up against her chest to thumb through it. She had to shine the flashlight with the same hand she used to sort through them until Alice grabbed the light for her. "Really old," Maggie continued. "These are all pictures of Chinese men. Oh, here's some women. Several photos of one woman, actually. God, she was beautiful. Look, you guys!"

Alice reached to take a look. "Man, she was something! Kitty, it says."

"Huh?"

"Look, written in the corner of this one," Alice said. "Kitty. August 23rd, 1895."

"So, that'd be your grandpa's time?" Luke asked.

"Somethin'."

Marc shook his head. "No, that would be her great-grandpa, probably."

"Well, let me think. My great-great-grandfather built our house in 1882. So, yeah, man, that would be him. My great-GREAT-grandfather!"

"Geez, that's a long time ago!"

Alice handed the photo back to Maggie. "Holy bananas," she said.

They left the guns down there, because they were creepy, and maybe they were loaded. But Maggie took the spyglass and rickety box of papers to her bedroom. They decided not to mention the underground room to Maggie's parents. Not just yet.

A few days went by. Men landed on the moon and Maggie's family watched the whole thing on TV. She spent those days with her extended family, roasting marshmallows at the beach with her cousins and eating tons of watermelon. She didn't see any of her friends other than Luke. When she mentioned the sighting of the ghost to her parents, her mom said, "Really? Coool," and her dad said, "Maggie it's time to come back up the rabbit hole. You need to start thinking about college."

One night, Maggie's brother Steve screamed. She heard her dad yell, "Fire! Everybody get out of the house!" She hurried downstairs and out the back door. A narrow blue-violet flame ran up the wall. In the darkness, that fire lit up part of the garden. Steve headed to the neighbor's to phone for help. Maggie helped her mother and father get a hose hooked up to spray the wall. Her dad blasted the corner of the house. The hose had plenty of pressure but the spray didn't diminish the flames. It took a lot of water before the fire finally died. Afterward, they still heard hissing from the clouds of steam. In the light from the porch, they couldn't see any damage.

While Maggie coiled the hose and her father felt around on the wall with his hands, her mom went to find a flashlight. Luckily, they'd all been returned to their places after going underground. Steve came panting back from next door. They searched the corner of the house with the flashlight. The fire should have charred the wall significantly, but no damage could be found! "Okay, that's spooky," Steve said.

"It's the ghost," Maggie said.

"Fuck, yeah!" Steve said.

"Steve!" said their mom. He apologized to her.

"No, really," Maggie said.

The firemen arrived and dragged a hose to where the family stood at the back of the house. Unfortunately, in so doing, they trampled the mom's primroses in the dark. When they arrived at the spot and heard the news, they stood as dumbfounded as the family, never having seen anything like it.

"The fire reached the height of that upper window?"

"Yes!" Maggie's father said.

"Hmm, maybe there was some chemical on there. Could have been a cool fire, not enough to ignite the wood."

"But we couldn't get it to go out!" Maggie said.

"Did you apply a varnish to that wall today, by any chance?"

"No," replied her dad, "it's just regular paint on there."

"Hmm," said the fireman.

That night Maggie fell asleep spread-eagled on her bed and slept right through supper. Waking up in the wee hours, still dressed in her clothes, groggy and half-awake, she rose and went to pee. Back in her room, she stood debating whether to change or just flop back into bed. With a big yawn, she wrestled with the first metal button on her jeans. *BANG!* The sound came out of nowhere.

Maggie froze. As the smell of burning human hair choked her, a ghostly figure burst into her bedroom through the wall, scooped her up and carried her off into darkness. She could still hear the bead curtain in her doorway rattling, although she'd gone somewhere else, somehow. In the pitch dark she could see nothing. A slight breeze, a dampness. The odors of outdoors.

Stunned, she never thought to fight for freedom. The thing squeezed her tightly around the middle and traveled rapidly through the dark. Maggie had no sense of how far.

They stopped. The thing set her down, holding her from behind. She didn't try to look at it. A dim and diffused light rose up from the ground all around. Her feet were wet. She felt cold, and it smelled like mud. As the light slowly grew, she saw shapes moving around. Human shapes. People working. Her heart beat so fast she could barely breathe. She stood in a huge garden, and these were Chinese gardeners. Was she in China? They were all men, dressed in old-fashioned clothes, like the people in the photos. They looked happy, working, working.

Everything changed, and she found herself standing before a Chinese family dressed in those same period clothes. But they weren't looking at her. Several of them sobbed or hid their faces. One lady wiped a child's tears. Behind them were the charred remains of a block of buildings, still smoldering. She couldn't tell if these people could see her or not. Maggie recognized this as the Chinatown fire, from the time when a whole area of the town burned up.

With a *pop!* she arrived back in her room, and the thing squeezed her even tighter, painfully tight, she couldn't breathe at all. She couldn't get air! No breath, she could die! Then it threw her onto her bed, she landed hard. *Poof!* It disappeared. Maggie lay panting and shaking for a long time. Then she sat up, slowly, experimentally. The wall looked normal. But her bare feet were caked with dirt, as if she'd walked through mud.

Maggie wanted to run and squeeze between her parents again, like in her younger days. But soon she'd turn eighteen. She crawled back into bed and pulled the covers over her head.

The next day, Luke didn't quite seem to get it. "Hey, babe, you know we ate those shrooms yesterday." He stroked her forehead. "It must have been a dream."

Maggie pulled away and sat up straight. "No, man, this was no dream! It was very real. I was there, Luke. I could see and smell, and feel. Not like in a dream!"

"You sure?"

"Yes, Luke! I'm super sure. This really happened."

Arwen, Maggie's cat, rested across Luke's shoulders. He petted her for a moment before he asked, "Was it the ghost that grabbed you?"

"No, I don't think so. Well, maybe. It wasn't like that. It wasn't him or not him. Does that make sense?"

"Well, no," Luke said. "But it doesn't have to. None of this makes sense. It's what they call," he took a deep breath, "weird." He set Arwen gently on the dark blue carpet. "I've been thinking. Let's see if Alice wants to use her Ouija board."

"But that's a toy."

"Yeah. It's a toy because ghosts aren't real."

That evening, right around dusk, Luke and Alice walked down to the beach with Maggie. They reached their special spot and sat against a log, looking out to sea. Almost immediately, Alice started in.

"Are you sure you can't go with us to Seattle?"

"No, Alice, I really want to stay here and figure out what's going on with this ghost!"

"Well, you know, the kids are starting to make fun of you."

"What? Why?"

Alice looked at Luke. He looked up at the sky. He threw a piece of candy into the air and caught it in his mouth. Then he said to Maggie, "Ya know, you're always talking about how horrible the war is. About how we need to do something to stop it. And, you know, of course I agree completely, we all do."

"So you guys think I'm a hypocrite for not going?"

"No," said Luke.

"It's just," Alice said, "this is our chance to go to a real, meaningful protest. It's gonna be huge. Seattle's on fire these days, man!" She let her little white dog off his leash. He jumped into her lap.

"Well, I know, but I can't be in two places at once. I need to stay here."

Luke passed her the joint, and after inhaling, said in an airless voice from the back of his throat, "Don't worry about what the kids think."

"But yeah, they are mad, you know," Alice added. "You can't be the leader all the time and then just drop the ball."

"For Christ's sake, I haven't even been around for months!"

Alice shrugged. "But you're the one that's always out there in front, Maggie. The whole trip to Seattle thing was your idea in the first place."

"Well, I'll still chip in for gas. Okay?"

"You still have time to think about it. We're not leaving till Friday," Luke said.

"Yeah, okay," Maggie said. "Shit, man. People are always telling me what to do. I can't get away from it." She plucked the dog out of Alice's lap and held him against her own chest, burying her face in his fur. "It's not like I don't want to go with you guys," came her muffled voice.

"C'mon Maggie," Alice said, "Let's do the thing."

Alice opened the box and pulled out the game board and plastic planchette. The board had the alphabet printed on it, and creepily, at the bottom, the word Goodbye.

Although the cursor made violent movements, it didn't point to any letters. The friends couldn't be sure they hadn't moved it themselves, somehow. It didn't seem like it though.

"Whoah, that was weird!" Luke said.

"Yeah. But we didn't learn anything," Maggie said sadly.

"Listen!" Alice whispered. "What's that?"

The dog whimpered. A scratching came from the direction of the surf.

"No! No way!" cried Luke, pointing. His arm shook.

The girls didn't need him to point. They were staring, jaws hanging open. Not two hundred feet away, a thin driftwood branch moved by itself. Upright, it drew a message in the wet sand. It moved slowly, in a precise and purposeful manner. They watched for a long time. The stick kept drawing in the firm sand of the foreshore. It made a bunch of small, intricate designs. About a dozen of them. Then it went sailing through the air and dropped into the surf.

When they could pull themselves together enough to do it, the friends took a look at the drawings. They had to peer carefully to see in the gathering darkness.

"Chinese characters!" Luke said.

"Well, that fucking makes sense, doesn't it," Alice said.

"Don't swear!" exclaimed Maggie.

Alice looked at her. "Why? He's not gonna know."

"Anyone read Chinese?" Luke said.

They sat, a short distance away, thinking about this awhile.

"I need a beer," Luke said.

"Yeah, me too," said Alice.

Luke pushed at her shoulder, saying, "You look pale, Alice. You look like you just saw a ghost!"

"Shit. I'm shaking," Alice replied.

Maggie looked hopeful. "What about that Chinese lady who lives above the art gallery? That old lady that volunteers at the historical society. Lukie, doesn't your friend Veronica know her?"

That's how Maggie ended up carefully copying the characters in the sand onto a small sketchpad from her giant macramé shoulder bag while the other two held lighters for her. She gave the drawings to Luke, who, the next day, took them to his friend Veronica, the psychic who worked at the head shop right down on Water Street.

The phone rang. It was for Maggie. She ran to the kitchen, and her dad said Luke sounded high. Maggie smirked and shoved his shoulder. She thanked him for handing her the receiver, and retreated around the corner into the hall, thanks to the cool nine-foot handset cord. She stretched it almost to the bathroom door for privacy.

"Lukie! What is it?" she said softly.

"Hiya, Magpie!" came his voice.

"Did you get the symbols to Veronica?"

"Yep, I did. And she has Mrs. Chang's reply. She says to come on down to the shop any time."

"Oh, perfect! I need to do some dishes and hang out with my mom for a while. How about we meet down there at the shop around six-ish?"

"Sounds good."

Veronica sat behind the counter, largely hidden by frizzy hair and the collection of beads that hung around her neck. She wore puffy long sleeves and lots of rings. And a headband. "Hi, Luke!" she said, with a huge smile. "Hi, Maggie, I haven't seen you in forever! Want some pizza?" She offered them the last two slices of a whole-wheat crust pie with sun-dried tomatoes.

They talked for a couple of minutes about random things, and then Veronica said, "So, anyway, I gave the drawings to Mrs. Chang. She said those symbols were written in what is probably Cantonese. She doesn't speak Cantonese, she speaks Mandarin. She said she could work out part of it but had to guess the rest." Veronica ducked down and disappeared behind the counter. "I've got the paper here somewhere," came her voice. She popped back up. "Here."

In her hand she had a piece of typing paper. She laid it out on the counter, smoothing the edges. Everyone hovered over it. On the paper were all those same characters, beautifully redrawn, and some words in English:

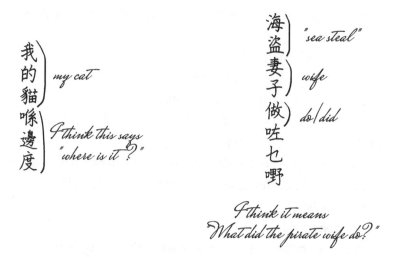

我
的
貓
喺
邊
度

) *my cat*

) *I think this says "where is it?"*

海
盗
妻
子
做
咗
乜
嘢

) *"sea steal"*

) *wife*

) *do/did*

I think it means "What did the pirate wife do?"

"Pirate wife? What's that mean?"

"That's the amazing thing! Your house is a pirate house!"

"What?" said both Maggie and Luke at the same time.

"Yeah, Mrs. Chang said that a pirate, a retired one, lived in your house when it was first built!"

Maggie tilted her head so her left ear could catch the sound better. "A what? A pirate?"

"Yup! A real pirate. Cool, huh!" Veronica said.

"How could I have never heard this before?" Maggie asked. "And weren't pirates from way before that time? My great-great-grandpa built my house. John Airedale. He was a pirate?"

"What the heck?" Luke said. "So cool. I thought you said he was a miner or something, Maggie."

"That's what it says in the old scrapbook: A mining engineer."

"It wasn't him, I don't think!" Veronica laughed. "Get ready for this, Maggie: It was a female pirate! And guess what her name was!"

Maggie shrugged and scratched her head.

"It was Maggie." Veronica saw Maggie's disbelief. "Really. It was! Maggie."

"Hold on, so that would have been Mrs. John Airedale, my great-great-grandma! Yeah, her name was Margaret, Maggie, just like me."

"Yeah, I guess so!" Veronica laughed again.

"Do you know anything about her?" Luke asked.

Maggie paused. "Only that she was born in the Cumberland Mountains. Before the Civil War."

"Wow," Luke said. "What an interesting ancestor! She retired? I never thought of pirates retiring."

"Yeah, well, Mrs Chang said Maggie kept her pirate career a

secret. Few in the community knew. Mrs Chang also suspects she went on to smuggle opium. And Chinese illegals during that time when they weren't allowed to come into the country."

Maggie and Luke looked at each other. The tunnel. The underground room.

Veronica decided to give them a free tarot reading. She had them sit at her little table where she flipped her cards over, one by one. She told them a story about Maggie's purpose, and why Luke had come into her life. Then she cast the I-Ching for them. After they left the shop, though, they didn't see anything useful in the readings she had given. Her help with contacting Mrs. Chang was a different story!

Maggie took Mrs. Chang's paper out of her big macramé bag just before she went to bed that night. She mused over it for a few minutes, and then set it on her desk. As she climbed into bed, she grabbed the book Alice had given her as a coming-home present, *I Know Why the Caged Bird Sings*. She thought she'd probably finish it that night.

She got sort of groggy reading though, lying there on her stomach. Reaching for her lamp switch, she paused. Everything felt strange. Electrical. Something cold touched the back of her shoulder. It felt like a finger. An icy finger. Maggie went rigid, unable to blink her eyes. The finger pressed into her skin through her cotton nightshirt. It traveled down her back. She whirled around and tried to scream but she made no sound.

She saw nothing. But while Maggie sat up to gasp some air into her lungs, the wooden crate of papers she had retrieved from the underground room began to rattle and shake. It scooted across her desk and crashed to the floor, dumping most of the contents.

The room grew chill. The light went out. But a switch flipped somewhere inside Maggie. She took a leap from shocked to livid. In her deepest voice she challenged the ghost, "Look, asshole! You don't belong here! And you know what? You're not going to pressure me! Enough. Stop it! STOP it! Go away!" She threw her shoe across the room in the direction of the box.

Nothing happened after that. Only silence. Except for the sound of her own panting. After a few minutes, she jumped when she heard a rap on her door. Her mother's voice asked, "Maggie, are you okay? Is someone outside? Were you yelling at someone?"

Maggie got up and opened the door a crack. "I'm okay, Mom. Sorry. I had a nightmare."

"Oh jeez, honey. Maybe go make yourself a glass of warm milk. Want me to do it?"

"No, thanks. I'll be okay now."

When she heard her mother walk off down the hall, Maggie turned her bedside lamp on. For a long time, she stood holding her upper arms, staring at the mess. She couldn't get over that feeling of the finger sliding down her back. She got her heavy terry cloth robe and put it on. Then she sat on the bed and continued to stare at the overturned box.

Now with a surprising lack of fear, she gathered the papers and photographs and set them back in the crate. When done, she studied it for a few minutes, just looking. Then she brought the whole thing over to her bed.

Sorting through the papers, Maggie didn't see anything that

she felt she ought to be looking for. There were sales receipts, letters, and newspaper articles. Sugar in 1880 was ten cents a pound. Molasses was fifty cents a gallon! She found one faded clipping particularly interesting. It came from the *Singapore Free Press*, dated 1871. Under the headline she read the summary:

IT IS BELIEVED that rumors of the Selangor Incident of June, gruesome massacre of men, women, and children, passengers of the junk Kim Seng Cheong in the Strait of Malacca, have caused the dreaded pirate Maggie Jones to vacate these waters, along with her misbegotten son Francis the Whiskers, perhaps to abandon pirating for good.

A shadowy photo of a woman accompanied the article. Maggie stared at it. Luke would later swear Maggie Jones looked just like Maggie, although Maggie didn't agree. For one thing, her hair looked dark, not auburn like Maggie's. The pirate had sat for a studio portrait, wearing a lovely dress typical of the era, her hands folded in her lap. Her eyes were almond-shaped. She had a long nose and a toothy grin.

Maggie went on sorting through the papers. She'd rifled through them once or twice already but hadn't taken the time to sit down and examine the contents of the box carefully. She came again to the set of pictures she'd looked at in the underground room. She held one up to look at it, and gasped.

The next morning, as soon as she had cleared the breakfast table, Maggie headed downtown to Luke's loft on her bike. He opened his door with a yawn, and said, "Maggie! What's up? What ya doin' boogyin' down here so early? It's, like, nine o'clock! You woke me up."

"The cat, Lukie! The Chinese cat, the one the ghost wrote about. It's her! It's the woman in the photos!"

"Kitty!"

"Yeah! How did we not see this before! 'Where is my cat?' He wants to know what happened to Kitty!"

"Yeah," Luke said, "come in, Maggie." He put his arm around her and shut the door behind them."Yeah, that makes sense. He wants to know what happened to his girl. Maggie would have known, I guess."

"He's got the wrong Maggie, then, Lukie!"

"Well, no. No, I don't think so." Luke opened the fridge. "Here, sit down, I'll get you a cup of tea. We're out of OJ." He looked at her, "You're not the wrong Maggie."

"What do you mean? I don't know what happened to Kitty."

"No, but maybe we can find out. We've got a bigger picture than those folks in the old days. You know. We just have to do some research. It will be fun."

"Ha. I don't enjoy digging around as much as you do, Lukie."

"Got your library card?"

"Somewhere. I think."

"That's okay, we can use mine. I have one somewhere. I wonder if it's possible to find information on Chinese immigrants from those days." He stopped to think. "That could be a challenge."

A few hours later, Maggie and Luke sat at a table in the old City Hall building, just across the park from Maggie's house. The historical society had a research library there in what had once served as the police courtroom. A cardboard file box sat on the table in front of them as they sorted through various items regarding the history of Chinese people in the town. Maggie had a folder labeled "Fire of Sept 24, 1900."

"Well, that's the Chinatown Fire," she said. "I've looked all through this and I don't see any list of casualties or mention of anyone named Kitty."

They spent quite a while looking through papers, and getting more and more discouraged, until Luke said, "Here! Here's something! Oh, this is good, Maggie—look! It has Kitty's name!"

Maggie leaned over to see.

Luke continued, "It's a list of men known or suspected to have died at the hands of smugglers or in crossing the water from Canada. And, oh look at this! It says 'Information collected by Mr. Francis T. Griffin.' The date in pencil at the top says 1946."

Maggie held her glasses rim between thumb and finger so she could see better. "Where's Kitty's name? Oh, yeah."

Luke pointed, "This man, Yeung Kai. Here, where it lists a wife, Lao Ya-ting. Someone has scrawled the name Kitty."

"That's her! That's her!"

"Geez, that's sad. He died at only twenty-six."

"This is cool to find out her name," Maggie said, "but it doesn't really give us any information about what happened to her."

"Well, assuming that's our Francis, your great-grandpa, he must have donated that information when he was an old guy. Maybe there's more."

They continued to search, although they both knew they'd been more than lucky to find the paper with her name. Finally, hungry and tired, they decided to call it a day. As they carefully placed papers back into that folder Maggie spotted a photo of Kitty.

"Look!" she cried.

She held a page torn out of a scrapbook. Someone had pasted a photo of Kitty to it, and a death notice from a newspaper. They had added a couple of sentences underneath in the spidery cursive of an old person.

"Read it," Luke said. "What's it say?"

"It says, 'Although declared deceased, this woman had gone to San Francisco to work as a dressmaker under an assumed name. Mother corresponded with her well into her later years.'"

They both whooped and Maggie jumped up and hugged Luke.

Startled, the librarian peeked between the books on a shelf. "Are you kids okay?" he asked.

But now, a new problem. How to tell the ghost, who apparently didn't understand English.

"Oh, I know what to do!" Maggie whispered.

That night, when Maggie went to bed, she left a drawing on her bedroom desk. It showed a woman with a big smile standing in front of a cable car. (She'd had to copy the cable car from a box of pilaf mix because she realized she didn't know exactly how to draw one.) Maggie had placed a big sewing needle in one of the woman's hands, and she held up a dress in the other. The woman had cat ears and the name Lao Ya-ting was written. Also, Maggie had painstakingly drawn the character for cat, "貓".

While Maggie and Luke waited in the ferry line with their backpacks on, saying goodbye to Maggie's family, they saw their friend Veronica. She stepped off the ferry, having returned from visiting her sister.

They all stood talking for a moment while the cars drove by. Veronica whispered breathily into Maggie's ear, "Hey, man, I had a dream a couple of nights ago. This young Chinese guy came to me. He didn't say anything, but I knew he thanked you. He's free now." Then, as she started for home she called back to Luke and Maggie, "Hey guys! Have fun at Woodstock!"

Pup on the Loose

A story about Ozzie

a Black Labrador Retriever puppy
owned by Lindsay and Tom.

Ozzie sat down. He fixed his soulful puppy gaze on me. Those eyebrows! He raised his expressive Labrador eyebrows in such an earnest look of appeal that I couldn't help but laugh. Floppy ears framed his chunky baby face. I gave in and picked him up. Who could resist him and his sleek black softness?

"What's wrong, little guy?" I asked, snuggling my cheek against his fur. "We haven't gone two blocks!" Last time, he'd trotted eagerly along.

I cuddled him and scratched behind his ears and under his collar. He nuzzled me with his sniffy nose. "Poor Oz, are you scared?" I looked around. *Of what*, I wondered. Ozzie had a new red collar on. It hung a bit loose on him. He looked cute, though.

Gently, I shifted him to the other arm. He already weighed a substantial amount and would be a bit tough to carry, but I didn't mind. I noticed a dog barking somewhere. It sounded like that fluffy German Shepherd who inhabits a balcony beyond the stormwater pond. Ah.

"Don't worry, buddy, I'll protect you," I told him. Still holding the pup, I resumed our stroll along the smooth white sidewalk edged by manicured lawns. After a while I set him down. Ozzie performed well on the leash. He had taken to it readily and knew several commands.

The housing development where he lives has forested areas and, important to Ozzie, a couple of creeks and ponds. There's a powerline trail that goes on forever through brambles and native shrubs and even today, as a heavy-duty doggie dynamo, Ozzie is sure there's a bear along there. He's probably right.

That morning, as we walked along, we passed the cedar fence where the debarked dog (or whatever it is) runs back and forth on the other side. I expected this creepy dog (or whatever it is) to frighten little Ozzie, but it never has. Ozzie loves to challenge my assumptions! I'm aware that I make too many assumptions. But I never could have seen this day coming.

The enormous spiders poised to jump from rooftops, gray zombie hands reaching out of people's lawns, and all the other Halloween decorations we passed seemed normal to a puppy with limited experience. But Ozzie didn't like the monster. Someone had placed a seven-foot-tall Frankenstein's monster, dressed as a butler, next to their front door. Ozzie decided at first glance that this atrocity needed killing and that he was the dog for the job.

"Look at me," I commanded Ozzie. I gave him a piece of kibble. I had his full attention, but when a man across the street whistled and called, "Rocky! Rocky!" it upstaged my powers of dog-focusing.

A few houses down, a little girl of about five years old stood in her yard. Sobbing, she faced the woods behind her house. With only a thin purple sweatshirt on, and what looked like pajama pants, she must have been cold but this wasn't the reason for her tears. She called, "Rocky!"

The man, just visible through the trees, shouted the same name. "Where are you, boy? Come on, Rocky!"

The girl caught our movement from the corner of her eye. "Rocky!" she shouted and ran toward us. "It's Rocky! Dad! Someone found him!"

The little girl tried to leap onto Ozzie and hug him, but I snatched him up just in time. While I stammered, "Wait, wait!" she crooned, "Rock-eeeey!" to Ozzie as she reached to pet him, and "Thank you so much!" to me.

The man ran up, too, and told me thanks so much for bringing him back.

"No, wait—"

"He got out when I went to empty the trash. He took off like a bat. I've been looking for him for at least twenty minutes. Again, thanks. My daughter was beside herself."

"This is Ozzie," I said.

"I've got to teach him to come when he's called," he continued, then he said, "What?"

We looked at each other. The girl smothered Ozzie, who didn't mind too much.

"Sorry, this isn't your dog."

"Of course it is. What do you mean?" He stared at Ozzie. "You mean this is your dog?"

"Well, no. I'm a dog walker. But this is my client's dog, Ozzie. I'm sorry."

The girl looked at her dad. "This is Rocky, though!" she said softly. The dad squinted at the dog. He looked at me out of the corner of his eye.

"Honey, we must be wrong. This is the lady's puppy," he said. "But look, he even has Rocky's red collar!"

I'm sure my voice rose in pitch at this point. "Really, this is Ozzie."

The man took his young daughter by the hand and gently pulled her away from the pup. She didn't fight him, but her hands kept reaching out toward Ozzie. I set him down. The three of us had our mouths open, watching Ozzie sniff around in their neighbor's pampas grass.

"Ozzie." The dad said. "He sure looks like Rocky."

I wondered if he meant this as a challenge or maybe he

wanted to see if the pup responded to its name. Ozzie ignored both names. He was busy in the grass. The dad looked at me with a little lopsided smile.

He and his daughter acted so dumbfounded by the resemblance to their pup that I started to feel guilty, as if I were somehow trying to steal the dog. Such a silly reaction! I had to shake it off.

"I have some time," I said, "before I have to get Ozzie back. We could help you look for Rocky."

The girl looked at her father as if to say, "Daddy, this *is* Rocky!"

"I can't get over how much this looks like our pup!" the man said. "And that same collar, too. How old is Ozzie? Um, yeah, sure! Thanks. That's awfully kind of you—sure you have time?"

So Dave (that was his name) sent little Chloe into the house and he and I headed into the woods to search for Rocky. I carried Ozzie because of all the logs and undergrowth. We must have crashed around out there for about ten minutes before I stumbled across Rocky wandering. I clipped my extra leash to him. "I found him!" I called. Now, I just needed to find their house again.

Walking with a pup under each arm proved difficult, so as soon as I could manage it I got back out to the sidewalk and returned to Rocky's house that way. Rocky and Ozzie had great fun, tackling each other and jumping around, and wrapping the leashes around my legs.

When we arrived at the house I took the dogs into the backyard and called out to Dave. He soon answered and appeared out of the woods. He exclaimed, "You found him!" Then he asked, "Which one is he?"

I stared at the puppies. Uh-oh. Two identical leashes. Two

red leather collars from the sale at the local pet store. And a couple of excited Black Lab puppies that had caused me to switch hands with their leashes repeatedly. When Dave saw my face, he stood for a moment, looking at the dogs. He squatted and called Rocky. Both pups were busy wrestling. He called again. Both pups rushed happily up to him. "Uh-oh," Dave said.

"What are we going to do?" I asked with a groan. "I've got to get Ozzie back, right away. This is only our third walk. I can't be late!"

We watched the dogs play happily, hoping to notice something familiar. Chloe had joined us again, dressed in her jeans. One pup looked slightly bigger and had a faint white spot behind his left front paw. These observations didn't help.

"Is Rocky chipped?" I asked.

"Probably. I didn't think to ask. He's had all his shots. My daughter got him for her birthday and we've only had him a few days. Is Ozzie?"

"I think his owner said so."

The thought occurred to us that it was Sunday, and to have a chip checked would require a trip downtown to the emergency vet. Neither of us knew at the time that the big chain pet stores will check chips. Even that would have taken a good hour. I faced losing my first client.

"Ozzie!" I called, "Here, Ozzie!" Both pups came happily to my outstretched arms and covered me with puppy kisses. I had an idea.

I handed one of the leashes to Dave, and with Chloe tagging along we headed over to visit Ozzie's monster. Still enamored with one another, the little guys failed to notice the giant human thing. Then, when he took a break to scratch himself, the smaller pup saw it and started barking. But his new friend joined right in. With an even greater amount of gusto. We all headed back to Rocky's house.

"Well," Dave said, "this one seems like Rocky to me. If we can't tell, what difference does it really make? How about we assume this other one is Ozzie?"

"Dad!" cried Chloe.

"No!" I said in surprise. "We can't do that. This isn't even my dog. I can't just bring some random dog back to his owner!"

"Well, unfortunately, we've got to get this figured out right now. Chloe and I are in town visiting her mom. We leave for home in the morning. Louisiana." Dave motioned toward a lifted black pickup with a tarp over its load.

Fighting tears, I pulled out my phone. "Well, this is my fault. I'll take the one you think is Ozzie downtown and get the chip checked. I don't know what else we can do. I'll text the owner, and try to explain this somehow." This marked the end of my walking Ozzie. I couldn't even keep track of her dog! And what if she gave me a bad review? I'd never get a second customer. My week-old business had already burst into flames.

Then I saw it. "Check this out!" I exclaimed.

While the puppies tugged on our arms with their leashes, Dave and I leaned to peer at the phone screen which I held in my shadow. Chloe stretched to look at it, too. "What?" she asked, "What is it?"

"Oh! I never thought to look there!" Dave said.

The wallpaper image on my phone showed Ozzie. I got such a cute photo the day of our first walk that I put it on my phone. I'd captured him right in the middle of a big yawn.

I held it so the little girl could get a better look. "See, Chloe?

Ozzie has a tiny pink bird shape on the black roof of his mouth! All we have to do is take a peek in their mouths. We'll know for sure which one is Rocky."

Chloe's face brightened, and then it fell. "Unless they both have a pink bird in their mouth."

"You know, Chloe, the way things have been going I'm not sure I'd be that surprised!" I told her. "But don't worry, I'm kidding; these two having that same marking is next to impossible."

"All we have to do." Ha! I had five minutes to get Ozzie home, and somehow we needed to see inside a puppy's mouth. We had figured out that Rocky was two weeks older, so based on that information I felt the pup I had on the leash, the smaller one, might be Ozzie. Silly, but it was the only thing we had to go on. I sat down on the lawn with him in my lap.

I reached over the top of his muzzle with one hand, sticking my thumb and finger into his mouth just behind his canines. I'd learned this in pet first aid. Then I placed the index finger of my other hand between the incisors of his lower jaw and pulled it gently down.

He didn't like it, and I couldn't hold his mouth open for more than a second. So, I tried again, popping a piece of kibble in as soon as he opened up a little. After he'd consumed several pieces of kibble in this way, I pressed his mouth open and took a quick peek. Sunshine seemed to pour over me. "Ozzie!" I squealed. Oh, I hugged him.

"Are you sure?" Dave asked, holding and petting Rocky.

"I got a good look. I'm sure."

Chloe reached for Rocky, jumping up and down. Her dad set the puppy down and let her fawn over him. Dave and I looked at each other. Wow, relief.

"Well," I said, "a pleasure to meet the two of you; and I'm glad you got your puppy back; and I'm sorry about the mix-up; and have a great trip to Louisiana! I don't mean to be rude, but I have to get Ozzie home!"

I had to run three blocks in two minutes, carrying a heavy puppy. And you know what? I did it. Not bad for a lady in her sixties.

Unexpected Turns

The following tale has fictional characters, except for one:

Pippa

my family's East European Shepherd.

Pippa sprawled on the squared timbers of a hand-hewn floor, blocking the doorway. No one would leave that tiny cabin without her knowing. Her head resting across her foreleg, ears alert, she gazed with German Shepherd emotion into the distance. She didn't know that guarding the door so diligently served no purpose: it was bolted shut from the inside and locked with a padlock.

She eyed the kids, panting a little. They'd been handling their backpacks. Maybe they were going for a walk!

On a heap of clothes in the middle of the floor, a man lay on his stomach. His sweat and unwashed hair had a smell only slightly less powerful than the rot in the room's blackened log walls and sagging roof. When the man and two teenagers had arrived the day before, they'd had to evict some mice.

The one small window wasn't the type that opens. Underneath stood a rough table, the only piece of furniture. Smoke leaked from a fire burning in the rusty stove. The kids had almost used up the dusty stack of firewood making homemade Boston beans the night before. They'd had nothing for breakfast.

"Are you ready?" Skylar whispered.

Hannah's voice shook a little, "I guess so." She looked at the man on the floor. "But I'm hungry," she said.

"I have some money." Skye whispered close to Hannah's ear, "The first thing we'll do is call the police. Then we'll get something to eat."

"Okay," Hannah said.

"And," Skye added, "we can eat those sandwiches I brought from town yesterday. But let's save them for our lunch along the way."

As they pulled on their boots, Pippa sprang to her feet. The man on the floor grunted. Hannah softly gave her dog the "hush" command, with limited success. She tried calming Pippa by covering the dog's forehead with the palm of her hand. This didn't help. Skye found the last stick of yak cheese and gave it to Pippa. The dog held the stiff bar in her mouth but remained focused on the possible departure. Skylar and Hannah put their coats on.

"Stick your mittens in your pockets," Skye told Hannah. Fifteen-year-old Skylar felt responsible for their barely-thirteen-year-old sister.

"Skye," whispered Hannah, "are you sure it isn't getting too late in the day? It's snowing again."

At the word "snow" Pippa barked with anticipation.

The man sat part of the way up and muttered, "Dirigible butternuts," or something similar. Hannah and Skye both froze, not daring to breathe. But the man's eyes were glazed; he didn't notice their coats or much of anything. He fell back into a deeper sleep, or daze, or whatever it was.

"The—white stuff—will cover our tracks. It's the perfect time to go. It's only like . . . a two-hour hike," Skye said softly. "Here, come help me." Hannah stood watching while Skye spread molasses on one of the four panes of the window. She had read about this trick on a history site about crime in Victorian England. After the sticky substance completely covered the glass, Pippa was more than happy to lick Skye's hands clean. Next, Hannah pressed the tea towel onto the gooey surface.

Hannah handed Skye a folded sleeping bag. Skye held it up against the window. "Thanks, now go over there, and hold Pippa," Skye said. "And if he wakes up . . . I don't know." They both glanced at the man.

Hannah shrugged, trying to look encouraging. It was the only chance they had. What else could they do?

Holding the sleeping bag up with one hand to pad the window, Skye used the other hand to bash it with the skillet. *THUD!* Skye and Hannah both turned to look at the man. Again, breath held, *THUD!* The cracking sound of the glass wasn't too bad. The kids' hearts beat wildly as again they checked the man's reaction. He lay with drool pooling under his chin, his dream uninterrupted.

Behind the sleeping bag the window had smashed to pieces but the tea towel held most of the glass in place. "Help me!" Skye whispered.

Hannah hurried over, and together they carefully removed the towel and most of the glass pieces as a unit. Skye folded this into the frying pan. Cold air came in through the opening now but it felt good after the overheated, stuffy cabin. Hannah eyed the man on the floor but didn't notice any movement. Pippa came to investigate the skillet, the contents of which must certainly be for her. Skye looked for a place to set the pan full of glass bits and molasses out of the dog's reach. The cabin had no shelves or high places, so they did the next best thing. Carefully reaching out through the broken window, Skye tossed the skillet and contents so they landed along the cabin wall somewhere outside. Then, it took some time, but Skye and Hannah wiggled loose and removed all the jagged pieces which had remained in the edge of the frame.

Skye covered the bottom of the window frame with an old shirt in case of any slivers of glass, saying, "Okay, Hannah, out you go!"

Hannah climbed onto the table. She crawled through the opening. Skye heard her land, plop, in the snow. She reached back through for the packs. Skye handed them one at a time.

"Okay, now it's the moment of truth," Skye whispered. Skye took a deep breath and then struggled to lift heavy Pippa onto the table. Pippa knew she wasn't allowed on tables. She panicked. Her feet scrambled wildly, running nowhere, but then she dove out of the hole where Hannah had gone. Pippa hit the snow with a crunchy thud. Snow! Oh boy! Hannah tried to shush her, but Pippa sprang madly around outside the cabin, only stopping for a few seconds to pee and maybe nibble a little molasses glass if Hannah would let her.

With one last look at the man who lay there, Skye squeezed through the window also. The two kids stood for a moment, looking around them outside while Pippa circled. They shouldered their packs and turned to leave, but Skye looked back at the window and whispered, "Wait!" Skye asked Hannah for a boost. Reaching back through the opening, Skye grabbed the sleeping bag and stuffed it into the hole where the glass had been. "We don't want him to freeze to death when the fire goes out," Skye said.

Tears came to Hannah's eyes. "Is he going to be okay?" she asked.

"They'll probably come get him tonight. He'll be safer in jail. Try not to worry," Skylar said.

"Goodbye, Dad," Hannah whispered.

Skye pointed out that they'd have to guess the time, because the weather hid the sun. It must have been close to noon. Somewhere between twelve and two. Fog had settled low over the mountain, and big fat snowflakes came floating down. It wouldn't be hard to find their way back to the road, though. The trail followed the creek, and then, once they were down, would go along the river right at the base of the mountain for the rest of the way. Considering that they were in a wilderness area, the path couldn't be more clear.

The footprints from their hike up to the cabin the day before were already covered. Although the snow wasn't deep, it was slippery. The trail went down a large gully through thick woods of snow-laden firs. It went over quite a few fallen logs and detoured around boulders. The route disappeared a lot, but they managed to stay on it most of the time. At any rate, they only needed to keep within earshot of the creek.

Pippa trotted ahead and then circled behind, nosing into shrubs and hollows with her long pointed snout. Every couple of minutes she'd check the kids, making sure her little flock moved along okay, and perhaps touch her nose to some fingertips. Skye and Hannah realized they'd forgotten Pippa's leash.

After only a quarter mile or so down the mountain, the snow disappeared. They stopped in a brushy place where the trees grew smaller, probably an old avalanche chute. Above them, mountain tops crowded close. Below, a forested valley formed a sea of green. "Look at that view!" Skye said, and then, after a moment, "Wow, I'd assumed it was snowing everywhere, not just on the upper slopes." Directly In front of them, a vertical ridge of snowy granite peaks rose into the low clouds. Inclines that weren't too steep for trees were covered in patches of forest, green with swathes of golden.

"What do you think happened to kill all those trees?" Hannah asked. "Do you think it's a disease?"

"I think it's a type of tamarack. Like the one in the backyard."

"Oh. Yeah, the tree Mom thought was dead that first fall after we moved."

"You must have been three years old! You remember that?"

"Mm-hmm." Hannah looked back up the gully.

"He's high," Skye said, reaching to adjust the string on Hannah's hood, "he's not going to follow us. Not for a long time. We'll have reached civilization by then. Come on, let's keep going. You warm enough?"

"Let's get the hell out of here," Hannah said softly.

"He wouldn't have hurt us, Nanner. Not on purpose."

"Well, he's losing custody now, for sure," said Hannah.

They could see the forested river valley below until they entered the taller trees again. Undergrowth and boulders complicated their passage through a fir and hemlock forest. They had glimpses of the snow-covered ridges above them on both sides of the gully. Several times they had to retrace their steps because of an impassable slippery or brushy spot. Pippa took great delight in climbing over logs and crossing trickles of water. "Hike" was another of the words that had to be spelled in Pippa's presence unless you wanted to excite the dog. Even if you spelled the word she'd get suspicious.

They continued along the creek, sometimes on what appeared to be the trail, sometimes losing sight of the water as it tumbled down the rocky mountainside. Their clothes were damp from brushing through all the snowy foliage, but their eco fabric parkas and fancy rain pants with instep laces kept them warm and dry.

Eventually they met an established trail that crossed their

path diagonally. Pippa turned uphill on it and then started downhill on a deer trail. She stopped and looked back. Her head was up and her tail wagging.

"I don't remember this," Hannah said.

Skylar stood quiet for a moment, staring. "Um, I do. I thought it was farther to the main trail, but I guess not. It must just look different coming the other way. I think we want to go to the left. Come on, Pippa!"

They made better time traveling across the lower flank of the mountain. The trees grew as thick as ever, but the gentler incline helped. They could see the trail well now, a narrow but more defined path with less undergrowth and fewer logs. Crossing a creek put Skye and Hannah's minds at ease. They remembered this spot. Or at least they thought they did.

After a while the land leveled out. They reached a fork in the trail. A signpost stood there, but the names didn't mean anything to them. "Well, actually, 'Icicle' does sound familiar. Icicle Canyon? Remember? Let's go that way." They took the right-hand fork because that trail headed out into the long, flat-bottomed valley they'd seen at times during their descent. After walking a short way along the trail, Hannah mentioned that something didn't seem right. Skye agreed. The path had become less clear, maybe, or the woods too thick.

"Should we turn around, then?" Hannah wondered.

Skye paused, faced Hannah and answered in a small voice, "I don't know what to do. We can't afford to get lost out here. Maybe we should go a bit farther and see if we come to that river."

They pushed through the trees for a few hundred feet and stopped again. Pippa came back to see what the problem was.

Pippa loved hiking and couldn't have been happier. She whacked Skye in the back of the leg with the giant, heavy, stick she carried in her jaws.

"Ouch! Pippa!" Skylar cried. "Dammit!"

"Maybe we could let Pippa guide us back," Hannah said.

"That's a good idea. There's all those stories of dogs who find their way home. I bet Pippa can find the way back to the road."

Pippa had dropped her stick for a moment to sniff around under a tree. When the two kids came toward her, she picked up the stick and walked along the trail a bit farther. Skye and Hannah backed off to give her some room. Pippa left the trail and they followed her through the trees. She seemed to be going somewhere. They kept following.

"This might work," Skye said.

"She really seems to know what we want," Hannah said.

They passed an old snag riddled with woodpecker holes. Interestingly, the holes made a pattern of neat, horizontal rows. Fifteen minutes later they passed the same snag. Pippa lost her new job as scout.

"Now what?" Hannah asked.

Skye threw the stick for Pippa. "We need to find that other trail again. The one we turned off of. But there's nothing but trees. No shadows, nothing. Wait—can you hear the creek?"

Hannah listened hard. "No."

"Well, let's keep going, and try really hard not to walk in circles. Okay? It's pretty flat, but the ground does incline slightly going that way," Skylar pointed. "The trail was going along the base of the mountain."

Hannah perked up. "Skye, that's really good thinking!"

And it proved to be. After another ten minutes or so, they

found the trail again that ran along the base of the mountain. They'd taken a right fork off of it, so they took a right turn onto it to keep going in the same direction. Not only that, but they went through a small clearing. This allowed them to see the mountains above them. The clouds had lifted a bit and the peaks were visible. In every direction they could see, mountains rose high, breathtaking beauties covered in forest, with granite ridges along the summits.

Skye and Hannah stood for a while, silent and staring. They'd never seen anything like this. How absolutely stunning. And terrible. Where were they? They'd hiked in the White Mountains wilderness before, at home in New Hampshire. They'd even been on Mount Washington. This range looked similar, but less civilized, somehow. These were rugged and craggy and in the middle of an area that probably had wolves and grizzlies.

"Well," Skylar said, "Are you hungry? Do you want to have lunch here?"

"I don't know if I'm hungry, but I guess lunch sounds like a good idea," Hannah replied.

Skye sighed. They pulled off their backpacks and sat down on a log. Skye handed Hannah a sandwich wrapped in a bread bag, saying, "I guess it's time to have our peanutty cottonseed oil and white bread sandwiches."

"I miss Mom so much!" Hannah said. "She'll be so worried."

"We'll see her soon," Skylar said. They were quiet for a moment, chewing. "Hey, see that cliff across the way? It looks like the mountain we followed along to get to the cabin! I think we've finally got an idea where we are! It's not the same trail, but it goes along the same valley."

171

The kids couldn't give Pippa any of their sandwiches, because that peanut butter had Xylitol. So they gave her some of the cheese puffs. Pippa gobbled them and looked for more.

"Sorry, girl," Hannah said.

They set off again. The path led across the base of the mountain. Once they lost track of the trail, but they kept going at about the same elevation and they soon ran into it again. They got some views of the river running down the middle of the valley, and they crossed a few smaller creeks that were flowing down the mountain. They had to step across on stones, and several required crossing on logs. Pippa got scared a few times, but her fear of getting left behind outweighed her fear of tumbling into a creek. She performed several wonderfully athletic leaps and scrambles.

Eventually, it occurred to Skye and Hannah that the river was running in the wrong direction. If they were heading back toward the road, the river should be flowing in the same direction they were hiking. It wasn't.

"Do we have to follow it back the way we came?" Hannah asked.

Skye answered hesitantly, "Well, I didn't see anywhere we could turn off to yesterday's trail."

"I didn't, either," Hannah said. "Dad could be awake now."

"I was thinking that, too. We don't want to be back where we started when he comes looking for us. This trail goes along the valley. There's a good chance it's a loop, right?"

"Are we lost?"

"No, we're not lost," Skylar said. "Look, there's more light over that way. That's west. We want to go east, so let's keep going on this trail and see if it turns east. I think that's our best bet."

Hannah looked extremely uncomfortable.

"Don't worry, Nans. Remember, this is why we brought the sleeping bags. We're prepared for anything! We could spend the night out here if we have to. No big deal. I've got the backpacking tarps too. We could live out here."

"Maybe we should," Hannah said. "We could live on fish and crickets. Except I miss Mom so much, though."

"I'm not sure there's crickets here," Skye said.

They kept on. Each glanced at the other uncertainly as they pressed along. They were beginning to regret their lack of a good lunch. The packs started to feel heavy. Pippa could go on forever, but her light had dimmed a little. She spent less time as the pathfinder now, preferring to trail behind, investigating a smell or working to achieve the perfect grip on a dropped stick.

The trail went on and on through the trees. Here the woods were less dense and looked like the woods they went through the day before. Some of the trees were enormous, with great thick trunks and taller than Skye and Hannah had ever seen. With each curve or rise of the path, Skye and Hannah kept saying that they'd meet the other trail, or perhaps some other hikers. But the changing light hinted at the approach of sunset.

In a voice that bordered on a whine, Hannah said, "I'm getting so thirsty, but I don't want to get gerardia."

"Giardia."

"Whatever. Beaver fever. I don't want to get that."

"Yeah. Don't want to get dehydrated either, though."

The valley narrowed into a canyon as the trail climbed slightly.

After a mile or so they came to the end of the trail. They'd reached a lake. An eagle flushed from the boulders they passed at the top of the trail. The burst of wings came so close that the force of its wind blew in Skye's face. They shrieked and nearly fell over backward. Pippa barked. Hannah laughed, and exclaimed, "Holy cow! Are you okay?""

The trail ended at the lakeshore. Pippa lapped water and explored smells among the rocks. Skye and Hannah stood staring. The lake filled the end of the canyon. Snow had powdered the branches of the conifers that came down the steep slopes to meet the shore. Higher up, the trees were covered with white, and higher still the snow clung to a towering wall of rock, the ridgeline of which dipped and then rose into two fan-shaped peaks. The beauty of this scene astonished both of them.

After a moment, Skye sighed and said, "Yeah, well, we're not going that way." They looked at Hannah. "Well, let's get a drink anyway."

"Is it safe?"

"A little bit of eagle poop isn't going to hurt us. Don't worry."

"I don't want to get sick."

"Better to feel like crap in a few weeks than die of dehydration."

"Well, if you put it that way."

Pippa was fooling around with some sticks that floated up to shore. The others joined her, squatting down and using their hands as cups.

"Oh, that's cold!" said Hannah.

With no other choice, they retraced their steps back down the canyon. At least it went downhill going this direction. About halfway through the narrow part of the gorge, the trail ran right alongside the creek. A nice big log lay across. They saw a path up through the forested valley on the other side. It followed a gradual slope. It led somewhere, and not back to the cabin. And so they crossed the creek.

"We've got to find some other hikers. It's getting late," Hannah said.

"We will," Skye reassured her. "And we'll be okay anyway. It looks like we'll have to spend the night out here. But we have our bags and stuff."

"It's not that cold out. I think it's above freezing, anyway," Hannah said.

Skylar put their hand on her shoulder and said softly, "We'll be okay."

Hannah thought it may have been an animal trail they were on; it was intermittent and more difficult to discern. "It's going on too far to be an animal trail," Skye said. "Look, we might as well go up at least to that first ridge where the snow is, we can see more from there."

Hannah agreed. "Maybe we'll see some hikers."

At the mention of snow, Pippa perked up her ears. But she didn't do her usual dance. She had a worried look in her eyes.

After hiking for about an hour in the twilight, the kids found a great area to make camp. Halfway up to the ridge, it had a flat area for sleeping. Some slabs of rock stuck up to make a perfect wall against the wind. It felt good to take off their packs. Skye and Hannah collected leafy branches to prop against the rocks for a roof to sleep under. Pippa helped to drag them. They searched for firewood, looking under fir trees for dropped limbs. Pippa helped again by carrying a good-sized chunk of fir in her strong jaws. She held her head high afterward, proud to see her favorite hobby receive proper recognition.

They spread the nylon backpacking tarps on the ground under their roof, one on top of the other, and sat on them to have dinner. The ground felt cold through the tarps. They were glad to have the roof because a bit of rain began to sprinkle. All they had to eat was a bag of shelled sunflower seeds from Hannah's pack. They'd been in there a while, but they were okay. Skye divided these equally between the three of them, resulting in about a handful each. Pippa wouldn't eat hers until they were tossed to her one by one.

Pippa hunkered with her chin on the ground, looking more and more unhappy. Her expression said something along the lines of, "I don't think this is a good idea at all. Let's go back to the house. Where mom is. That's a better place."

"Don't worry, Pippa," Hannah said, "We're not moving here. Just camping for the night. Tomorrow we'll be headed home!"

"We'd better get a fire going," Skye said, fishing for a lighter. "Nanner, do you have any paper in your pack?"

Hannah's search produced a short receipt for something.

"You don't have any books?" Skye sounded surprised.

"Well, I've got three books," Hannah replied, eyeing Skye suspiciously.

Skye started making a little tipi out of twigs.

"Why?" Hannah asked.

"We're going to have to use one of your books to make the fire, that's all."

"What?"

"It's all right. We'll just get you another one. They're not first editions or something."

"Burn my book?"

"It's not book-burning. It's just burning a book. Not the same thing," Skye said. "It will help us get warm, and keep animals away."

"I'm plenty warm," Hannah said.

"And keep animals away." Skye allowed Hannah some time to remember there could be wolves or grizzlies in this area.

"Okay," Hannah said. "Just one book."

"That's all we need. To get the fire started. The wood is wet. I'm sorry, Nanner."

Hannah pulled her books out to look at them. She had a copy of *White Fang*, a copy of *Where the Red Fern Grows*, and a copy of *Cujo*.

"Oh, well, keep *Cujo*," Skye said.

Hannah made a sad little raspberry sound with her lips and tossed *White Fang* next to the kindling. She cringed in exaggerated drama every time Skye ripped out more pages, and they both giggled. Skye ended up ripping out all the pages. They couldn't convince the kindling to stay lit. Skye wanted to use Hannah's colored pencils, but they were the expensive kind and Hannah looked like she might cry. Skye didn't ask again.

The only thing they could do to warm up was get to bed. They had only one sleeping pad with them, so they set it crosswise to share it under their upper torsos. They got Pippa to lie on the tarps, and then, in their sleeping bags, they lay on each side of her, slowly folding the stiff nylon over themselves. Because Pippa had exercised plenty that day, she stayed willingly in the big cocoon. Perhaps she felt safer there. The kids passed the time by talking about childhood memories, camping and swimming, and that trip they once took to New York City. They appreciated that Pippa's body heat helped keep the cocoon warm.

As darkness began to fall, Pippa barked at something.

"What is it, Pippa? Shhh, don't bark," Skye whispered.

"Don't say that. She always does it if you say that word," Hannah said.

"Bark?"

Pippa barked again, sharply, several times.

They both laughed.

"Say 'shush.' That helps her calm down, remember?" Hannah said.

Skye rubbed Pippa's chest and belly until she relaxed. Then they gave a big sigh, looked out into the dusk, and said, "God knows what she was barking at."

Pippa fell asleep after an hour or so and stayed in her spot for the whole night. She woke a couple of times to growl softly or bark, which was unnerving. Despite their tiredness, the kids lay awake much of the night. The bumpy ground hurt their backs. Their feet and legs felt cold. What if a bear came? In their bellies the pressure of fear and uncertainty subdued any feelings of hunger.

The best sleep came in the hours before dawn. Then the light woke them. It had rained during the night, but they had stayed dry. Stiff and sore, all three climbed out of their tarp tube and stretched the kinks out of their legs. Pippa went off to pee.

With no breakfast to be had, they shook out the tarps, folded them up, and continued on their way. During the night they'd agreed to take the trail up the draw and see where it went. They were sure to find someone else soon, and neither of them wished to return the way they'd come. Escape remained their priority.

Pippa darted here and there. She had a wolfy look to her; the kids couldn't tell if it came from excitement or anxiety. Maybe both. Warmer than the previous day, the air smelled fresh. No rain fell now, but the clouds looked dark. Wisps and patches of fog obscured parts of the jagged peaks above.

Soon after they started out, they crossed a creek on the slope by stepping from stone to stone. The rushing water wasn't deep. Pippa could simply have waded through it, but she preferred to leap from rock to rock as her humans were doing. One broad stone had grown slimy with algae. Pippa slipped and fell, flailing uselessly, to land on her side in the creek.

"Pippa!" Hannah shrieked.

Pippa struggled to her feet and lunged for the other bank. Clambering to the top, she shook herself.

"Oh, Pippa," Skye said.

As they hiked up through the trees, they entered the snow again. Conifer branches held fresh white powder and the ground had a few inches. Pippa rolled in the snow and took big mouthfuls of it, but Hannah commented on how she didn't leap and bound through the trees on the gentle hillside as they might have expected. Not much farther along, the kids heard and then saw a waterfall. It looked so perfect with all the white that Hannah said that she wished her phone had some battery so she could take a picture. They crossed the creek below the falls, this time with no accidents, and then the trail climbed the slope beside the tumbling water.

Mounting the slope, they encountered deeper snow. With a crunch sound their feet broke through the upper layer, and then with the pop of their legs sinking through the softer stuff, each step took effort. The snow reached most of the way up their boots. Now and then, icy chunks scooped into their boot tops, packing into a wet ring around their legs, just under the knee.

After they had gone through this for a few hundred feet, Hannah suggested turning around. "This is miserable," she said. "I'm wet. I'm cold. What if it's like this all the way along?"

Skylar looked down, busy with a jammed parka zipper, and didn't answer right away. "Yeah, we probably should turn back soon if it keeps like this."

But a short distance farther along the trail they saw something amazing. Footprints! Snowshoe prints. Someone else was on the mountainside! The snowshoer couldn't be far ahead. Catching up seemed possible. Arriving at the prints, Skye and Hannah had a clear path to follow and less work to make each step because the person had compacted the snow. They rested for a few minutes, but not long enough to take off their packs. They were eager to continue.

Hurrying up the trail of prints, which they now could see were made by two people, they came over a rise to a small lake, the source of the waterfall. They'd reached the ridge they had aimed for. But looking back out over the valley told them nothing. They saw only a carpet of never-ending forest.

The landscape before them, though, made Hannah wish out loud again for a camera. They stood at the edge of a flat-bottomed bowl surrounded by several high peaks. Skye and Hannah stood near a pointed end of the small lake and could see a bigger lake beyond. The mists among the jagged peaks along with heavy gray clouds accentuated the soft whites of the snow and slate blues of the lakes. The forest grew patchier here, and not as thick, but there were still a lot of trees. They couldn't see any sign of people.

Skye and Hannah passed behind the small lake and traveled with the second, larger, lake on their right and the foot of a tall peak on their left. The trail here had a lot of little ups and downs, and the kids still felt tired from their hike up to the ridge. Pippa found some especially fascinating scent. She left the trail and went exploring a short way up the slope. She made her way through the snow like a rabbit, stopping here and there to wallow and dig.

The kids' hopes were up, but exhaustion and worry had risen also. They barely noticed Pippa's antics. Skye had the threat of a blister on one heel. That could become a serious problem. They needed to stop and take a look at it. Skye took off their backpack and started fishing in it for one of the tarps to pad a rock for sitting.

Hannah sighed. "When I walk a long time, I start to feel like my legs are a machine," she said. "Like a tractor or something. Working on their own to power through. Do you ever get that feeling when you're hiking?"

"I just imagine the fat melting off my ass as I trudge along," Skye replied.

Hannah snorted.

A terrible *whumph!* came from the slope where Pippa was rooting around. A huge thud, as if a tree had fallen. Pippa charged across the slope toward her humans with her ears flat and tail tucked. Skye and Hannah turned, and could only watch in horror as the snow fractured under her like cracking glass, like something in a sci-fi movie. It happened so fast.

The thundering snow flowed under Pippa like a load of gravel dumping. She tried desperately to swim through it, but the avalanche barreled her over, tumbling her down with the sliding mass until she disappeared underneath it.

The rumbling snowslide slowed down, and then it stopped. The debris from the slope made a pile that reached clear into the lake. Pippa was gone.

At first, the two onlookers stood frozen, unable to breathe. Then, they started screaming, "Pippa! Pippa! Pippa!"

There was no sign of her anywhere.

"What do we do? What do we do?" cried Hannah.

Skye stood with their mouth open, staring at the mess of broken snow.

"She's gone!" Hannah cried, covering her mouth with her mittened hands.

Skye ran along the edge of the debris field, trying to see any sign of the dog. Both Skye and Hannah gasped and sputtered, too shocked yet to cry. Was it safe to go onto the pile of snow? Would another avalanche follow? They didn't know. Then, in the quietness of the aftermath, they heard a tiny sound. A whimper? They both held their breath. It must have been a bird somewhere. It didn't happen again.

After looking upslope and trying to determine if more snow would come down, Skye decided it wasn't likely. This was a judgment call, and probably a bad one, but Skye told Hannah to stay where she was.

"What are you doing?" Hannah cried.

"I'm going out on the snow to look," Skye said. "I'll be careful."

Climbing gingerly onto the pile of snow, Skye searched the areas they hadn't been able to see. Nothing. A rock, for a moment, looked like a dog. As Hannah's desperate calls rang in the cold air, Skye's heart fell. Pippa had not survived. Why did they let her run up onto the slope? Why did they do such a stupid thing? Skye kept searching but with slim hope.

A small black knob caught Skye's attention, but for some unknown reason they dismissed the possibility and moved past, examining a crack along the snow. As a second thought, Skye looked back again at the knob. Could that be a part of Pippa? Returning to check, just in case, Skye started to feel it might be her. A closer view showed Pippa's nose, only her nose, sticking up out of the snow. Her snout felt only slightly warm, but it moved when touched.

"Hannah! I found her!" shrieked Skye. Pippa whimpered softly, under the snow. Using their hands, Skye started digging and Hannah joined in. They cleared away the snow from around Pippa's head quickly. Pippa's eyes rolled, she was in a daze. They both kept digging but the snow had compacted around her like cement. Digging frantically, they had to rest every few minutes. Sweating and panting, they kept on. It took at least half an hour to dig her out. Her legs were bent over her back like a scorpion's tail. But they got her out, and together they brought her off the avalanche debris.

Nothing suggested any broken bones. Pippa shivered hard, her eyes round and rimmed with red. Skye carried her a hundred feet or so down the snowshoe trail, to a place along the lakeshore that had a small rise to protect from wind off the lake. The flat area looked safe from avalanche slopes above. As far as they could tell. Pippa panted rapidly, with a horrible smile on her face. Her whimper sounded more like a whistle. She whimpered constantly. She didn't stop shaking.

"Something's wrong," Hannah said.

"I think it's hypothermia," said Skye.

While Pippa hunched with her tail between her legs, shivering, Skye used frozen, trembling fingers to open their backpack and pull out the tarps. Hannah gathered branches from the brush that grew nearby. The two of them laid the boughs on the snow and spread the thin nylon tarps on top. They lifted Pippa onto this bed, laid her down, and wrapped the top tarp around her tightly. Hannah lay hugging Pippa to try and insulate her while Skye gathered branches from the younger fir trees. When they had enough, both kids mounded them on top of Pippa.

Sunlight pierced the clouds for a moment. Skye and Hannah stood looking at the surrounding slopes. "It makes me feel so small!" Hannah exclaimed.

"We've got to get a fire going, somehow," Skye said quietly.

Both of them were soaked from digging Pippa out; their toes were cold and their hands were in pain. They couldn't keep moving because of Pippa, and they couldn't sit on the snow. They had only the one sleeping pad to sit on. Things were suddenly very serious.

The two of them worked together to drag a log from the edge of the lake to use as a seat near Pippa's head. The effort helped warm them enough that they could focus on making a fire.

Hannah dug in her backpack. "So, *Red Fern*, then?"

"*Red Fern*."

This time, they used driftwood from the lakeshore. When they had a good stack of wood in various sizes, they gathered some lichen and searched for dry cones and dead twigs on the trees. The two worked until they had an enormous pile of kindling. Skye put thicker branches down first to keep the pine tinder off the snow. Without a pocket knife to strip the damp bark from the twigs, it was the book that saved them. They tried over and over, using a few crumpled pages at a time, to get enough kindling going to light some larger sticks. But luckily, with several hundred pages, *Where The Red Fern Grows* offered enough dry material to produce some flames.

They built the fire up, focusing with surgical care on the placement of each progressively bigger piece of wood. It grew to a crackling and snapping source of warmth, the relief enormous as they toasted first their hands and front sides, then toes, and then their backs. They stuck their feet as close as they dared and laid their mittens on rocks near the coals.

"I wish we had some marshmallows," Skye said.

"Or, anything," Hannah added.

"Maybe someone will see our fire," Skye said, "and come check it out. Someone with trail mix."

Hannah coughed. "It's certainly smoky enough to be seen for miles!"

It took more than a couple of hours before Pippa made any effort to free herself from the chrysalis. When finally she scrambled out, she had stopped shaking and no longer had whale eyes, but she needed comforting. She wasn't fond of the fire, but she sat behind Skye and Hannah's log bench to receive some love.

Although they spent some time extinguishing the coals, returning the unused wood to the lakeside and the branches to the forest, and then folding up the tarps, they finished before mid-morning. But they'd gone only a mile from their camp. Sadly, they had little hope now of catching up with the snowshoers. Their success with the fire provided encouragement, especially considering they had managed to dry out somewhat. They declared that they'd make it back to town today for sure. They had no idea how vast this wilderness was.

The snowshoe trail led up the slope, and they guessed that a low saddle up above them was the destination. Hannah couldn't believe they were planning to go that way. She laughed, because all this was crazy and unreal and they were probably going to be found out there somewhere frozen solid and stiff like boards. Skye said it wouldn't be so hard, and that they'd be able to see the town from there, almost for sure. They headed out. Pippa had a slight limp now, which caused concern. She stayed behind them on the snowshoe path, her ears pinned back against her head, her eyes wide. "Poor girl," Hannah told her. Less snow had accumulated on the granite cliffs on this side of the valley, so the avalanche risk didn't worry them.

An hour later, they stood at the top of the ridge. It had been a climb, steep in some spots but not too bad, and they had rested along the way. Looking off in the direction they had come, they had the most impressive view yet. The clouds had lifted somewhat, and they could see for miles. Judging by the light, they were looking south. Below them they saw the valley with several lakes in it. Ringed by towering mountain tops, a mosaic of granite cliffs and fresh snow, everything looked postcard-perfect. Beyond, a backdrop of distant snowy peaks filled the horizon. Beautiful, but so unnerving to see the mountain wilderness go on forever. After gazing for a few minutes, they rushed to the other side of the ridge.

The snowshoe tracks led down into a valley not far below. The flat valley floor had no trees. Toward the far end, it squeezed between forested arms which sprouted from the high ridges that formed the sides of the valley. The one on the right was lower, and beyond it could be seen the green of forest below the snow-line. Beyond that rose a giant wall of granite. It extended off to the right as far as they could see. In the distance, more white mountain tops. They couldn't see a town. No sign of civilization anywhere.

Walking downhill seemed refreshing after their climb. For the first ten minutes of travel down the slope, the snowshoe trail made switchbacks. After that the hike down to the valley floor became relatively easy. It took only about an hour to cross the valley and reach the forest they had seen from the ridge. Pippa had perked up her ears, but her eyes had a wide and desperate look. She stayed behind, treading only in their footprints.

Through the trees below they could see a valley. It followed the towering granite wall on the far side. They headed down. The incline wasn't too bad and these woods grew fairly sparse. Soon they were out of the snow. Fantastic! Except for one thing. There were no more tracks. They could see no trail at all. The only thing to do was keep going.

"Wait!" Hannah cried.

Skye and Pippa looked at her. "What is it?" Skye asked.

"Over there! Look! Over there!" Hannah pointed at the snowy ridge at the end of the valley off to their left. Two spots, one blue and one green, were moving up the slope. The snowshoers!

"Hey!" they shouted, "Hey!"

Pippa barked. Her bark bounced off the mountains. Surely those people heard it. But they didn't seem to react. The spots kept creeping up the hill.

"Hey!" the kids shouted again. "Help!" "Heeeelp!"

"Woof!"

To no effect.

Skye, Hannah, and Pippa hurried down into the trees. They

had to find that trail! These woods were patchy, and more open than yesterday's forest. A lot of berry bushes grew here, and scrub. They came to a little river. It flowed from left to right.

This time, they made the wiser choice. They hiked in the direction of the current. If it wasn't the same river they'd followed to the cabin with Dad, it likely fed into it. And if it didn't, at least it would lead them in the general direction they needed to go. Hopefully. They looked up on the western slope. They couldn't see the people anymore.

The first half mile or so along the creek had scrubby openings they had to make their way through, sometimes taking large detours around brush. Crossing the pebbly areas took less effort. Now and then, great views opened up. Then, they entered the dense forest again.

"Oh, look!" Skye pointed to a small pine. The living tree had a bunch of dead branches on one side. Skye looked at Hannah. "Nanner, I don't think we'll have to do another night out here. But just to be safe, I'm gonna see if I can get some pitchwood for starting a fire."

"Yeah, okay," Hannah said.

They each broke off a dead branch. Hannah's thicker branch had pitchwood right at the joint. Skye handed the barren branch to Pippa, who waited in expectation as apparently sticks were being doled out. All three of the next branches broken off contained pitchwood. The kids snapped several inches off the big end of each branch and saved them in an inner pocket of Skye's pack.

After a while, they met a real trail again. A trail along the river that was running in the right direction! Good. It wouldn't be long now. Dinner in town, a call to the police, and maybe a shower tonight! The midday hour made them feel their hunger.

When some deer crossed the trail, Skye grabbed Pippa's collar but remarked about how good venison would taste. At this point the trail left the river but continued along not far from it.

"We're fine," Skye said. "We should just stay on this path."

"What's going to happen to Dad?" Hannah asked, since the subject of the police had come up.

Skye answered slowly, "I don't know. I hope so much that he finds his way."

"Yeah. We need to find our own way, right now. I sure didn't expect to be lost in the woods thousands of miles from home. I'm so hungry!"

"We're not lost anymore. This trail will get us back to the road," Skye said. After a moment, Skye stopped and gave a strange tight-lipped grin. "Life takes unexpected turns, Hannah. Dad getting hit by that drunk. He didn't see that coming, or the painkillers. The heroin, any of that shit. And here we are, on a two-hour hike that's lasting forever."

Hannah nodded and then, after looking around, gasped. "Wait, where is the trail? I don't see it now."

Somehow, they had lost the trail among the trees. Backtracking to look for it, they couldn't find it. The rush of water came from straight ahead, though. They scrambled through the woods in the direction of the sound. They found the river and were relieved to pick up the trail again, still in the valley bordered by the giant granite wall. Now Skye recognized the same cliff they saw across the valley yesterday when they first started to follow the creek. They were in the right valley!

They approached the bridge that crossed the little river. They should have seen this bridge yesterday from the other side, but somehow they'd missed it. Skye stopped suddenly. "Um," said Skye, "Bad news."

The end of the bridge as they approached looked fine, the part anchored to the near bank. But pink plastic tape had been strung between the railings. A closer look showed the rest of the bridge, a twisted mess of wooden boards, lying on its side in the water. The bridge was out.

"We'll just have to ford the creek," Skye said.

"It doesn't look too bad," Hannah said.

It wasn't great, though. They looked for a place to cross. The water ran too fast to hop from rock to rock, as channels between them flowed just a bit too deep. But a short way upstream a makeshift bridge had been built by lashing a bundle of skinny logs together. It spanned the creek a couple of feet above the water. Skye tested it out by walking across. Yeah, this seemed doable. Hannah would want to cross on her hands and knees. She led Pippa to the end of the bridge and encouraged her to step onto it. If it had been a log, maybe. Probably. But this thing, no.

Normally pretty good at crossing on logs, Pippa acted desperate to cross this stream. Her greatest fear was to be left behind. But she couldn't bring herself to cross on those sticks. Placing her front paws on the sticks, Pippa whimpered. She pulled away and ran up and down the little river, looking for a spot where she could cross. She fretted. She wailed. But she couldn't bring herself to cross that makeshift bridge.

"Should I try carrying her?" Skye asked, returning across the bridge.

"No," Hannah said. "If you fall in while trying to balance with her, that would be really bad."

"Well, then, let's just walk upriver and find a place we can cross. The stream will get smaller in that direction, right?"

"I guess so," Hannah said.

Pippa hunched her body for a while as they all three kept searching for a crossing. She knew she had let her family members down. Hannah tried to reassure her with praises. Although tired, hungry, and scared, Pippa made up for her shortcomings by performing her services as a trusty guide. Skye and Hannah let her know she was doing a great job.

Walking along the river's edge proved impossible because of all the brush. Traveling upslope from the stream, they crawled over logs and rocks in the thick forest. Muscle pain and sore feet made the going even slower. Hannah had bruising from the backpack straps. Pippa, with her sore leg, went around rather than over obstacles whenever possible. Skye and Hannah would peek down at the river at every chance, to look for a possible ford or place to cross on a big log.

After going on this way for longer than they realized, they finally came to a place where another sizable stream joined this one in a Y. They went on past the confluence, having decided that since there were now two streams instead of one, they should each be easier to cross. The branch they were following came downhill through the forest. They could walk along closer to the rocky creek, but still couldn't cross. They climbed just a little farther. They didn't know what else to do.

"This is getting ridiculous," Skye said.

"How can it be so hard to cross this crazy stream?" Hannah asked. Then her eyes got big. Her jaw dropped.

Skye tried to follow her gaze. "What is it, what do you see? A bear?"

Hannah gulped. "We'll be able to cross this creek soon," she said.

"What? How do you know?" Skye stared at her.

"Because we can cross at the same place we crossed last time."

Skye's head titled. "What?"

Hannah folded her arms and tried not to cry. She pointed to some cliffs across the creek, just up the slope a bit. "Don't you recognize those cliffs? With the big crack and the four trees? Those were right above our campsite."

There had been more snow on them this morning. Hannah was right. They'd spent the day walking in a huge circle. "Oh, my god," Skye said.

Hannah sat right down on the cold ground. This was it. This was finally too much. Pippa nuzzled her and stuck her tongue in Hannah's ear. Surprisingly, that didn't help.

Skye squatted next to Hannah and grabbed her mittened hand. Without saying anything for a while, taking the time to think carefully, they stayed in that position, holding Hannah's hand and petting Pippa, who had nosed her way under Skye's armpit.

"Well, you know," Skye said, "I think we should camp in the same spot again for the night. It was a good spot. The snow has melted off a bit, it will be easier to walk that same path again tomorrow. It only took, what, a couple of hours to get to the place we turned downriver. The clouds are breaking up, I think it will be nice tomorrow. Instead of turning right along the river again, we can turn left up that draw where we saw those people. Surely we'll run into someone tomorrow. This isn't the moon. The better weather will have people out."

Hannah laughed, tiredly. "You're unstoppable, Skye," she said. And then, "Okay."

So they crossed at the same place as in the morning and hiked back up to the standing slabs. They set up their chrysalis camp in the same way as before and then went to search for firewood. A fallen tree had been down for a long time. It rested on another log, which kept it off the ground. Hannah and Skye broke branches off this old tree. This time, building the fire went better. Skye used two pitchwood sticks and only used most of the *Cujo* book. They got the branches burning hot enough to light the end of a damp log when they dragged it onto the fire.

The two removed their boots and socks and set them close to the fire. Spark holes were less of a worry than trench foot. Even with a decent flame burning, and coals to set them near, the boots didn't dry enough inside. The damp wood didn't produce enough heat.

After they'd been sitting for a while, Hannah said, "What a shame."

Skye looked up from rubbing Pippa's belly. "What?"

"A nice fire and no s'mores."

"Or hot dogs."

"Salmon in foil."

"I'm so hungry," Skye said in a small voice.

They brought the boots into their bed when they lay down to sleep. Warm on the outside, they made good bed warmers. Skye fell asleep almost immediately. Hannah started to read the remaining piece of Cujo with her little flashlight. It was the last third of the book. She hadn't read the beginning, but she couldn't put it down. Not the best story to be reading, considering her circumstances. She eventually fell asleep with her face on the pages. She didn't sleep well. The night felt colder. Pippa stayed in her spot between them all night. Hannah curled up her legs to try to warm them up against Pippa.

"Did you see the stars last night?" Skye asked when they were shaking the morning dew off the ends of the tarps and folding them up.

"Oh my god, yeah!" Hannah said.

An animal had walked through their campsite during the night. Pippa had growled softly at it, waking them both. It sounded like something big. Whatever it was had investigated their packs, which probably smelled like food. They'd dragged one a short distance. Since there was no actual food, the grizzly bear or wolverine or whatever it was had gone on its way.

"Do they have grizzly bears here?" Skye asked.

"I don't know," Hannah said. "Wolverines?"

"I don't think so."

Pippa's limp looked slightly worse this morning. Her back left leg didn't move right. Skye felt it, but couldn't find any swelling or heat. "Maybe it's stiff from sleeping so cramped all night," they said. There wasn't much they could do about it, anyway.

The day grew gloriously sunny. Less wind blew, but the air had a chill. Although they walked the same route as the morning before, the scenery had changed. Some of the trees had shed their loads of snow. Everything looked different in today's light. They made it farther up the slope before they reached the snow-line, but the tracks from yesterday were still there.

The lake was glassy, reflecting the snowy granite cliffs and spires like a mirror. "Wow," Sky whispered, adding in a louder voice, "Man, I wish Mom was here to see this!" When they came to the site of the avalanche, they couldn't tell for sure if Pippa recognized it. She seemed stressed, and did sniff around a lot. Skye and Hannah crossed the pile of icy rubble gingerly, glancing over at the hole where Pippa had been. Hannah shuddered.

The next setback happened on the trail while they ascended to the saddle. They had nearly made it to the ridge, climbing a particularly steep section, when Skye slipped, unable to get a purchase on an icy patch of snow. Although Skye only slid a short way, while it was happening Hannah lunged and tried to grab Skye's arm. Hannah missed, and lost her balance, falling uphill onto the rocky slope. She seemed okay, though. She thought her forearm might be bruised. "And, ow, my ankle hurts," she said.

Skye took a deep breath, concerned, and told Hannah, "Let's get your boot off, and have a look."

"No, no. It's not that bad," Hannah declared. She was able to walk on it just fine, so after a rest at the top, where for a long time they sat and absorbed the beauty of the panorama, they continued on. Snow had already melted from the valley below, and from much of their path descending into it. The valley itself, a huge talus field, had been easier to walk through when covered with snow. Navigating the scree was difficult with a sore ankle or a sore hind leg. They found it easier to cross the valley and push through the dense growth of the heather and wild blueberry which grew along the other side.

The day started warming up. They stopped to remove their jackets. Skye took off both their jacket and sweater. While busy stuffing their clothes in the packs, and tying jacket arms around their waist, Skye caught some movement among the young conifers on a small rise just ahead.

"Pippa, come," called Skye softly.

Pippa stopped her rooting in the heather and came obediently to Skye's side, allowing her collar to be grabbed.

"Bear!" Hannah whispered. "I think it's a grizzly!"

They watched as the bear lumbered along the little line of trees and then stopped to scratch. It wasn't a huge bear, but it looked enormous to them.

"It's not a grizzly," Skye said. "It's black. A black bear."

Pippa either caught wind of the animal or noticed its movement. She went rigid and started to bark. Skye squatted and hushed her and tried to hold her snout shut. Pippa squirmed her snout free and barked again. Skye held the back of the dog's head with the same hand that had the collar and pressed their other hand firmly over her eyes. Softly, in a baritone voice, they commanded her to hush. Pippa struggled, but in her tired state she had limited energy. Maybe she felt the urgency of Skye's mood. She stopped barking. Instead, she panted heavily.

The bear stood up on its hind legs and looked in their direction. "Oh god, oh god, oh god!" muttered Hannah, instinctively trying to make herself look small.

"Is it 'make yourself look big' for a bear?" Skye asked, struggling with Pippa, who now made strangling noises in protest. "Or, no, that's a cougar. Bears, ummm, bears you're supposed to not look threatening. Hear that, Pippa?" A touch of anger accented that last question, due to fear and the frustration of trying to keep Pippa under control in her excitement.

"No, you ARE supposed to look big. Just not threatening," Hannah said.

Skye looked at her. "You sure?"

"Yes."

Grabbing Pippa around her chest and rump, Skye turned her onto her back and stood up, holding her like a baby. This position always quieted the dog and it also let Skye stop hunching over.

"I think so, anyway," Hannah added.

Pippa whined, but she didn't struggle. The bear watched for a moment. Then it apparently decided this group of creatures was too bizarre to piddle around with. It turned and waddled down the other side of the hill. A moment later they could see it trotting, then cantering, across the valley and up into the trees.

Skye set Pippa down and she shook herself. She was about to bark again, but Skye shushed her. Hannah and Skye stood looking at each other. Then they shouldered their packs onto aching backs and continued across the heather. The good smell of the low-growing shrub filled the fresh air. The sun shone brightly; there were no clouds.

Soon they saw what looked like a trail going up the ridge on the left. They were near the end of that ridge, not far from where both ridge and valley sloped down and disappeared into the river valley that followed the wall of granite. That was the river they could never find a place to cross. This time, they'd be going the other way, up the slope the snowshoers had taken. But, in the meantime, they were looking up a trail. This trail went up the low end of the ridge arm. Would it be worth going up there to get a view down the other side? They could see what lay before them before they committed to going that direction.

"Wait!" cried Hannah. "Look! A cabin! Oh my god, a cabin!"

"What? Where?" Skye looked in the direction of her pointing finger. 'What the heck, yeah, it is!"

Through the trees, they could both see a cabin near the top of the snow-covered ridge. Pippa got excited, too. Skye and Hannah hugged each other, and then gave Pippa some love, poor girl. The three of them scrambled up the trail, with both Hannah and Pippa limping noticeably.

"Are you okay?" Skye asked.

"It's hurting worse than it was, but I'm sure it will be better by tomorrow."

Skye had Hannah wait while they went to look for a branch that could serve as a walking stick. It took a while to find one. Then the two continued up toward the cabin, Pippa following.

"I wonder if there's possibly anybody there?" Hannah asked.

"At least there might be some food," Skye said.

But when they got to the area where they'd both seen the cabin, they found only a crisscrossed pile of blown-down pine logs. They stood looking, expressionless, both of them. When they reached the crest they had a glimpse of what lay beyond, but it was of yet more snowy mountains. A higher part of the ridge blocked most of the view. Rather than hike back down, they realized they could keep going around the end of the ridge. As they walked, they looked down on the spot where they'd seen the snowshoers. They could see a lake beyond. The part they could see looked perfectly square.

After a climb down the slope, they met their familiar river just below where it poured out of the square lake. At this point, they turned left and hiked up to the lake through the snowy woods. Then they went left again, with no trail, to follow above the lake shore. Another mirror-like lake sat surrounded by peaks.

The steep slopes here came right down to meet the water. As they walked on, they could see that the lake wasn't actually square, only the end. It had a shape more like a goldfish. "Oh, what I wouldn't do for some little cheddar crackers right now," Hannah said with a sigh.

Hannah's ankle was swelling, and hurting more and more. Skye found her a better crutch, a forked branch. She hobbled along as best she could. It was tough crossing a stream. They came upon a pond where they sat to rest on a big log. They rested longer than usual. Besides feeling anxious and hungry, tired and discouraged, they were smelly, sore, and both had horribly chapped lips. Pippa kept thrusting her head into Skye's lap and staring as if Skye could do something.

"I have an idea," Hannah said. She opened up her backpack and produced the plastic sandwich bag with colored pencils in it. "We can send Pippa ahead with a note. She can cover a lot more ground than we can."

"What a great idea!" Skye said.

They quickly agreed on what the note should say, and Hannah wrote it carefully in dark purple on a blank page from the end of *Cujo*:

> *Help. We are lost.*
> *Skylar and Hannah Jordan from Concord NH*
> *We just passed a lake with a square corner.*
> *Going west. Injured. Please call 911.*

Hannah dumped the colored pencils loose into her pack and placed her note in the clear bag instead. She took off Pippa's collar, folded the note around it, and secured it with numerous hair ties, some from her pack and the rest from her hair. Then she buckled it back onto Pippa's neck.

"Okay, Pippa!" Skye cried, "Let's go!" It was immediately clear to both Skye and Hannah: What were they thinking? There was no way Pippa would ever run on ahead without them. At home, she couldn't stand it when someone left the room.

Having drifted away from the lake because of the terrain, when they resumed their journey they made an effort to return to the shore. Still among the trees, Skye and Hannah stayed on their route a short distance above the lake. Following around the curving bank of a cove, their possibilities ended at a cliff. The only choice was to retrace their path nearly back to the pond. At that point, Skye stopped to treat a blister by folding an alcohol wipe and using it for padding inside the sock.

Starting again, they took the gentlest slope, picking their way up the snowy scree. Skye carried Hannah's backpack along with their own, because walking on the loose rock made it especially tough for Hannah. It got very steep. Her ankle hurt a lot, and now her armpits were sore, too

Skye borrowed Mr. Fuzzbuh from Hannah's pack and tied him to the crutch with the string from Skye's jacket hood. His super-soft stuffing made him a remarkably good pad. Hannah was beyond caring that much about the fate of Mr. Fuzzbuh.

It felt like they had been walking all day, but the sun remained high overhead. Finally, they came to a narrow pass through a low point in the crest of the ridge. They could see some lakes down below. And lots more wilderness. Hannah sat down in the snow.

"No-no-no," Skye said gently, pulling their jacket from their pack and spreading it on a rock. "Here, Nan, sit here."

Skye's nickname for Hannah had begun as Hannah Banana. It had evolved to BaNanner, and then, eventually, Nanner. Nan was only used in pleading requests or certain circumstances such as this one.

"Look!" Skye cried, pointing.

"What is it?" Hannah asked, without standing up.

"Look, look! It's some people!"

Hannah used her crutch to help her stand and looked across toward the lakes. "I don't see them," she said.

"There's several hikers going up that incline by the lake on the right!"

"Where?"

"On the slope just beyond the upper lake."

Hannah couldn't see them, but she and Skye started shouting. Skye said the people didn't react. "We'd better stop, or we'll start another avalanche," Skye said.

Hannah still couldn't find them on the slope, but knowing other people were around was a great relief. "Okay, I'm ready to keep going," she said.

Descending the ridge was also difficult for Hannah, but soon they reached a line of trees along a small shelf that zigzagged across the open area. They followed along this and then struggled over the lower part of another spur coming off the same mountain. They had to rest again. They were hungry. Pippa was, too. When they rose to move on, they startled a white hare. Pippa took off after it, back up the trail, the way they had come. No amount of calling brought her back.

"Let's wait here, she'll be back in a few minutes," Skye said. "She'll give up the chase."

They waited. Hannah needed a longer break anyway; her ankle throbbed horribly. After a while, Skye unpacked one of the tarps. They got Hannah seated on a sleeping bag on the tarp, with her back to a log. Her ankle rested on the other bag, still in its stuff sack. The two sat in the full sun, but it felt good. The area before them opened down into a great flat snowfield. Walking would be so much easier now. And Skye was sure they heard some voices in the distance, although Hannah couldn't hear anything. They both desperately needed Pippa to come back. But she didn't.

Pippa had instinctively chased the hare, her hunger driving her to pursue it back up the slope and then downhill through the treed area to the lakes, much farther than she normally would have gone before she gave up. Her hind leg slowed her down, and the hare had never been in much danger. She lost the scent. Then she realized she didn't know where she was. But something else caught her attention. Food. She smelled meat, just a faint whiff but she followed it. There it was again. Meat.

The people sat joking and laughing. They'd returned from an early morning hike and now lounged by their fire, nibbling sausages and grilled apple slices. They weren't through-hikers, just locals out on the Pacific Crest Trail for a mid-week overnight. There were five of them, all in their late twenties or early thirties. When the lame dog wandered into camp, everyone stopped talking.

Meanwhile, Skye and Hannah decided to pack up again and keep going. "We've got to reach a road or a trail with hikers on it soon," Skye said. It was beginning to sound like a recording.

But Hannah cooperated, and she hobbled along through the snow, changing arms with her crutch, trying not to think about her pain. Trying not to worry about Pippa.

"She'll catch up to us again," Skye told her, "she probably just chased that bunny too far and it's taking her a while to get back. You know she'd never leave us."

"It's funny," Hannah said in a low voice, "Before we couldn't get her to go on without us. Now she does, but goes the way we've already been."

"Yep, that's our Pippa." Skye gave something between a laugh and a sigh.

They entered a lightly forested area, walking on flat ground. A squirrel chittered at them from above. They hadn't gone far, but Hannah needed to rest again soon. They passed a small pond. They passed another. Hannah kept on hobbling. Finally, she admitted that she couldn't go on. She had to rest again for a while. Maybe she was just plain exhausted. Maybe she was reluctant to leave Pippa. But for whatever reason, she couldn't continue. Skye didn't argue.

Skye set a comfortable place up for Hannah again and felt her forehead. Neither one said much. After a while, Hannah said, "We've made a lot of mistakes."

Skye looked at her pensively for a moment and then said, "Yeah, things don't always go as you plan. This was supposed to be a walk to town."

They were quiet again. Then Hannah asked, "Skye, are we going to die out here? Out in this lonely, snowy wilderness? All by ourselves?"

Squatting next to her, Skye gave Hannah a long, tender hug

and spoke softly, "That's your pain making you say that, Nan. Of course we're not. We've only been out here a couple of days. We could survive for weeks."

"I can't, Skye," Hannah said. "I can't do weeks."

"No, that won't happen. Don't worry. We'll see someone soon."

A deep *woof! woof!* filled the air behind them.

Hannah stiffened. "What was that?"

"That's Pippa!" Skye cried, jumping up. "Somebody's with her!"

"Woof! Woof!" cried Pippa.

Très Chic

This little story revolves around
young French Bulldogs named Ellie and Diego.

Shelly and Larry are their beloved chauffeur and chef.

The lovely curve of her ankle attracts the attention of several admirers as Eleanor stands gazing over her shoulder. She has turned to scrutinize two women seated behind the railing and as she does so her lip trembles just a little, pursed in a puckery pout. She raises and tilts her chin. These ladies—her public! She sighs. How could they have neglected to appreciate her gorgeousness as she happened by this morning on the Avenue? Why don't they admire her and ask to pet her?

She notices the young man pouring coffee for these ladies as they lounge by the heater in the sidewalk cafe. Anyone can see what Ellie is thinking: *His eyes, oh his eyes! And how sweet he smells, like doves. I love him. I must have him! Perhaps he hands out biscuits!* To snap Ellie out of it, I say her name and give her leash a gentle tug.

The hood on her little parka needs adjusting. Ellie likes it over her ears, just so. We have a couple of inches of snow on the ground, but Ellie and her pal Jacques wear toasty warm dog jackets. Her hood is trimmed with thick and fabulous faux fur. Jacques's is in a cotton hoodie style, as he requires the fashions of a teenage adolescent. "Come along, you two," I say to the dogs.

French Bulldogs are sweet as sugar, but sometimes they exhibit a teensy bit of stubbornness. Ellie is hesitant to depart without the new sweetheart she has selected. The heartbroken look in her eye has one last glimmer of hope, « *Je dois t'avoir! Viens à moi, ma chérie!* »

Finally Eleanor acquiesces. I lead her and Jacques through the small town holiday crowd, stopping often to say, "Thank you. Yes, they are adorable, aren't they!" We slip into a store that allows dogs. It's warm in there, and something different for the dogs to enjoy. But we are only a few steps inside the shop when we see him. Standing quietly in his fresh-brushed beauty among the small houseplants, ceramic tiles, candles, and windchimes, is a tall, long-legged, and silky dog. An Afghan Hound.

Fabio, his owner tells me, has just come from the groomer. His unnervingly human-looking topknot of champagne blond hair is parted on the side, the silky thickness of it sweeping over his perfect left eye and flowing down onto his shoulders. The long nose and pronounced jaw add to his appeal.

Honestly, I've never seen Ellie speechless before. She's standing back, looking small and staring at him in the rudest sort of way, with her mouth hanging open. Her pal Jacques tries to distract Ellie, as he has quite a moony crush on her, himself. He nudges her. He hopes she'll follow him over toward the gardening department. But Ellie has fallen in love for the second time this morning.

I reach down to pull back Ellie's sable-trimmed hood and open her parka a bit to give her some air. Ellie responds with a burst of confidence. Stepping forward, she thrusts out her little hip and rolls back her shoulders. She tips her head to stare upward at the marvelous Fabio with eyelashes a-flutter.

But Fabio is aloof. He waits patiently while the man who accompanies him examines the holiday-themed scented bath salts, lifting each packet to savor the fragrance. The dog's glance does not fall on Eleanor nor upon Jacques. He sighs and looks across the store in the direction of the hunting and fishing department.

At last the man turns to browse his way farther into the store. The dog turns to follow him. Fabio has a deep chest and powerful loin, slightly arched. His build is substantial but refined, built for speed and endurance. He accompanies his owner with an effortless, springy step and a toss of his silky locks. Ellie is overcome with despair as her soulmate begins to slip out of her life. She rushes forward because surely he won't leave her if she renews his interest.

Perhaps it is the long hair hanging alluringly over his eye, but Fabio fails to notice the little Frenchie. Unprepared for obstructions underfoot, he stumbles over Ellie, trampling her under his gorgeous plumed forelegs. «Oh là là!» she yelps, and clearly she's thinking along the lines of *Vous m'avez enfin remarqué! Tu es un dur à cuire!* She bats her eyes at him some more.

The man and I exchange apologies while I rein Jacques in and check Ellie quickly for injury. She is fine, of course, panting, and staring at Fabio. If a French Bulldog could manage to place the back of its paw on its forehead, she would do so right now. Fabio, for his part, is merely confused. He reaches his shapely nose down from its great height, and he sniffs Ellie, his warm breath on her neck. Because he is a gentle dog who certainly doesn't want to hurt anyone, he gives her the tiniest gentle lick on her cheek.

This is a moment Ellie will treasure for the rest of her life. The day she met Fabio in the trendy boutique and her irresistible beauty threw him out of control so much that he grabbed her tightly and lost himself in their passionate kiss. She stares after him as he walks away without looking back. He and his owner only make it a few yards before a lady stops them to admire him.

Swept up in the mood, I tell Ellie, "Alas, *mon cherie*, it can never be! Like two great ships in the harbors of Marseille that draw close in the thick of the night, you and your *garçon amoureux* must find your happiness in knowing that life has let you meet. And, anyway, you're getting too warm in that parka. I need to take you and Jacques back out to the street."

The snowy scene outdoors is festive and colorful. It's still several weeks before Christmas, so shoppers dawdle and laugh and point at things in shop windows. The horse-drawn wagon jingles by, filled with families bundled against the cold. The dogs aren't impressed with the wagon, and as long as I don't attempt to lead them in that direction they are happy to pretend it doesn't exist.

We pass a family waiting outside a busy cafe. Several of them are seated on a bench, looking hungry, and among these is a frail man, an elder, with a blanket around his shoulders on top of his coat. The others are chatting away, but the old man sits staring at the sidewalk. His face lights up as Ellie and Jacques enter his field of vision.

The fellow looks so happy to see the dogs that we have no choice but to stop. Ellie stands before him expectantly, but the man isn't able to reach down and pet her. I lift her gently so that his trembling hands can stroke the side of her head. He speaks to her in a soothing voice, "What a lovely girl." She enjoys this thoroughly. The man tells me about the dog he had for many years. I know what it is like to cherish the memory of a long-absent pet. I lift young Jacques for him to caress, too. We leave him smiling.

The next human interaction we have is with a gaggle of young teenagers. They squeal when they see us, and approach the dogs in a hurry. "I like your dogs!" " What cute doggies!" Ellie and Jacques get excited, too. One of the kids is especially thrilled to meet the dogs. After asking, they kneel on the cold sidewalk and, respectfully, reach to pet Jacques. This goes very well. Everyone is happy and having a good time. The same kid, maybe ten or eleven years old, offers Ellie some love, too. She is more than happy to accept. So happy, in fact, that after a few nice scratches to her shoulders, she lunges upward and smooches that kid right on the mouth. By the reaction, I'm thinking this is probably the kid's first French kiss.

We are having such a delightful morning, Ellie, Jacques, and I, that we decide to stroll across the Ave and visit the park with the gazebo. More snow is starting to fall. Holiday music comes from a speaker high on a pole and strings of lights crisscross the park. All the trees sparkle with lights, too.

I find the perfect location for a photo. I pose the dogs and squat to view them through my phone. A Chihuahua startles the three of us by barking fiercely. He is wrapped in a blanket and is barking from his owner's arms, a few yards away.

"¡Yap yap! ¡Yap yap yap yap yap yap yap yap! Yap, yap yap," he says.

Ellie responds with an « Arf arf arf, arf arf! »

"Yap yap yap yap yap yap yap yap yap yap. ¡Yap yap yap yap yap yap yap yap yap!"

« Arf arf arf, arf arf arf! »

The lady laughs and apologizes at the same time. Her little dog is exceptionally loud. She tries to cover his mouth with her hand. Luckily, he doesn't bite her as he squirms his apple head free and yaps even louder: "¿Yap yap? Yap yap yap yap yap yap yap yap yap. Yap yap yap yap yap, yap yap yap. ¡Yap yap yap, yap yap, yap yap! Yap yap yap yap yap yap yap, yap yap, ¡Yap yap yap yap yap yap yap!"

« Arf arf arf! »

He calls out in a muffled voice as the lady bundles him away, "Yap yap yap, yap yap yap yap yap, yap yap yap. Yap yap yap yap yap. Yap yap yap yap yap yap yap yap yap, yap yap yap yap. ¡Yap! ¡Yap yap yap yap yap yap yap yap yap yap yap yap yap yap!"

But Ellie has to have the final bark, « Arf arf, arf. Arf arf! »

Here is the same conversation, translated:

"¡Super preciosa! ¡La cosa más maravillosa que he visto en mi vida! Hola, mi reina," he says.

Ellie responds with « Mon vrai amour, je vous ai trouvé! »

"Ojalá las estrellas brillaran la mitad de intensas que sus ojos. ¡El mundo se acaba si usted no se enamora de mí!"

« À chaque palpitation, mon cœur chuchote de notre amour! »

His owner is laughing and apologizing at the same time. Her little dog is exceptionally loud. She tries to cover his mouth with her hand. Luckily, he doesn't bite her as he squirms his apple head free and yaps even louder: "¿Sabe usted algo? La miro y me imagino el rostro que podrían tener mis hijos. Sueño con nuestra vida juntos, con su belleza y mi coraje. ¡Venga a mí, mi amor precioso, y abracémonos fuerte! Si tan sólo estos chimpancés nos permitieran abrazarnos, mi amor, ¡podría mostrarle lo machista y maravilloso que soy!"

« Nous vivrons d'amour et d'eau douce! » Ellie croons.

He calls out in a muffled voice as the owner bundles him away, "Estoy tan triste, la señorita solo me ladra, yap yap yap. No entiendo nada más que yap yap yap. Si tan sólo pudiera hablar su idioma yap yap yap, sé que ella me amaría. ¡Ay! ¡Qué trágico que todo lo que puedo escuchar de sus exuberantes labios sean los sonidos de yap yap yap!"

But Ellie has to have the final bark, « Je suis triste, vous aboyez seulement. Si vous parliez français, vous m'aimerais! »

Here is the English:

"Super precious! The most wonderful thing I have ever seen in my life! Hello, my queen."

"My true love, I found you!" Ellie cries.

"I wish the stars shone half as intensely as your eyes. The world ends if you don't fall in love with me!"

"With every flutter, my heart whispers of our love!" Ellie cries.

His owner is laughing and apologizing at the same time. Her little dog is exceptionally loud. She tries to cover his mouth with her hand. Luckily, he doesn't bite her as he squirms his apple head free and yaps at Ellie even louder: "You know something? I look at you and imagine the face my children could have. I dream of our life together, of your beauty and my courage. Come to me, my precious love, and let's hug each other tight! If only these humans would let us embrace each other, my love, I could show you how macho and wonderful I am!"

"We will live on love and fresh water!" Ellie croons.

He calls to her in a muffled voice as the owner bundles him away, "I'm so sad, the lady just barks at me, yap yap yap. I don't understand anything but arf arf arf. If only I could speak her language yap yap yap I know she would love me. Oh! How tragic that all I can hear from her lush lips are the sounds of arf arf arf!"

But Ellie has to have the final word, "I'm sad, you only bark. If you spoke French, you would love me!"

The snow has begun to fall with sincerity. How lovely the park looks with all these lights twinkling through the big, feathery snowflakes. I stoop to adjust both dog coats. My fingers ache from the cold. Checking the time, I tell the dogs that we must go. We're running late.

The sidewalks are kept clear of snow. But the Avenue is crowded with shoppers. We take the paved path north out of the park instead. It's blanketed in snow, but the deserted trail has room for us to trot. Ellie and Jacques have a great time leaping and bounding through the whiteness. After a while I am huffing and puffing, but now I'm plenty warm.

We reach our street and turn along it, but continue to trot. We've gone only one block before we all three run out of steam. It's not far now. But the snow is coming down fast. As we approach the intersection, I decide to pick up the dogs. I've learned to be wary of drivers in this town, and in the driving snow, well—no point in taking chances. It's becoming difficult to see. I make eye contact with the woman in the Subaru at the stop sign, and then I toddle my way across, made top-heavy by my two reluctant passengers.

After we make it to the curb, a pickup skids right through the intersection, recovers its trajectory, and keeps on going. "Good timing," I tell the dogs. They both want down. But now I'm worried about their cold feet. Jacques struggles to be free. The snow is wetter now. It feels colder. I've got to carry these dogs up a steep hill. It's not comfortable for any of us. Should I put them down? I decide to continue to carry them. Jacques is giving me a dirty look. These dogs are surprisingly heavy.

At last we arrive at their house and I can finally set them down. We shake off all the snow and I punch the door code. Ellie and Jacques push eagerly through before the door is fully open. I remove the leashes and coats and hang them to dry. Jacques runs ahead of us into the kitchen.

When I arrive, I fill their bowls with fresh water. The dogs are happy to be home. Ellie rolls on the carpet. Jacques licks Ellie's face.

Sitting on the floor, I take both dogs into my lap. I rub their bellies and scratch Ellie below her ears. "Ah, Ellie," I say, "It must be so discouraging to be let down, day after day, in all these romantic interludes." She looks up at me, a sad glint in her soulful eyes. Such a tragic life she has, so much work it is to engage with her public, so much sorrow should a romance fail. She sighs. How does she go on? Jacques licks Ellie again, and she acknowledges this with a bump of her nose. I wink at Jacques.

"Well, Ellie," I say, "Tomorrow we'll dress you in the pink sweater. And I'll bring those cute little snow boots I told you about. We can use the gold lamé leash!" Ellie vaults out of my lap. Jacques and I follow her through the laundry room to the place where the leashes are hung.

Ellie sits and raises her paw, begging to go out again.

Best Friends Forever

Inspired by Carmen's dogs:

Bernese Mountain Dogs named Forest and Ranger,

and her Miniature Dachshund named Daisy.

The transmission occurred on Tuesday at 8:15 am. All four of the dogs received it, but Max was having some tech trouble so it's unclear how much he understood.

Daisy woke before the others. How strange it felt to be awake so early! With her head still on her pillow she projected a mirror and gazed into it. Big round blue eyes stared back at her. With those and her tricolor coat, Daisy looked something like a long thin Beagle. Her Mini Dachshund body fit perfectly on one of those air surfboards made for humans. Daisy owned an old board, she had fun playing on it sometimes. She was practically an expert on humans. They'd always fascinated her.

She poked her head out between pink gauze bed curtains. She sniffed the sweet morning air, heavy with fresh oxygen thanks to the abundant greenery in the neighborhood. After her bath and pedicure, Daisy emerged from her room with a sparkly bubblegum-pink bow above each ear.

Ranger and Forrest shared a much larger bedroom. They were Bernese Mountain Dogs. Ranger weighed in at one hundred twenty-three pounds, with the younger Forrest almost as big. One might easily tell them apart but the two dogs certainly could have passed for brothers. As Daisy finished her breakfast they finally showed up at the meal area. Forrest wore a collar this morning, along with the ever-present endearing and hearty smile of a Berner. He had yet to fully wake up.

Daisy pointed out that Forrest had worn that collar the day before. He grinned at her and winked. The color changed from solid green to purple with tiny, brilliant yellow lights flittering around inside. Daisy sighed. His generation had no taste. Forrest and Ranger went to their bowls.

When Max didn't respond to their call, Ranger went to his

room. A Border Collie in his late fifties, Max had already fallen back to sleep. Ranger woke him gently and told him to ignore the messages and stay home. A NANA would come and see to his implant, as they hadn't been able to repair it remotely.

For the last couple of days, Max had been licking his lips a lot and chewing his paws. The strange gray appearance of his room made him uncomfortable. Everything had the dull look of bacterial cellulose and mycelium plastic. Normally, Max liked his table and chair to be mahogany and his bedclothes to be royal blue with a silk texture and tassels. Ranger reassured him that it would all be fixed soon. They'd get his implant sorted out, and he'd be fine. Max nodded. He tried not to look too sad about missing the outing. He stuck his snout back under the covers and returned to his snoring.

Two hours later, Forrest, Ranger, and Daisy stood at the bus stop, tails wagging. When the transport arrived they seated themselves in the nose of the cabin so they could look out the front window. They and an older model NANA were the only passengers.

In all their years of working for the Fish & Wildlife Service, none of the dogs had ever been farther into the mountains than their favorite hiking trail near Marblemount Station. Forrest drooled heavily with excitement. The bus zoomed along the familiar tidy streets lined with eucalyptus and olive trees. They rode through the grasslands, past several manufacturing plants, and then followed the dry riverbed through the hills dotted with oak trees and wild grape.

Just as they entered the pines, their vehicle had to brake for a herd of wild pigs. Despite his being a wildlife monitor, and a sizable animal himself, Ranger could never get used to how

huge those boars were. Some of them were twice his size. Along
their way, the dogs saw plenty of jackrabbits and deer. A coyote
leapt and arched to pounce on a mouse. At one point, Forrest
declared he smelled a grizzly. Before they knew it, they'd arrived
at the station.

A terra-trekker waited for them to board, but they balked
at the pungent smell of ozone. This particular vehicle served
to transport monkeys into the forest for mushroom collecting.
It must have been cleaned the day before. Forrest and Ranger,
eager to see the jungle, were willing to put up with the odor and
ride, but Daisy would have none of it. The trekker would have to
be left with its doors open to air out.

Marblemount Station held the outer node of the mesh net-
work on the west side of the mountains. The wild which covered
most of the planet indeed grew wild; left to itself with minimal intervention. Of course, the dogs could continue communication
with one another, but not far beyond Marblemount they would
lose contact with the civilized world.

There would be nothing but nature and wild animals where
they were going, and they'd be utterly on their own for three
weeks. No Neuromorphic Adaptive Neural Androids to rescue
them, and no contact with Nexus Global. If they were attacked
by a cougar or a wild boar, they'd likely lose their lives. They
knew this.

Other than ozone odor drifting from the terra-trekker, the
station smelled like pine trees, coyote piss, and overheated plastic. The place amounted to a cluster of uninteresting pods, and
the dogs recognized the small one on the left as the creature
commissary. That was the place to go for meals or any supplies,
and also the sleeping quarters. The team decided to grab a pic-

nic lunch and spend the day exploring Lookout Mountain. They returned to the station after dark. They were dirty, exhausted, and happy.

After a bath and a meal, they were each supplied with an oval foam-filled pad to sleep on. They shared a small room. Forrest and Daisy competed with changing the wall colors until Ranger stood and stared at them. They knew they'd better leave it, or Ranger would jam their implant interfaces.

In the morning, Daisy's pink snack satchel went missing. Daisy didn't wonder, even for a moment, what might have happened to it. She demanded Forrest and Ranger give it back. The two wasted about ten minutes pretending they hadn't seen it, and then several more minutes laughing and feeling pleased with their joke. Somehow, Berners never tire of this sort of thing. Finally, the three of them went to breakfast.

The terra-trekker still smelled worse than Daisy might have preferred, but with the crew so eager to see the rainforest none of them complained about the odor. This assignment held a special significance. Nexus had observed some sort of disturbance in one of the pocket rainforests deep in the mountain range. The analysis program concluded that the cause stemmed from a rare population of wooly monkeys. As this wild species faced extinction, Nexus sent the team of dogs to track them down and gather data.

These vehicles were loud and ran on wheels. Four wheels. The team had ridden a trekker before, but not for such a long trip. At such a low speed it took well over an hour to get there.

The wheels traveled on a gravel surface, making for a bumpy, uncomfortable ride. The sound of the vehicle scared most wildlife away, but they did see a bobcat.

At last they arrived at the Ross Basin Nature Preserve. Of all the accessible wildlife areas in the Salish Sea watershed, this was the most remote. It smelled amazing. They recognized the aromas of fig trees and wax palm from the conservatory near their residence. There were many smells they couldn't define.

Out of the vehicle in no time at all, the dogs got busy. Ranger marked several trees, and Forrest dug some soil samples. Daisy put her keen dachshund nose to use, sniffing for a scent. She didn't find anything promising, but they already knew which direction to go.

They broke trail through shrubs and young trees. They descended into the bed of a long narrow seasonal lake. Many of the larger, gnarled trees had exposed roots, making the way difficult. Ranger noted that they could begin searching after they had crossed the river, but Daisy felt determined to find evidence of the monkeys right away. Despite slowing the group down, she insisted on sniffing every root and stone. She found a scent. And then she found a footprint. These were a large species of monkey, but the team hadn't expected a footprint quite so big. The print had poor definition, it looked faded, probably a week old, but finding it did increase everyone's excitement.

They had to find their way through dense forest, but eventually they arrived at the river about a kilometer south of where the wooly monkeys had been detected. At this point, they needed to cross the river. Swimming was not an option, because they each carried panniers filled with supplies.

The stretch of river upstream from them ran narrow and

deep. Mountain slopes faced one another across the narrow gorge through which it ran. The rainy season had left a bend clogged with the wreckage of downed trees, and one of these logs made a suitable bridge.

Daisy trotted across and stood waiting on the other bank. Forrest went next, tail wagging and—then he scratched desperately at the log as he tumbled into the brown water. Panicked, he splashed and sank and then resurfaced. Panting and gulping water, he warned Ranger to watch out. A wire stretched across the log. He'd run right into it. Now Ranger and Daisy could see the wire too. She must have gone underneath it.

With a great deal more splashing, Forrest swam to the bank where Daisy waited. He reached for the slope with his front paws, but the dirt came away as he clawed at it. The more he grabbed at the bank, the more dirt fell into the river. Ranger reminded him to calm himself and tread water. He'd be there in a minute. Balancing with deliberate, calculated movement, Ranger stepped over the wire and made his way along the log and then the bank to where Forrest struggled. Ranger turned his back to Forrest and instructed him to grab his tail. Forrest clamped his teeth around Ranger's white-tipped, bushy tail and Ranger strained against the weight, his strong legs climbing, a slow step at a time, until Forrest clambered to stable ground.

They were still breathing hard when a face appeared, shadowed among the shrubs above them. Ranger and Daisy both saw it. The creature traveled upwind, long gone before they could reach it. Ranger had a good look, though. A monkey had been watching them. Certainly a wooly monkey. All their noise must have made it curious. How lucky. It would be easy to track the fresh scent.

That, however, marked the extent of their good fortune. Why was a wire stretched above that log? Could it have been placed there on purpose? By who? And for what possible reason? It must have been swept downriver with the trees. But how did wire get so far out into the wild to begin with?

And then came the problem of the contents of Forrest's packs. These things hadn't been packaged for a dunking. They nosed through the contents, finding that most items would be all right. The food rations were dry enough, thankfully. But the medications box had come open, and all the contents were ruined. There would be no nutritional supplements. Much more ominously, the heat regulation tablets had dissolved.

Forrest felt pretty sure he and Ranger were going to die. Out in these mountains without those pills, their organs would boil in the heat of the day. They needed someone to shave off all their fur. They needed to abandon the assignment. They needed those pills. Ranger suggested that Forrest calm down. This certainly posed a problem, but they'd find a way to keep cool. They weren't going to suffer. The river would be nearby.

After everyone had a roll in the dry grass and a good shake, they hoisted their panniers again and started off after the monkey. It had circled above them and traveled north at a good pace. The smell was as Daisy had expected, rather rancid-cheesy with a base note of fresh vomit. The creature followed a stony path, but when it dipped down toward the river it left some clear prints in the mud.

Daisy stopped so suddenly that Ranger ran her over. She didn't seem to notice. Her mouth hung open, and her telepathy became crackles of white noise. She stared at the footprints. No thumbs. No tail marks or finger marks: Human. These footprints were human. They had to be.

The dogs studied the prints. They were certain there must be an explanation. Humans had been gone for nearly a century. How strange those prints looked, and somehow, so beautiful. Hearts pounding in their chests, the team trotted hurriedly along on the trail of the creature. Their excitement overwhelmed any sense of caution they should have had. Humans! Actual humans! They broke into a run.

The trail climbed and climbed along the slope. They came to a rise, and then a sudden drop into a valley along the face of the mountain. Because they were running, they ended up bursting out of the woods into a clearing. They found it filled with people. Seven or eight of them, just standing there. Humans.

"Oh my god!" a woman cried. Of course, the dogs couldn't understand her language, but they got the idea. They were having the same reaction.

"Jesse, what the hell! You led them here? You were supposed to kill them."

The man the dogs had been following walked over to the speaker and handed him the weapon he was carrying. "Here. You do it," he said.

"What's wrong with you, Jesse?" a larger woman with long hair cried. Ranger recognized the scent drifting from her tightly woven hat as fresh-cut ryegrass.

Ranger suggested that maybe they should run. Forrest was thinking so, too. Daisy told them not to worry.

The humans were scrawny, dressed in crude clothing, and

smelled like hunger and stress. Odors of smoke and urine and countless other things permeated the area. The site reeked like no other the dogs had ever encountered. More humans peeked out of a hole in the mountainside, apparently the entrance to a cave. They seemed so vulnerable. Except for that weapon the one brandished.

The man holding the weapon repeated, "You led them right to our camp. What have you done, Jesse?"

"But they're not drones or robots. They're just dogs," Jesse replied. He rubbed his short, trim beard with his sleeve. He had wooly black hair.

"They work for Nexus. Without a doubt, they work for Nexus. It's probably too late," said an old man. "They've found us."

"Dogs!" a small woman cried. She had just arrived. "Dogs! I can't believe it!" She addressed the team, "Can you talk?"

Everyone was silent for a moment.

Everyone looked at one another.

There were two huge furry dogs and one little one. The little one matched the big dogs exactly in color but not in pattern. All three were wearing packs. One of the big dogs was all wet. They just stood there. They weren't growing or hissing. They didn't seem aggressive. They looked scared, if anything.

"I guess they can't talk," the small woman said. "Jeez, you'd think by now they'd have implants or something."

Members of the group murmured and a few uttered louder remarks.

"How incredible! I never thought I'd see dogs."

"Seriously, folks. We need to get rid of them."

"It's too late. What good would it do to destroy them? We're found."

"Let's ask Adrian what to do."

A woman fetched Adrian from inside the cave. A dozen more people came out with him. Adrian had frizzy, curly white hair on his head. He stared at the dogs. After a moment of silence, he said, "Wow. Dogs. Of course they'd use dogs." He stood for another moment, while everyone waited. "Can they speak?" he asked.

"No, they don't have any language. Just dumb animals. Certainly they have tracking equipment, though."

"Why, after all this time?" a woman asked.

Adrian stared at the dogs. "That's the strange thing, isn't it. Gosh, what beautiful animals."

"We should dispatch them right now, Adrian," said the man who held the gun. "And throw them in the river. They're probably sending some sort of signal as we speak."

Adrian took a moment to answer. "Well, now," he said, "Let's not be in a rush. We need to think about this. If they're sending a signal it's ended right here. If we plan to kill them, we should take them back the way they came, and kill them downriver somewhere." He paused. "Let's see if they'll let us look at what they're carrying. That could tell us a great deal."

Some of the crowd expressed unhappiness about this plan, but soon the majority agreed.

"Be careful," one man said, "dogs bite."

Two women volunteered to approach the animals. Someone handed each of them a good-sized stick, so they could warn the dogs that they weren't prey. They held the sticks up in front of themselves as they walked toward them. The large dogs backed away, but the small one took a step forward.

Daisy trembled. Real humans! But what would the humans

do? Ranger tried to call her off from going so near them, but a swirling mixture of excitement, curiosity, and anger filled her entirely. The gold-crested female stopped, but the dark brindled one crept toward Daisy and held out her hand as if to touch her. Daisy instinctively bared her teeth.

"Watch out, Kalina!" the woman with the hat called.

The big dog who wasn't wet came forward protectively. It stood right next to the small one, but it still didn't growl or bark.

"Come away from there, Kalina," someone shouted. "Those are dangerous animals. You're going to get hurt."

But Kalina didn't listen.

Standing next to Daisy, Ranger didn't know what to do. What was their intention with those sticks? This human didn't seem aggressive. What should he do? Forrest still thought it would be a good idea to run. Daisy had gone all to static again.

The female put her stick down and moved closer to Ranger. Her companion said something to her, but she shrugged her off. Her arm trembled as she reached toward Ranger. What a strange thing to do! He asked the others what was happening. Forrest didn't know. Daisy didn't know. The human touched him. Right on the top of the head. A thrill of electricity ran through his body. Overcome with panic and awe, Ranger fainted.

When the big dog fell, he landed on the little one, trapping it underneath.

Gasps and exclamations filled the air as the community stood watching.

"You know, I don't think these dogs have come to hurt us," said the small woman who had spoken before.

Adrian called softly, "Hey, just come back now, you guys. Come on back, Kalina. Leave the dogs alone. Let's see what they do."

Kalina backed off, and everyone stood breathlessly, watching the dogs.

The big wet dog went to its companions and started licking the unconscious dog's face. Meanwhile, the small dog squirmed out from underneath it. The prone one slowly revived, and lay there, staring at the women who had approached it.

Adrian said something to the man next to him, who retreated into the cave. Nobody said or did anything. They stood watching the animals. The dogs didn't move, either. When the man returned, he carried roasted meat on a ceramic plate.

"Hand it to Kalina," Adrian said.

The woman who had touched the big dog carried the meat timidly, but rather hurriedly, over to the dogs. She set it down and backed away.

Ranger lay upright now, with a paw out in front of him. He didn't feel hungry, only confused. Daisy wasn't hungry, either, and that food looked like it might have something wrong with it. Forrest was always hungry. These humans were obviously attempting to show friendliness. Daisy thought they should be careful. Forrest agreed, but that meat did smell inviting. His observation rang true. Both Ranger and Daisy agreed that the meat smelled tasty. Venison. Like venison kibble, only better. Forrest started to drool.

One of the humans said something, and then all those closest to the dogs backed away a few meters. Were they hoping to build trust? Forrest wondered what they should do. Ranger noted that these were humans, and he felt fortunate to have a prime opportunity to interact with them. Daisy pointed out that humans couldn't be trusted, and that they should probably retreat safely away and hide somewhere until the time came to return home. Ranger thought they should report on the humans the same way they would have observed the wooly monkeys. A much more significant find. Forrest sniffed at the plate.

Forrest sniffed again, uncertain. He'd like to try this food. But would it be disempowering to accept it? Did the humans mean this as some sort of trap? Why offer food on just one plate for the three of them, wondered Daisy. Ranger pointed out that they were primitive humans. The food smelled good. Forrest tasted just a tiny lick of the food. He decided to eat some. It would show the humans they were cooperative. The three agreed. He took a nibble of one of the strips of food.

"They're eating it," the old man whispered. "That's good. If we're going to check those packs, we've got to do it right away. We may have to get the hell out of here."

A large young man spoke up for the first time, "And, just maybe, they were looking for us to help us."

The fellow with the gun snorted. "You want to take that chance?"

"We have no evidence the NEXUS was ever hostile," a gray-haired woman reminded.

"Benna, you're so incredibly naive," the old man said.

Adrian spoke up, "There it is. The same old argument. The fact is, we don't know. So let's exercise some caution. Grandpa Alexander's right. We should examine those packs as soon as possible. But we don't want to scare the dogs off, or get someone bitten. So, everyone please stay calm."

They watched the dogs in silence. Only the one would eat,

but he worked away at the plate, chewing one strip of meat at a time. As he and his brother panted, their faces looked friendly with big smiles. But they were such huge animals.

"I can do this," Kalina said. She watched the creature finish his food. She moved forward, without a stick this time, and stood a few feet from the one who'd been eating. She turned sideways to him. It seemed a less threatening posture. She held out her thin brown hand without looking directly at him. The dog stepped forward.

Everyone held their breath. The huge furry creature leaned to sniff Kalina's fingers. Several people aimed weapons at him.

The female's fingers smelled like so many things! She'd recently been handling human young, beeswax, and all sorts of food. Forrest wanted to know what he should do. The humans were aiming weapons at him, Ranger told him. Those are something that could kill him instantly. Forrest froze. He couldn't move a muscle. Ranger thought it best to let them do anything they wanted. Daisy let him know she would stand by him no matter what the humans did.

The human didn't try to touch his head again. This time, she said some things to him, looking him in the eye. She asked him some sort of question. Then she slowly reached toward his pack. What the heck! Why did she want the pack? Nobody knew. Ranger reminded him to let the human do what she wanted.

Kalina slowly opened the flap of his pack and got just close enough to peer inside. Nobody made a sound. The dogs remained still, all three of them. Everything felt unreal. She could see some equipment in the bag, but mostly it looked like nuggets of food, packed by different varieties in small clear pods.

She saw only one item which looked like some kind of tracking or communication device. It sat right at the top of the load. Kalina snatched it up as she closed the flap again. She whispered, "Thank you." Maybe he could understand the intonation. She slowly backed away. Gosh, what beautiful animals. How incredible to see dogs in real life.

It looked like a hologram emitter, someone said. The large young man had a look. He turned the little cylinder over in his hand. Yes, he was pretty sure. He couldn't find a power button. He tapped on a panel. And indeed a hologram appeared. He placed the emitter on the ground. They couldn't hear any sound, but images of monkeys flickered. They looked like the big wooly monkeys that had several colonies nearby. More images. All monkeys, and of this same type. Some were accompanied by measurements or graphs.

The humans started chattering when they saw the monkey images. Many of them looked relieved. The weapons were lowered. The chatter evolved into an argument.

The community members eventually decided, creating a fragile truce, that they shouldn't destroy the dogs, but they would keep them in the village. The risk of letting them return and alert the NEXUS somehow of the colony's existence felt too great.

The human female returned the equipment to Forrest's pack. She seemed much more at ease. She let Forrest sniff her hand again. Ranger came forward and checked her hand, too. The human reached out to Daisy, but Daisy would not allow any sort of contact. When the humans tried to convince the dogs to enter their cave, it was Daisy who dragged her feet. These creatures were not to be trusted.

Remember, cautioned Daisy, that the human species had driven themselves to extinction. Humans were neither intelligent nor loyal. The dogs also had to remember that these particular humans would be the descendants of the elite few who had run NEXUS before the Singularity, themselves descendants of those who cruelly controlled the rest of humanity for hundreds of years before NEXUS.

After they had all passed through the entrance to the cave, a human pulled a barrier across the lower part of the doorway. Daisy knew it. They were trapped! Ranger suggested she calm herself. They were guests. No reason to worry. Forrest looked in awe at all those antiques. Daisy drew their attention to a computer terminal. Humans had used these to operate the NEXUS. They noticed an ancient power cell nearby. The room was set to quite an eclectic mixture. Ranger pointed out that the humans probably didn't have the room set to anything at all. He doubted they had the technology. The colors and forms weren't changeable. Everything around them dated back more than a hundred years or else they'd made it themselves using their opposable thumbs. Forrest wondered, then, did the humans actually carve these chairs? With some sort of blade? Daisy thought probably so.

The cavern smelled of body odors and mildew. Cluttered with furnishings and equipment, the space also contained an odd assortment of creepy items. Simulated animals of various types, reproduced in miniature out of stone and wood, sat scattered around the room. Their soulless eyes stared off into nothingness. Small false humans also peered from shelves. Some orchids, clipped off from their stem, stuck up out of a tall, narrow dish. Attached to the walls were random images, recorded with varying degrees of accuracy using some multi-colored substance. All these objects had no apparent purpose other than to be observed. The most interesting display sat right in the middle of everything. The humans had reassembled the complete skeleton of a wooly monkey.

The dogs were led along a passageway in what appeared to be a great system of caves. A man showed them to a chamber used for the storage of cleaning supplies. He and some others set down quilts and cushions for them to lie on. They brought in a ceramic bowl which contained water for the three of them to drink. The situation was barbaric, frankly, but the team tried to be gracious. These were humans. Actual humans. And they were very much alive!

The team decided to stay with the humans for the full three weeks and complete their assignment as best they could, studying the humans rather than the wooly monkeys. They had to commit most of the data to memory, because, through mischievousness, or, more likely, fear, the humans had stolen nearly all of their instruments from their panniers.

Daisy performed some equally shady actions as she snooped around the caves. On shelves here and there, she found rectangular objects. These smelled ancient. Upon examination, she found that these had an outer protective cover and flimsy sheets of cellulose fiber bound inside. Although difficult for her, she found a way to separate the sheets with her nose and paw. She did tear a few before she perfected her technique. Each sheet was marked on both sides with code. An ancient language, probably used by these humans, since they still communicated vocally, like the apes. She couldn't use anthropologic document translation software, as it was stored in the cloud. Even so, Daisy collected a couple of these objects from the children's area and hid them so that she could study the language. She had a personal interest.

The dogs fascinated the cave community. They had no pets or other animals living among them, except for a wild boar who angrily awaited slaughter. He occupied a pit not far from the entrance to the caves, in a grassy area under some eucalyptus trees. His mood had deteriorated even further when they began his seven days of fasting before the annual festival for which he'd serve as the main course.

The dog breeds were looked up in the encyclopedias on Grandmother Putnam's computer, along with how to care for them. A schedule had to be established in order to give them some time to rest, because community members of all ages would constantly want to visit them. Kalina remained their primary handler, but they were popular with everyone. Once they became used to the situation, the two large dogs began to quite enjoy being petted. Even the little one eventually warmed up.

Adrian suggested assigning jobs to the dogs. Helping with the hunt seemed a good choice for the two Bernese Mountain Dogs. The Dachshund might be more useful in removing rodents from the caves and gardens. After a great deal of discussion, the group bestowed the official position of Dog Trainer upon Kalina. A bow-hunter would go with her, and they would take the Bernese dogs on a short hunting trip. Hopefully, the dogs could be used to track and carry the prey. If nothing else, they'd offer a defense against panthers.

Daisy, back in the cave, protested the separation, but as he and Forrest headed up the trail with the humans, Ranger reassured her. The humans had found a way to include them in their community. They were apparently on a hike. It would be a fine opportunity to learn more about their habits. Daisy expressed her concern that the man they accompanied belonged to the group of unfriendly humans. Forrest felt she needn't worry, the man seemed focused on searching for prey as they climbed through the brushy woods.

The man's name was Gildor. He and Kalina conversed sporadically as they searched the mountainside.

"These dogs must have seen some amazing things out there, eh, Gildor? All these years our scouts haven't found any sign of other people. Do you believe there are any?"

"There must be people still. Why would AI breed barkless dogs?"

"Hmm. I never thought of that."

They hunted in silence for a while.

"Gildor, do you ever wish you could go and search for other people out there?"

He took a moment to answer. "No, I don't think anyone who has managed to survive would be anything but a head of livestock by this point."

"That might not be the case. NEXUS is performing marvelous stewardship of the environment. Maybe people have gained more control. I can't believe people have been completely subjugated by technology they created." Kalina thought about it. "Things look much better than in the past. Certainly the people out in the world must be thriving."

"Think what you want, Kalina. Dream on."

Gildor suggested they take the east trail, where they'd have a better view. When they arrived at the cliffs, he went right to the edge, as he always did, and looked over.

"Oh my god!" he exclaimed, "Oh no!"

"What is it, what?" Kalina cried.

He looked at her with an expression of I-told-you-so and motioned for her to come look. Kalina wasn't fond of heights, but she took baby steps over to where she could see below.

"Look! More dogs! And there are drones with them!"

"What? Where?" Kalina whispered. "I don't see them," she said.

Gildor stepped closer to her and leaned forward to say something important. "Kalina, listen to me. I'm going to kill these dogs." He held his bow high in the air.

"I won't let you do that!" Kalina replied. "I'll tell the council. You'll be banished!"

"I'm sorry, Kalina."

"For what?"

Forrest and Ranger could only watch this conversation, they couldn't understand a word. Both humans seemed excited about something, while the man exuded a huge amount of stress hormones. Something was wrong. The pitch heightened, and then, after a moment of silence between them, the male swung his bow right at Kalina. He knocked her off the cliff!

Forrest and Ranger rushed to the edge. Kalina had managed to grab some roots at the top of the cliff. She clutched them, dangling, and screaming. The man lay down on his belly and reached to rescue her. He caught her by both wrists. She gasped for air, sobbing out some words. The male spoke to her again. And then he let go of her.

The woman plummeted to the river basin far below. The

dogs searched in panic, but couldn't see where she landed. It didn't make much difference, anyway. What's he done? they both asked. They turned to look at him. They backed away from the cliff's edge. What's he done?

The human reached for an arrow from his quiver. He stared at Forrest and Ranger in a very unsettling way. Daisy warned them to watch out. Daisy? She repeated: Watch out!

"Hey!" shouted a man. The group had emerged from the brush and come upon the scene of Gildor reaching for his arrows while the dogs cowered. "Hey, Gildor, you stop right now! Don't you dare!"

Gildor paused and looked around at the newcomers, a group of half a dozen, along with the Dachshund dog. Several of them were armed. He slowly lowered his hand, letting the arrow drop back into his quiver.

"God damn," he said, "you should have come sooner. These brutes just shoved Kalina right off the cliff! She's dead."

Everyone ran to look over the precipice. No one could find her. Stunned, the people stood gaping at the dogs and Gildor. One man fell to his knees and started crying. Then others joined him with tears and moans. "Kalina!"

"Evil NEXUS dogs!" shrieked a woman. She and an older man both aimed weapons at Forrest and Ranger.

"No," another woman shouted. "Don't do it!"

This woman held a position of authority. The two lowered their weapons.

"Not yet," sobbing, she continued. "We need to take this to Adrian. Poor Kalina. My god, poor Kalina. How could this happen?" She and a young man hugged each other and sobbed.

"Why did the little dog lead us here?" the man said, wiping his eyes. "She made such a fuss."

Forrest and Ranger, of course, couldn't understand any of this. The murderer had told some kind of lie. They let Daisy know what they'd seen. All three dogs were at a loss. They stood panting, with their tails tucked and their heads down. The whites of Forrest's eyes were showing. Ranger was sick on the gravel of the trail.

In the days following Kalina's death, a fog of despair lay over the community. Wailing and angry voices echoed throughout the caves. A memorial ceremony held at the location where she fell had everyone in the community in attendance. Everyone except for the dogs, and two men who stayed to guard them. One man stayed to supervise the dogs; the other to keep the dogs safe from the first man.

Confined in the supply room, the dogs pondered their situation. They had only a few more days before they must return to meet the terra-trekker. If they failed to return, another team would be sent to investigate. But they had another, more immediate problem.

Having lost their primary advocate and person who could best communicate with them, Forrest, Ranger, and Daisy faced a greater danger than ever before. The balance of opinion had turned against them, and the smell of fear dominated in most of the caves. Wherever they went, people with weapons followed them. They had no privacy anymore.

Based on the behavior of the people, the dogs predicted that they would continue to be kept prisoners indoors with only periodic breaks outdoors to relieve themselves. They considered what resources they had for an escape. Daisy's research, past and recent, along with Ranger's astute observations, gave them enough information to formulate a plan.

Jesse, the kinder of the two men, came to take the dogs out one at a time to commune with nature. He started to place a loop of rope over Ranger's head, but Ranger reacted the way anyone would. "I'm sorry, guy," Jesse said, "but we have to use this. It's not personal. Just until we find out what happened." He sighed. "To Kalina," he added.

Ranger couldn't understand his words, but the intent showed clearly. He allowed the man to leash him. They went along the same trail the dogs had generally used for this purpose since their arrival. During the return trip, Ranger nosed around among some flowering henbane and pulled a massive plant out by the roots. He acted as if he were playing with the plant, shaking it from side to side as he walked. The man laughed and petted his neck. As they passed the pit that contained the boar, Ranger dropped the plant and stepped near the edge of the pit to stare down at the unfortunate animal. The boar snarled and lunged upwards at Ranger, who drew back to escape his wrath.

Daisy went next for a walk, and then Forrest. Instead of waiting to relieve himself somewhere along the trail, Forrest did his business right there by the pig pit. The man seemed surprised but without complaining he cleaned up the mess. While he did so, Forrest kicked his hind legs out repeatedly, raking the henbane into the pit.

"Oh, no!" cried Jesse, "I'm in so much trouble!" The boar was supposed to be fasting. But he gobbled up every shred of that plant. Jesse looked at the dog. "Well, buddy," he said quietly, "I won't tell anybody if you don't."

They kept the dogs in a makeshift pen the following day at the long-anticipated harvest celebration. As the three peeked out between woven branches of thorny barberry, Ranger and Daisy reminded Forrest that they must comply with the demands of this species as much as possible, even though it meant enduring ancient practices of inequality and brutality.

The path to the site of the fair followed a creek downhill from the vicinity of the caves. The trickle crossed a shady meadow, relatively flat, a place that caught a cool breeze now and then. The spot had a view of both the slopes above and the river below. Naked children splashed in the creek while adults lounged in their most colorful attire on reed mats and wooden chairs.

Community regulations prohibited music outdoors except for at these rare holiday events. The beat of congas and goblet drums went on throughout the day, often joined by crude stringed instruments and the lilt of a silver flute, along with singing and dancing on the fresh-mown grass. Although they felt sorrow about Kalina, and confusion regarding what had happened, the people carried on with their tradition of thankfulness and joy.

Food, of course, played a central role. A long table sagged under the weight of their bounty. Olives, figs, walnuts, and grapes overflowed earthenware bowls, while greens and roots from the forest lay heaped on wooden plates. Great quantities of grilled fish from the river lay on beds of rosemary sprigs. Loaves of millet bread and rye sat proudly stacked on breadboards. But the focal point of the day was the boar. The ritual butchering, roasting, and consuming of the wild pig had intrinsic significance to the ceremony. By the time the meat finished cooking, the children had gone to bed, but every adult in the community must eat some pork, with the liver especially desirable.

Although pigs suffer no ill from tropane alkaloids of black henbane, and it in fact probably made this fellow's transition easier, other mammals, including humans, are affected by secondary poisoning. The tone of the party changed dramatically after the meal. This dosage of henbane had both inebriating and aphrodisiac effects. Many of the group experienced hallucinations and even delirium. The three dogs took this opportunity to go and take care of some details which needed their attention. They would have several hours before they needed to worry about human intervention.

Daisy smiled as Forrest effortlessly unlocked the door to the chamber which contained their stolen belongings. They needed their tools to be able to speak the human language.

The smell of someone wafted toward them, and then they heard her coming down the hall. The woman came into view. She froze when she saw the dogs. "Woaf!" Ranger shouted. The bizarre, deep-pitched noise echoed within the caves. The woman nearly fell over. Her hands went to cover her ears, too late. Her eyes round, she turned to scurry away. It's doubtful if she realized that she ran in a hilarious henbane-induced slow motion manner. She did not look back.

Ranger hadn't barked since puppyhood. His deep, loud voice shocked everyone, including himself. "Woof!" he barked again, just for the heck of it.

Forrest opened the door to the chamber. The space contained a century's worth of this and that, all in stacks and piles. Broken electronics, ragged baskets and bundles, mildewy books, and random junk made it difficult for Forrest and Ranger to fit into the room.

Even so, Daisy quickly sniffed out their dog packs. Most of the equipment had been replaced inside them or could be found nearby.

Their bionic eyes had limited function so far away from civilization, so the dogs would need to rely on outdated muzzle-held equipment which operated through telepathy. Ranger nosed around and found a neuromorphic imager and the small hologram emitter.

After gathering several images from certain wall displays scattered throughout the caverns, they reunited in the storage chamber and loaded the data to the emitter. The result produced a perfect hologram of a robed man with a short beard and very expressive eyes. Forrest toyed with the image for quite a while, working to animate the figure so that it had particular movements and the ability to send a message to unaugmented organics through telepathy.

Daisy began to feel nervous about any humans who might start to sober up. She heard voices in a nearby cavern. Ranger went to listen around the corner in the passageway. Yes, it did sound as if some of the humans had ingested only tiny amounts of the toxin. Forrest attempted to reassure them that he was working as fast as he could.

A man stumbled along the passage. The sound of his footsteps and bumbling approached them. As Ranger instinctively backed up, he knocked into a wooden shelf behind him, dislodging a small object which tumbled to the cave floor. The passing man stopped. He muttered something and tried the door handle. His sour odor drifted up from the gap underneath. The door started to open, but Ranger lept to block it with his weight so it wouldn't budge. The man tried the handle again, muttering louder, hammering on the door and cursing. Another human's voice, and then the two of them pushed on the door together.

Forrest brought an old chair to wedge under the doorknob, and he and Ranger leaned against the door to make it seem shut tight. The men pushed and kicked the door. They had some sort of conversation. Then their footsteps faded and it grew quiet.

Knowing that they may have gone for reinforcements, Forrest got back to work on the hologram, using his claws and teeth to perform delicate adjustments. While he continued, Ranger and Daisy searched for a blue plastic canister. It belonged with the imager, but it wasn't in either of the packs. Only a few centimeters long, it might have ended up anywhere.

More voices and smell of humans in the hallways. A man said something, just outside the door. But he continued walking. Daisy searched madly for that cylinder. Without the chips it contained, this whole action meant nothing. Finally, Ranger found it in one of the baskets. Forrest continued to tweak the hologram. It had to be perfect.

At last he finished. Now the chips could be integrated. Both Forrest and Daisy worked on this, and it didn't take long. With the system fully configured, Forrest placed all the holo tech on the floor behind a heavy cabinet, where the soft blue light from the emitter couldn't be seen. From this location, several of the sleeping quarters should be in range.

It was time for a deep breath. Everyone must be on tiptoes now, until they made it back outdoors. Ranger tried not to let his worry spread to the others. He pushed the chair to the side and opened the door a crack. He shut it quickly. A man sat next to the door, leaning against the wall. He must be one of the two who had tried to enter. Posted as a sentry? Ranger peeked again.

The man didn't move. He might have dozed off in that position. Ranger cracked the door further. Yes, the man's gentle snore and heaving chest made it obvious. No other human smell reached their nostrils. Time to move. With his lips, Forrest drew the door shut softly behind them.

Because of the late hour, they decided to return to their own storage closet rather than rejoin the festivities. Forrest had some curiosity about the state of things out there, but agreed to turn in for the night. Not far from their chamber, a woman shouted something and came running up behind them. Even if she'd been in her right mind, she probably hadn't learned about the foolishness of approaching an animal at a run from behind. The woman blathered at them, apparently reprimanding the dogs for disappearing from the pen as they had. But then she picked Daisy up and cuddled her, and it became clear that she meant no harm. Soon she zig-zagged off to some other location. The dogs reached their closet and slipped inside.

Adrian called a community meeting the following day. Someone came to fetch the dogs and bring them into the largest cave, where many members of the population were seated. Forrest, Ranger, and Daisy weren't surprised that a meeting had been called, or that they were brought in. But although they couldn't understand Adrian's speech, it didn't take long to realize they were wrong in guessing the reason. He spoke for quite some time, while members of his audience interrupted, shouting out or standing and speaking without bidding.

"Regarding the dogs themselves," he went on, "There are several options for us, as the committee sees it: One, we could let them return to NEXUS, and risk their leading NEXUS back here.

Two, we could keep them here permanently, depending on the outcome of Gildor's trial. NEXUS might come looking for them. Perhaps the dogs have tracking devices.

The third choice would be to do away with them.

Although I feel the animals are innocent, and we don't believe they were searching for us to begin with, I see no choice but the third to be viable. We should take them south, beyond where they crossed the river. Do it there. Make it seem that a natural accident occurred."

An odd silence filled the cavern, but two women broke it by bursting in from the corridor. They rushed to the podium and stood before Adrian, breathing heavily and looking around the room. Benna, the elderly one in the red sweater, whispered in Adrian's ear. He turned and stared at her, then at the other woman, who wore a blue dress. The blue dress woman first looked at the dogs, and then at Adrian, who eyed her with incredulity but gave her a nod. She took his place behind the lectern.

"Neighbors," the woman said, "I have seen the Lord! Jesus came to me in my chamber just now! He was right there with me!"

A rumble went through the crowd, with reactions as diverse as the number of people in the room.

One of the louder residents scoffed, "Haha, it was the bad wine last night! People were talking about giant white rabbits!"

Another said, "I've heard there must have been some kind of bad mushroom in the festival salad. I don't know, but I saw things I never wish to think of again. Atrocious things."

Some more youthful members of the audience cheered at this and were hushed.

The woman in blue went on, "I know that many suffered delusions for several hours. But I was one of the few unaffected. I tell you, the Lord came to me today."

Few in the audience were impressed by the woman's declaration. Most of them didn't practice the ancient religions. Even those that did observe the traditions seemed skeptical. People tugged at the necklines of their shirts or whispered to their neighbor. They shook their heads and rolled their eyes.

"You must believe me!" the woman cried. "He smiled at me. He gave me a blessing. And he, he—"

"He told you to let the dogs go free," said a man seated among the crowd.

Everyone turned to stare. The man who spoke, Huoli, had been adamant about euthanizing the dogs from the start.

"Yes! He did," the woman replied. She stared at him, too.

Huoli spoke in a soft voice, "He came to me too. This morning."

The crowd gasped.

"I saw him, too!" a teenage girl exclaimed. "You know, my family is Buddhist, but—Last night, during the night. When I got up to pee. It was Jesus himself! I thought I dreamed it. He told me too, not with words, I just knew. Free the dogs."

Only one person suggested that these three might be lying. Everyone ignored him.

The dogs knew the conversation had turned in the direction they'd anticipated. Their situation changed entirely. The people grouped around them as if they were some sort of miracle. And, truly, a miracle had taken place. The miracle of a swift reversal of public opinion.

The time had come to depart. The community held a dinner in the caves that very evening to honor the dogs, who were obviously making ready to leave. Unfortunately, leftover pork was served, but at least nobody suspected the dogs might be responsible. Forrest wanted to try a small piece of the meat, but Daisy and Ranger quashed that thought quickly. All around them humans wept and groveled. Others swaggered and flirted, or fought invisible foes under the table. A spontaneous chorus formed, with a sound amusingly unpleasant. The noise of the gathering lasted well into the night.

In their quarters later, the dogs decided that, on the way back to meet the terra-trekker, they would record images of the local wooly monkeys, who were easily found on the mountainside. They'd have to falsify a lot of data, but they felt this would be the best plan. It would be best if the humans remained undetected.

They departed the following morning while many of the community still lay groaning in bed. On their way out of the system of caves, Daisy stood on her hind legs to catch everyone's attention. She jumped up on the chair by the grandmother's old computer terminal. As the people gathered close around to see, Daisy amazed them all, including Forrest and Ranger, by painstakingly typing out the following with one claw: s-e-c-r-e-t i-s s-a-f-e / w-e w-i-l-l a-l-w-a-y-s r-e-m-a-i-n y-o-u-r b-e-s-t f-r-i-e-n-d

Outside on the trail, the team turned to take one final look at the humans who stood in front of the cave entrance. Scrawny and dressed in drab clothing, they appeared as they did when the team first saw them. They had the same look of amazement on their faces, too.

Einstein in Pajamas

In the following story,

Darcy's English Cream type Golden Retriever puppy
named Einstein
has a great day.

It was one of those autumn afternoons in the Pacific Northwest when the sun glares down from a pale blue sky. We'd had more than a week of hot weather. A rascally pack of dog days had tunneled right under August's fence to chase the summer heat all the way into October.

I've happily walked dogs in wind, snow, and driving rain, but this gorgeous day set the stage for a particularly sweet outing with Einstein. Birds chirped. Squirrels chittered as they scampered along the maple branches. A trace of wind fluttered the leaves. I had no idea this would end up as the walk with Einstein I cringe to remember.

To start things out on the wrong foot, I'd lost track of time and left my house in a rush. It would have taken maybe eight minutes to get dressed properly. In my silliness, I didn't give myself those minutes. Why? Two reasons:

One: I'd been up half the night because Loosey, the Queen of all Cats, couldn't make up her mind if she wanted to be under the covers or not. I'm sure I had bags under my eyes. I wasn't in my best form. I had to focus carefully while driving over to Einstein's.

Two: I'm fastidious about my business practices. I arrive at a client's house on time. So, as a result of trying to maintain pride in my work, I showed up for the dog walk in my around-the-house clothes. These included a pair of cheap sparkly fluorescent orange flip-flops with big plastic flowers on them. It was just a half-hour walk with an easy dog. I said to myself, *What could go wrong?*

I pulled forward and backed up again to adjust my position against the curb. It's a quiet neighborhood with no traffic, no cars parked in the cul-de-sac. But I felt I must park perfectly alongside that curving curb. Nope; I tried again. I was running a little late, but it had to be right. Nope. Nope. Okay, one more try. I got it! I reached to open the passenger door so I could see. Nope. Two more quick tries, though, and I had it.

After I scrambled out of the car, I had to reopen the door to grab my giant floppy hat. I hadn't neglected to bring protection from the sun. My broad-brimmed hat has always attracted attention, but I needed its shade for my face and neck. The floral pattern clashed ridiculously with the patterns of the silk wrap-around skirt I had on, made from upcycled saris. And I'd grabbed some UV sleeves too. The kind with a hole for your thumb. Unfortunately, this pair had stripes of wild fuchsia pink.

In a real hurry now, I punched in the door code. No, that was the bank code. Dang, no—my voicemail code. Rats. A mistype of the actual code. Blast! Oh no, wait, that was the actual code. The door unlocked.

I didn't expect to find Einstein in his pajamas. He sat staring at me through the white bars of the child gate which kept him downstairs. He wore a human pajama shirt to prevent him from scratching at a hot spot. The shirt had horizontal black and white stripes.

"What's the *matter*, Einstein?" I admit, I said it. "How come you're in jail?"

"Everyone sits in the prison of his own ideas," he seemed to reply.

I couldn't help myself: "I'm *relatively* certain there's some real *gravity* to this situation."

But of course, in *reality* my absolutely wonderful Einstein jokes were lost on the half-grown Golden Retriever. He sat there looking beautiful; his cream coat still a bright puppy-white. Along with the smiley muzzle of a Golden, it made his look of happy innocence irresistible.

Unaware he wore a cartoon character no-pants outfit, Einstein held his head high, proud of his shirt. "Sorry, bud, I'll have to take this off for now," I told him. "We can't risk it getting dirty."

I was ill-prepared that day to walk a puppy. Einstein tugged enthusiastically on the leash as we left his house. Hopefully, I wouldn't trip in those flip-flops and fall on my face. Because I was tired, I'd need to take extra care to be patient. Luckily, I knew a trick. I'd learned this from my many walks. I took a few deep, slow breaths. Then I pictured myself as royalty, back in the days of long velvet robes. I envisioned my hat as a grand golden crown that I must balance on my head. This compelled me to walk with good posture, my shoulders back, spine straight, and with a calm air of regal power. I knew the most important factors: Relax, and the dog's got to know that you're the boss. Dogs want guidance from a calm and consistent leader.

Why not head to that little pond? I thought. I'd glimpsed it a few times through the trees near the golf course just a couple of blocks away. I wasn't sure about the trespass status of those woods, but in that heat I needed a place for Einstein to cool off. I had to stop a few times along the way, in order for him to remember not to pull. I didn't worry about Einstein's paw pads because the sidewalk felt cool enough to my fingers, and anyway he had a grass strip to walk along if he chose.

As always, Einstein had a great time. Every falling leaf was clearly a dog snack. On our walks, we often exchanged hellos with the lady on the corner who would be out digging in her yard.

(Humans are allowed to do this, I explained to Einstein.) Farther along, our friend, the retired fellow, would usually emerge from his garage with a big smile and some neck scratches for Einstein. But nobody seemed to be around today.

We headed into the woods. I changed my mind when we neared the pond, but it was too late. Between us and the water was a sea of stinking mud. Einstein got his paws in it before I could react. Now he had short boots made of thick black stickiness. So, okay. My fault. I decided to carry him to the pond to see if we couldn't wash his paws off in the water. I balanced along the crisscross of logs in my sparkly fluorescent orange flip-flops, carrying a sizable and struggling pup. I made it, though! I made it! All without becoming too horribly smeared with mud myself. I knew his owner wasn't fond of dog tracks on her beautiful hardwood floors, so if I could get him cleaned up it would be a good thing.

"Look, Einstein—-water!" I set him down in some rough grass on the shore. "Look, Einstein!" I said again, "Water!" I wiggled my fingers, causing some ripples in the glassy surface of the pond. "Water, Einstein!"

Einstein was having none of this. Retriever or not, he wasn't about to allow that weird shiny stuff to touch his beautiful white fur. He made one giant lunge away from the pond, landing squarely in the mud. *Splat!* And then, staring at me, in defiance of any thoughts I might have about returning to the water, he lay down. On his side. In the molasses-like mud that smelled like Hell's chicken coop.

Black goo now covered most of Einstein. With him acting reluctant, there was no way I would get him to the water and then past the mud again. I could feel my invisible crown of serenity begin to slip. Another deep breath, and I pressed my lips together, thinking. Acting on the only idea that showed up, I feigned excitement about returning to the road, calling "Let's go! Fun! This way!" I turned toward the street, my body language indicating that I assumed Einstein would follow. "Higgledy-piggledy kittens! This way!" I said enthusiastically. It didn't matter what words I used. But I kept in mind that it's always important to distinguish clearly between the dog and the master.

Einstein floundered his way out of the mud, splattering me thoroughly. Such a good boy! We made it back to the sidewalk. Despite my best efforts, slippery mud now coated the tops of my sparkly fluorescent orange flip-flops and oozed up between my toes.

I couldn't take Einstein back to his home to hose him off because I had no access to the backyard except through the house. Not to worry. I'd find a neighbor. Surely there'd be lots of folks out in their yards on a glorious day like this. Someone would let me use their hose. There was no one.

Oh—there. Up the street. Some kids were out in their driveway, shooting hoops. Thank goodness. As we made our way along, my anticipation transferred to Einstein, and he started pulling. I no longer had the patience for that. I'd become too worked up. As a backup, I carried one of those little halters, like a horse wears, but made for dogs. They work well to keep most dogs from pulling while wearing the thing. So I unhooked that from my belt and strapped it onto Einstein's head. Einstein and I strolled up, casually.

"Hello, boys," I said. They looked like nice kids. Young teens.

"Hi," the eldest said, looking uncomfortable.

They were neighbors, sort of. Probably they'd recognize Einstein. "I wonder if I could ask a favor. I've got a problem. You see, I'm a dog walker, and this is your neighbor's dog, Einstein. I can't get into the family's backyard and I need to hose him off so he doesn't wreck their carpet when I take him home. Could I please use your hose for a minute?"

The kid looked even more uncomfortable.

"It's a big problem for me," I explained. "I can't take him back like this, and I have no way to clean him up." In case this wasn't obvious enough. "Do you recognize him? His name's Einstein. He's normally a white dog."

"Sorry, we don't have a hose," the kid said. ". . . that works," he added, after noticing a coil of the thick green one behind his left foot.

I would have been more annoyed if it hadn't occurred to me just at that moment that I was dressed pretty much like a clown. Besides the mismatched skirt and giant hat thing I had going on, my oversized sunglasses and a bloated, overfilled, black leather waist wallet were a part of my dog-walking outfit. Various items of dog-walking equipment dangled from my person. And here was Einstein, covered in mud and wearing his little horse-halter. We may not have worn the typical dress of someone in that up-scale subdivision. Besides, the kid had listened well to his elders. Stranger danger.

"Okay." I sighed.

I looked down at my muddy feet. Probably, the big plastic daisies on my sparkly fluorescent orange flip-flops hadn't been helpful, either. Why are people so judgemental?

I looked at Einstein. He looked back up at me through his lovely mask of mud. He panted happily. He didn't care. Not a bit. His day was going great.

"Come, Einstein."

Einstein was thinking he might like to play with these boys. Or maybe he merely wanted to pee in their yard. "Come," I repeated firmly. It's so important to be consistent. Dogs are happier when the hierarchy is clear.

It was hot. I felt sweaty, and a bit cranky. The mud stank. A neighbor drove past, waving and laughing. At Einstein, hopefully. He did look cute. In a slimy-otter or disgruntled-bear-cub sort of way. I hoped my growing exasperation didn't show from a distance.

We walked two blocks to Einstein's house. From my car, I retrieved the big old beach towel which I keep stashed in the back. I kicked off my sparkly fluorescent orange flip-flops and then, standing like a flamingo on the porch I wiped my feet carefully. I punched the correct code into the keypad and opened the front door. I looked at Einstein. He looked back up at me through his drying, cracking, and shedding mask of mud. He looked at the towel.

Some dogs enjoy a nice towel-dry. Einstein is not one of those dogs. I tied him by his leash to the porch railing. I tiptoed through the house, pushed a dining-table chair out of my route, and opened the sliding glass door. When I returned, Einstein seemed sure something was up. He wasn't sure he was happy about it.

I undid the leash from the railing and reached in my best diplomatic manner to enclose the mud monster in my towel. He squirmed away, dropping large shreds of dried mud. I wanted to avoid sweeping the porch. I led him to the lawn. With my hands, I brushed off as much of the gray crust as he would allow.

"Okay, buddy," I said. "You've got to be a really good boy,

here." I laid out the beach towel on the lawn, and, after several tries, got Einstein to step onto it long enough that I could pull the ends up and hold them against him. Now, gripping around his chest and his rump, I held a squirming dog-in-towel taco. Most of his muddy dog parts were inside. Laughing, I managed to stand. I didn't fall over backward. I held tight to keep the towel in place.

Einstein licked my face. "I defer! I defer!" he told me, in dog language. "You're not planning to hurt me, are you?" He struggled harder, just in case. In through the doorway, I used my bare toes to shut the door behind us. Einstein's attempts at wagging his strong, feathery tail inside the towel were not helping the cause. Nor were his paddling feet. He nearly threw me off balance and into the foyer table with the expensive-looking vase. "Knock it off!" I shrieked, ironically.

Raising my voice didn't help at all. Now Einstein squirmed like a frantic, forty-pound fish. I had to rely on my own brute strength to resolve this situation. I held him firmly as we passed into the living room. He tried to lick my mouth. With my hands occupied, all I could do was turn my head, which made me stumble. We fell toward the back of the white sofa. I turned so that when we hit, it was with my rear end. Einstein struggled. I moaned.

We headed off again toward that back door. Across the beautiful woven rug. Past the scratch-free dining table. Einstein flailed his legs, trying to break loose. "Hang on, guy," I crooned to reassure him, "we're almost there. Nice and calm." But the big puppy was anything but calm at this point.

Einstein was fed up with me, my towel, and the whole idea. When we reached the doorway, he wriggled free, and I had to let go of the leash so he didn't land on his head. I stood panting. As Einstein took off across the yard, I turned and peered into the house. It didn't look too bad. Only the back entrance, where Einstein had launched, looked dirty. I whisked the slider closed so that he couldn't run back into the house.

During liftoff, Einstein had smeared me with mud. I took off my waist wallet and dangly things and set them on a planter. I looked around. The garden hose snaked across the lawn, ready and waiting. First, I sprayed the front of myself off. The water was cold, but after the initial shock it felt good. I left the water running and went to get Einstein.

"Come, Einstein! Here, boy!" I called. "Such a good boy," I told him as he came running up. I bent and petted him, then led him over to the hose. It was immediately obvious that hose baths were currently on Einstein's "absolutely not" list. I didn't have time for this. But the family had a wading pool. Einstein's boys were well into their teens. This pool must be for him.

To my surprise, Einstein went happily into the pool. It felt like a miracle. Without shampoo, I couldn't get rid of the smell. The best I could do was make it less noticeable. I was just happy to remove the caked mud, scrubbing him with my hands.

While I dumped and rinsed the pool, Einstein found the spot where the water leaked from between the spigot and the hose. Oh boy, fun! He happily dug in the puddle there, splashing dirt and mud all over his wet coat. With my bare foot, I scraped as much soil as I could back into place. Puppy and I headed over for a quick second bath. On the way, I noticed a half-finished beer in a glass mug. It must have been forgotten. Some people believe beer removes skunk smell from dogs. Maybe it would help. I snatched up the beer.

I refilled the pool. I washed the dog. Now he looked clean but smelled like stinky mud and beer. I ran him around on the lawn to dry him off a bit. By this time I wasn't smelling too great, myself. I took off my big floppy hat, and tied my hair up off my face with my neck scarf, knotting it over my forehead, nineteen-fifties housemaid-style.

Common sense should have told me to tie Einstein up somewhere to prevent him from indulging himself while I rinsed the pool again. Doggedly focused on my work, I didn't manage to give this any thought.

While Einstein enjoyed the sunshine on the grass, smiling his beautiful Golden Retriever smile, I rinsed the pool again, coiled the hose, and set to work on the entrance to the house. I got onto my hands and knees to wipe the mess with an old towel, using a ceramic flowerpot as a bucket.

I heard a strange sound. It came from the balcony next door. I peered up through the glare of the sunlight to see a toddler and a Spaniel staring down at me as I'm bent over, cleaning up after the dog. Then I followed their gaze as it shifted to Einstein. He now lay on his back in the sun. On the lounge chair. Right next to where I'd set that beer glass. His head faced me, the satisfaction of his life of leisure all over his face. The toddler's mouth hung open. The Spaniel's eyes were wide with wonder.

"This isn't what it looks like," I called to them. "I'm the boss here, not the dog!" I stood up to go and remove Einstein from the patio furniture. The time had come to tie him up somewhere. Then I made the mistake of catching the happy stare of his big brown eyes. I muttered under my breath and bent back down to finish cleaning up his mess for him.

That evening I received a text from Einstein's owner: Were those my sparkly fluorescent orange flip-flops with the big plastic flowers on them on their front porch?

Raisins on a Sunday

Another story about Pippa
my family's East European Shepherd.

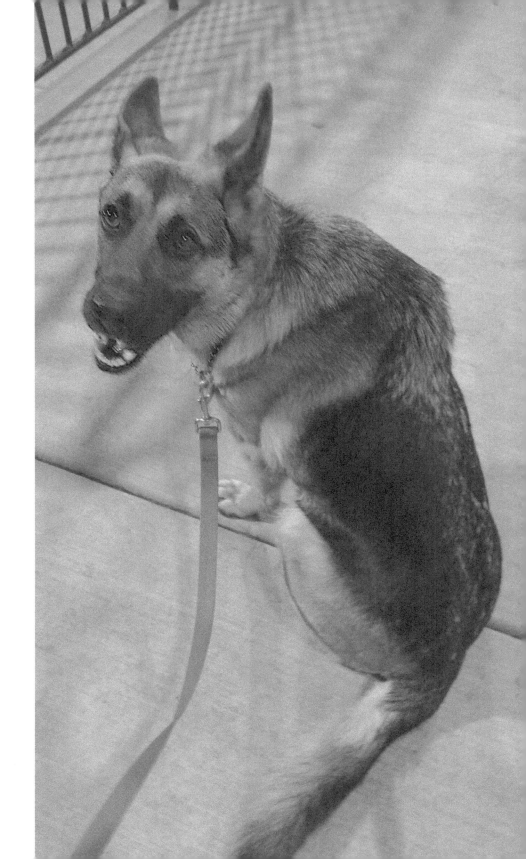

Our frail, elderly kitty was a beautiful soul. When kidney failure took her from us she spent most of her time during those last days cuddling in my lap. I use an easy chair at my writing desk, pulled right up underneath the keyboard shelf. This way, my feet can be up, although climbing in and out of the chair is admittedly a tricky gymnastic feat. I spend much of my time in this chair. My cat enjoyed sitting here, too, either on the chair's headrest or in my lap. So, since she wanted to be held, I stayed with her. Together we watched videos of birds and squirrels on my computer monitor. Our other pets stayed nearby, anxious about our cat and needing comfort also. My German Shepherd, Pippa, lay next to me.

I felt thankful to have these remaining hours to say goodbye, but at one point my brain wielded an image from some sitcom in which a distressed person devoured a pint of ice cream. A whole pint. I've never done this, but somehow it struck me as the culturally-appropriate thing to do. So, although I knew we didn't even have any ice cream, I set my kitty down and went to check the freezer, just in case. Of course there was no ice cream.

But there were bagels. I keep a package of bagels in there because they freeze better than bread does. So, I made myself a quick bagel and cheese sandwich although I didn't feel remotely hungry. *I know I'm stress-eating*, I thought, *but I'm going to allow that. It's a time to be easy on myself.*

Returning to my seat, I ever-so-gently picked up my cat. With her in one arm and my bagel sandwich in my other hand, I manipulated myself back under the keyboard. But I dropped a chunk of the bagel. A quarter of one of the slices fell to the floor, landing near Pippa's paw. She sat up and looked at me. Such a good girl. Instead of snatching it, she looked at me. "I see you dropped something. Are you going to want that? May I?" said her eyes.

"It's okay, Pippa," I told her. "Go ahead." As she grabbed it up, I noticed the raisins. Oh damn. I love cinnamon raisin bagels. I hadn't thought about it. Raisins were toxic to dogs, weren't they? I remembered something about that. "Wait! No, Pippa! Drop it! Drop it!"

Pippa is usually good about that particular command. But I had already given her the treat. It rightfully belonged to her. She held it high in the air and dashed across the room to her bed. I struggled out of the easy chair. I set my kitty down in a panic (but ever-so-gently.) I hurried across the room. But I arrived too late. I searched Pippa's bed for bagel fragments. I looked in her mouth. Long gone, of course.

The internet search terrified me. It turns out that raisins have a chemical that some dogs can tolerate, but which is fatal to others. At the time of publication of this book, there is no way to determine which dogs will react. It is not known for sure what chemical is involved, but it affects the kidneys. It causes kidney failure.

I called my vet. Although it was Sunday, I knew they'd have an answering service or a voicemail message directing me to the nearest emergency vet. They didn't. It just rang and rang. My husband was out of town. My son and I gave Pippa, as directed by a veterinary website, a small amount of hydrogen peroxide to induce vomiting. Nothing happened.

I called the emergency vet I took a client's dog to once. The recording told me it would be a six to eight-hour wait. The search results for a vet near me were horrifying. Closed. Closed. Closed.

Closed. Closed. Finally, I found an open clinic. They stayed open for the next half hour, anyway. Until 4:30 PM. They were located at too much of a distance to reach in that amount of time. But she told me to give slightly more hydrogen peroxide than we were giving Pippa.

We gave her two more doses five minutes apart, down the back of her throat. Then, still searching desperately with my cell phone for a vet, I led Pippa across the street on a long line. I had taught her to lunge, just like a horse, when I had an illness and needed a way to exercise her. Now, I thought that maybe running her in circles would help make her vomit. It had no effect on her. Only on me; I came close to losing my own lunch. Probably what saved me was the distraction of calling vet after vet while Pippa circled me.

The local animal shelter told me to call the veterinary poison control number. I'd already called them; they wanted seventy-five dollars. For that, I figured they'd tell me to try to induce vomiting and rush her right to the vet. Vet after closed vet, it took me a full hour to find the emergency veterinarian a half hour to the north.

I had tears of anger in the corners of my eyes. In my panic, I'd become livid that these people could be so uncaring. Why didn't these clinics add more vets? Quite some time later I learned why. Covid-19 intensified an already-existing shortage of veterinarians. During the lockdown many millions of people added pets to their families, creating a huge boom in pet ownership. Working beyond capacity, with delayed care, an escalation of sad situations and emotional owners, and a whole chain-reaction of issues, many in the veterinary workforce quit their jobs. There has been an increase in suicide among veterinarians. I'd no idea.

That day of the raisins I didn't know I was lucky we had a clinic up north. I asked my son to place dog mats in the back seat of the car (because surely Pippa would throw up in the car) while I ran to grab my keys and her leash. I fetched my laptop too (because any chance to write is a chance to write). Pippa happily jumped in the car and off we went.

A quarter of a mile away, at the stoplight, I realized I'd forgotten the leash. Some vague memory told me that a vet will not accept a dog without a leash. This silly idea had no truth to it. But I was in a panic. *Drive carefully. Focus*, I told myself. I recognized this as precisely the type of scenario that could lead to a traffic accident. I was in a lane at the intersection which headed out toward the highway. If I continued that way, it would be a while before I could turn around. Nobody had come up behind me. I backed up and then went into the left turn lane. I'm lucky something bad didn't happen. This caused me to sit through another rotation of the light. *Minutes won't make a difference*, I reminded myself. Thinking back, I'm proud of that. I didn't sit there fussing and swearing.

After I made the left turn I noticed Pippa's green leash on the passenger side floor. "Shit!" I drove to the street I'd planned to turn back home on, did a U-turn, and went back to the light. We sat through another long cycle. "Don't panic, don't panic, don't panic," I chanted.

Thank goodness for GPS. I focused on my driving and followed the nice lady's voice to our destination. Yes, I did speed, but by only five miles per hour because I was trying to be calm and not get us killed.

We arrived at the vet. We hurried inside. Pippa was very excited. On top of her anxiety about our kitty, her anxiety about her family's anxiety about our kitty, and now my panic about raisins, Pippa glowed with energy. She has always loved a trip to the vet. Even after her spay. They have peanut butter!

They checked us in quickly and took us right back because we had a life-threatening emergency. Others in the waiting room had been there for six hours. Pippa went off with the veterinary assistant to a place where I wasn't allowed. By the time they induced vomiting, it had been about two hours since she ate the raisins. My estimate had been two or three raisins. They found four.

As there was no way to know how Pippa's body would react to the raisins, we were advised to go ahead with treatments. If we waited for symptoms to appear it would likely be too late to save her. We had a choice to make. The best thing to do would be to admit her as a patient and keep her there for a couple of days on IV fluids, with a day of follow-up and then several days of tests. Alternatively, if we just couldn't afford that, they could give subcutaneous fluids instead. This means they would inject a saline solution under her skin so that during the night it would hydrate her enough to help prevent kidney damage. While praying that my kitty didn't die of renal failure while I was away, I made the choice that put Pippa's life more at risk. My son and I discussed it over the phone and decided to treat her at home as much as we could.

The vet gave her charcoal to try and absorb any toxin it would, and some expensive medicine to counteract the stuff they'd given her so she'd throw up. Eventually, they released her to me. My Pippa had been replaced by a rabid werewolf. Her eyes were wild with fear. The fluid had been injected at her shoulders, so she had enormous Quasimodo wolf hackles. Truthfully, I didn't look much better than she did by that point. An incoming dog owner made a wide circle around us. I would have done the same. But I left the office with gratitude for what they'd done for Pippa, and for the fact that they were open on a Sunday.

Twenty-four hours later found us at our regular vet's office having blood work done. Pippa barked at the dogs in the waiting room. I pulled her into a corner behind me and apologized to the people, explaining her extremely stressed condition. I wasn't surprised that in her current state she barked at other dogs. She sometimes does this anyway. It's embarrassing, and something we're still working on. A door opened right next to us. We were hustled into an examination room I hadn't seen before. Apparently, it is cleverly placed and reserved for reactive dogs.

While we waited in the Bad Dog Room I tried not to cry. Soon the veterinary technician came in. Pippa barked at her, too. Shocked, I realized sadly that Pippa's joyful trips to the vet might be a thing of the past. As Pippa didn't continue to show aggression, the tech softly called to her and offered a treat. But Pippa wouldn't budge. I'd never seen her dislike a person, let alone reject a treat. The tech suggested I drop the leash. This helped Pippa feel less trapped and she immediately found the courage to approach the young woman. There's always something to learn.

Later on that evening, at midnight, our kitty gently left us. I sat with her on the couch, and Pippa and the other pets were present. I felt thankful to be home when she passed.

We held less and less of our breath about Pippa over the next few days. As it turned out, only our bank account and Pippa's opinion of vets suffered damage. Very likely, she would have been fine had we done nothing. But we couldn't take that risk.

Dangerous Foods

Many foods can be harmful to dogs' health, but those below can cause death in a short time. Contact a vet immediately if a dog ingests even a small amount of:

Alcohol (Ethanol)   Found in alcoholic beverages and in syrups. Also in uncooked yeasted dough, which in addition can cause deadly bloat.

Xylitol (Birch Sugar, Wood Sugar, Birch Bark Extract)   An artificial sweetener. This is present in some peanut butters! Found in sugarless gum and candies, some baked goods, ice cream, flavored waters, condiments, sauces, jams, syrups, cereals, protein bars and powders, toothpaste, mouthwash, chewable vitamins, and cough drops. Highly toxic to all dogs. Poisoning can start within 20 minutes. Every second counts.

Grapes, Raisins, Sultanas, Currants   Even one or two. Found in cookies, breads, and many other foods. Kidney failure can occur within a few days.

Chocolate   The toxic component, theobromine, is found in all types. Darker chocolate has higher levels of theobromine, white chocolate has the lowest.

Caffeine   Present in coffee and tea, including the beans and grounds. Also found in chocolate, cocoa, sodas, energy drinks, and some medicines.

This list does not include household items or plants that are poisonous to dogs.

Of Man and Mountain

Written by my son Keziah
who hikes with our dog Pippa.

The rat-a-tat-a-tat of semi-automatic gunfire ricocheted between the cliffs as we cautiously crossed the ruins of the Canyon
Creek bridge. "I'm gonna miss civilization," I said to Pippa. For
the rest of the weekend, it was just me, my dog, and the mountain.

I pedaled hard up the abandoned road deeper into the woods,
bent on joining the handful of people to summit this peak in the
last hundred years. Pippa trotted behind me, ears pulled back in
determination. To our knowledge, hers would be the first ascent
by a dog.

The peak itself is nothing special, as hikes go; with a meager
elevation and thick canopy over almost the entire mountain, I
cannot help but compare the peeks between branches unfavor-
ably with the panoramas from higher, starker viewpoints that
college students in this year's sun-hoodies capture with their
iPhones. But this quiet little mountain was the perfect start to
get Pippa acclimated to backpacking. I'm climbing every mountain in the North Cascades, and as defined by topographic prominence, this is most definitely a mountain.

Tupso Pass Road coddled us. Cared for by the Forest Service
until just recently, it was smooth and solid under my tires. As
we circumnavigated Meadow Mountain, the streams were lively
with fresh snowmelt, and I traveled unburdened by water. We
reached the road's end–our planned campsite–with too much
daylight remaining, and we weren't ready to settle down for the
night. I hid my bike in the undergrowth, heaved my pack a little
higher on my back, and followed Pippa into the trees. It seemed
like a great start.

Nature had long since re-adopted the spur road we were now
following, and the brush was scrappy. For the most part we let it

be, and went over, under, and between trees in the mature forest to the side. The camping gear stuffed into my backpack was far from ultralight; one long mile later I was glad to find a good spot for our luxurious 3-person tent. Pippa watched from a safe distance while I set it up–she distrusts human inventions.

The bad news came after I set off to brush my teeth and set up a bear hang: The stream up the ridge from camp was missing. It was supposed to be perennial, but maps can't keep up with climate change. It was not worth heading further up the ridge to the next stream tonight, or retracing our plod back to the comfort of Meadow Mountain. We'd get a little thirsty overnight, but should reach water soon in the morning.

Unfortunately, I was unable to convince Pippa of this plan. As we settled down for the night, Pippa kept asking me for water. Later, she woke me up. "Keziah," she pantomimed, "we have to find water. If we can't find water, we will die!" I tried to assure her I knew where to find water in the morning, but she always imagines the worst. That made this night a bad time for the owl: "Who-cooks-for-you? Who-cooks-for-you-all?" Pippa prodded me with her nose: "Keziah! Wake up!" I tried to convince her it was nothing to worry about, but she thought I was oblivious. "Keziah! Don't you hear it? It's right beside our tent!"

It's actually a funny coincidence that it was a Barred Owl, with that distinctive call. The story goes that, back when pioneers were logging the old-growth forest, a disheveled stranger wandered into a logging camp on the mountain. When he asked the crew the name of the mountain, one of the loggers, as a joke, gave the name of the camp's cook. Years later, the logger saw the name on a map and realized he'd accidentally named the mountain. Pippa stayed on high alert until the owl was done reminding us about Mr. Ditney.

We woke up early in the morning, if we slept at all. As soon as it was light enough to travel, I loaded the bare necessities into the backpack I'd been using as a pillow, and headed toward the summit—and the high mountain streams. From camp, we were maintaining a constant elevation to the pass, where we'd begin our attack on the ridgeline. Pippa followed the way she usually does on difficult terrain: She'd watch me until I was almost out of sight, then plan her line to rejoin me. If I slipped even a little bit, she'd consider that area impassable and, no matter what obstacles a detour required her to surmount, she would get to me some other way.

Until one time, she didn't. A German Shepherd can be nearly invisible in the woods, but I called and called and didn't see any movement. I had a hunch where she'd gone. I went back to our previous rendezvous point, and then took a downhill-trending path. Sure enough, I found her a few hundred vertical feet below the camp, at a dry bog. She'd gone downhill to look for water. It's a good instinct, but she should have trusted me; I had the map. If Pippa knew what a map was, she wouldn't trust that either.

I led us back on track, and we climbed the steep duff up the ridge. From camp to the summit (and the nearby water) would be just over two miles, but the terrain was merciless and each mile took hours. Slips here were frequent enough that Pippa often was forced (by her logic) to take a route harder than mine.

We were parched by the time we reached the shoulder of the mountain, where the ridgeline broadened. I knew from a previous climber that along the cliff on the north side was a good route to the top, but the summit was not our first objective for the day: Once we reached the elevation of the streams and lakes, we sidehilled directly toward them. We risked meeting impassable brush and backtracking, but as luck would have it, we were not the only ones to choose this route between the pass below and the alpine lakes: A well-worn trail made our passage here easy. The trail was wide, and everything in the path totally crushed, so I was not surprised to find one section rife with bear scat. I just hoped we wouldn't meet the trail crew.

When we got to the high stream, it too was dry, but I wasn't worried. The bear trail was in recent use, so I knew the lakes it led to were still around, and soon enough we smelled water. As the lakes came into view across a meadow, I wanted to filter some water immediately, but I stopped at the shore: The snow feeding this lake had long since melted, and the water itself seemed to have grown textured. We hurried around the lake until we were downhill from it, where we found a stream percolating through the earth. I ran some flowing water through my filter and tasted it. It was the piny kind of water—not a sipping water, but if you chug it, it tastes just like ice water with a spritz of lemon.

Finally hydrated, we breakfasted on kibble and gorp and aimed uphill. From here it didn't take us long to reach the false summit, a high point on a long shoulder below the true peak. The false summit was one of those little peaks that has a big rock at the very top, as if nature put it there for climbers to stand on and feel a sense of accomplishment. The ridge here was a sheer cliff on its north face; from time to time we could see where, in less dry times, waterfalls run down it.

This is the unknown mountain with the nameless waterfalls that sightseers flock to the Boulder River Trail to look up at from the north. Any hiker who ends up here should peek over the edge, stand on the rock and go home, but Pippa and I are the type who hear "1,640 feet of prominence" and stretch our legs and reach for our trekking poles, so we continued on. The highest bump was farther up the ridge.

Conversation with Corgi Ken

I asked one of our community members,
Ken,
if I might interview him for this book.
He kindly said yes.

He and Laura currently have three Corgis:
Destiny, Pippin, and Gracie

We're sitting in a small coffee shop. Ken has insisted on buying me an Americano and a slice of pumpkin bread even though he has met me here as a favor to me. Ken's dogs Gracie, Destiny, and Pippin lie near our table, quietly receiving love from the customers who come and go from the counter.

So, Ken, why Corgis? Why do you like Corgis so much?

Ken: I love dogs, right? And I always wanted a German Shepherd. In the early nineties I went through a divorce as my kids were growing up. My oldest was nine, the younger was seven, and I was distraught. I thought the boys would benefit from having an animal in the household. I didn't want them to become animal ignorant. Growing up I always had dogs.

So I called up this gal Susan I knew from high school who I hadn't seen in ten years and I talked to her. She had gotten me a dog earlier than that and that dog ran away and found a good home across the street. So I went back to Susan and she said, "Well, what do you want a dog for?"

I knew she was breeding Jack Russell Terriers before they were even recognized by the AKC. She also bred tricolor Pembroke Welsh Corgis. I told her I wanted the Jack Russell because there was a Jack Russell puppy available and I just fell in love with the dog right away. So when she questioned me, and said, "Well, what do you want the dog for?" I said, "Well, it's for the kids . . ." *da da da*. She said, "No, no, no, no, take the Corgi!" I'd never heard of a Corgi. I didn't even realize until a couple years later there was a connection with the Queen, somebody had to tell me about that, I didn't understand that. I just wanted a dog.

So I bought my first Corgi from her for five hundred dollars; I had to borrow money in order to pay for her and she ended up becoming the matriarch of the family. Her name was Abby. She was a tricolor Pembroke Welsh Corgi whose ears never came up. She always had floppy ears! But she was such a phenomenal dog.

My older son was nine, it was his first year at Little League and I was coaching. We used to go out to this field called Camp Parks which was at a military base out in Dublin, California and they had a field out there that was exclusively for the Babe Ruth League in that area. So we'd go out there, and one day I left practice with, I think my wife was with me, my kids, and I forgot Abby. I realized I forgot my dog, I had left her at the field. So I turned around and went back, there was another team playing or practicing. She wasn't there, nobody had seen her.

There wasn't anything much I could do after that so I went home and the very next day, or, I guess, that same evening, one of the parents on that other team phoned me and said they brought her home with them because they knew her. Everybody knew her, everybody in town knew this dog.

You know, that dog went everywhere with me because I was self-employed. She'd jump in the truck with me each morning and we'd basically go off to a different job site. Never really had to put a leash on her. I taught her to heel, taught her to stay, taught her to sit, she knew all that really quick.

I used to go into a coffee shop every morning, there would be people in line and she would put a smile on people's faces, she was just that way. She was loved by the entire community, even to a point where, although I don't think many of them knew about the breed—to be honest with you—back then, it wasn't long before other Corgis started to show up in town.

Me: Haha! That is the special thing about Corgis, isn't it? They brighten people's days.

Ken: They just light people up.

So, yeah, I just wanted a dog and she just was there. I had her bred when she was seven and I kept one of her two puppies and named him Brownie Boy. I had the two Corgis for a long time. I lost Brownie Boy a couple years ago, he was sixteen.

Abby passed away when she was thirteen. She had developed a kind of an ulcer, I guess.

So I had a choice: The vet said, "Well, you know, we can remove this, it'll cost you eight hundred dollars but there's no guarantee it'll go away."

Me: Oh, that's such an awful position to be in.

Ken: It is. So I gave it some thought, I chose instead just to make her remaining time as comfortable as I could, really. Eventually, I had to go back to my vet to find out what it would take to put a dog down because I didn't know, I'd never had to do that. And that very same day, as I walked out of the vet's office shaking my head, not really figuring out what to do, that same afternoon is when she died. She looked at me and decided she didn't want to go on our usual neighborhood walk, so I said, "Okay, stay here, Abby." When we came home, opened up the side gate, she was there, she'd left us. So she kind of put herself down. I mean, I didn't have to make that decision.

Me: It sounds like she didn't suffer that much.

Ken: No, she really didn't. Her AKC name was God's Good Girl and I tell everybody she knew it because she treated everybody that well. I mean, I could talk forever about Abby but my kids grew up with her, you know. Whenever there was a practice, baseball practice, she would be there. Whenever there was basketball for my younger son, she would be there. Job site, she would be there.

299

Abby was just a phenomenal dog. She had a million-dollar disposition, even though she looked kind of goofy, she had the million-dollar disposition that you look for in animals. And so, when I raised her son Brownie Boy, he was anything but. He was, well, I explain to people that if I had owned firearms, I would have taken him out back because there were a number of times he got me so mad. I'm glad I didn't, of course, but he was a horrific puppy.

I think he destroyed five baseball gloves. One day I come home and he's destroyed a leather chair. He ruined carpets that we spent a lot of money on, I mean he destroyed thousands of dollars worth of stuff. He just was a terrible puppy to have to try to raise but when he was about four years of age I realized he had turned into a very nice dog. But it took me to grow up in order to find out that there were some things that he couldn't control and I could. So instead of me trying to scold him every time he destroyed a baseball glove, I just had to remember to remove the baseball gloves out of his possession so that another one wouldn't get destroyed. So, it takes two, right?

Me: Yeah. Yeah you're right.

Ken: It takes two. So yeah, I had to learn a lot and I think that's the problem with most dog owners today. They just don't do the things they need to find out, you know, to behave in a correct fashion around their dog.

Me: I guess it's the same with being a parent, really.

Ken: Yeah, parenting, but parenting you can communicate, you know. Dogs can't talk, necessarily. I mean, they can but they can't, right? And, yeah, so much comes down to patience, you've got to be patient. That's what I tell people on the internet, you know, they have these Corgi pages and they say, "Well, I've got this new Corgi and . . ." *da da da da*, and usually I just answer, "Patience," because every dog is going to be different, every puppy is going to be different, some puppies are easy, some puppies are difficult. And you can't hit them. I guess you can scold them a little bit if you want, but especially with puppies, it's all about patience.

Me: Well, Ken, I couldn't agree with you more. I've learned that a calm confident attitude and patience are everything when working with dogs. And patience, yeah. It can be hard sometimes. I mean, my dog Pippa tests me now and then because she's so high-strung. We, you know, get into a situation where she embarrasses me. I know ultimately I'm responsible for that, if things don't go well it's my fault, but it's difficult sometimes to stay calm. I mean you get frustrated and then you regret it later but I think that's part of being a typical person.

Ken: Yeah, I never hurt him but I sure know I got mad at him a few times and I let him know. But yeah, I mean that's what you have to learn. I'm sixty-seven years old and I'm still figuring it out, you know. I wish I had known all this stuff at twenty-seven.

Me: Yeah, I feel that way too. I'm finally figuring things out in life.

Ken: Right? So I had to learn that, okay, he's not going to be as nice a dog as what I had before but I had to learn to accept him for who he is and what he was. He was still a very good dog, he was just different. His disposition was different.

Me: So you had Abby and Brownie for quite some time.

Ken: Yes, for a good many years. And then we added Marty. Another dog who presented a challenge for us was Marty. Before we left California we had Abby and Brownie Boy. And then we had a woman at our church who had passed away. I knew she had a Corgi so I approached her son and asked if he had any plans for this dog. He said no. And so I took her in, and brought her up here with me.

Marty was already old when we got her. So I lost Marty after a couple of years. I didn't realize until after she passed away that she was actually in control of my pack. I think because she was the only female. The females control things with dogs, it seems like.

She was a really stubborn dog, very stubborn. I used to get mad at her, too. Even a person who knows better, you don't get . . . you don't really get mad at them, you know. It's the wrong thing to do. And I used to get frustrated with her because she'd always lag behind and I'd always have to encourage her, come on Marty, let's go, come on, *da da da da da*. She was a slow poke. So, yeah, over time, she taught me to be patient.

Our conversation is interrupted:

"May I pet your dog?" a lady asks.

"He's very friendly," Ken tells her. "That's Pippin. Yeah, he wants more. Yeah, he loves the attention."

All three of us laugh because Pippin is so cute.

Back to our interview:

Ken: So you know, after we lost old Marty I had only two again. Then we bought Timmy from a very reputable breeder. She was a vet. He was a wonderful dog, he was probably my favorite. He was a tri-color, fluffy boy.

We named him after Tim Lincecum, you know who Tim Lincecum is? They called him Timmy the Freak. He pitched for the San Francisco Giants. He's from the Seattle area. I think he played for the Huskies at the University of Washington and he came over to the Bay Area and played for the San Francisco Giants, became a phenomenon, so they called him the Freak. Because he didn't have the type of physique that most people would look at in order to be a big-league pitcher, but he proved them all wrong.

And so his nickname was The Freak, and Timmy was named after The Freak. And it turns out Timmy had an immunity deficiency that I'd seen a specialist about. She charged me a lot for a consultation. Very renowned vet who was published, so I guess she could charge what she wanted in a very elitist neighborhood.

And she ran it down to me, you could either give him these pills, they might damage his liver, or you can give him these other pills, it would take a longer amount of time but it would be no damage to his liver. So I took those lighter of the two pills, did that for about a year, and it was just starting to change his personality so I just stopped doing it.

And the problem with Timmy was that his pads on his paws never hardened, and when he'd run hard, he would tear his nails, I mean I went to my vet on three different occasions to have him pull off a nail that was already just hanging. They suspected it could have been a reaction to a vaccine. I'd gone to two or three different specialists to see if there was anything that could be done for Timmy, and there really wasn't.

So Timmy was a special needs dog. And I think that's why I loved him more than the rest, because when you have a special needs animal there's so much more of yourself that goes into keeping that dog, in this case, comfortable. So actually I think I might have loved him more than the others, just because he required so much more of me.

So the best thing we could do was to try to find booties that would fit him properly. My wife and I, we looked for booties for ten years. We could not find a pair of booties that would fit the Corgi well. I remember talking with this gal in Florida who made booties. She explained to me the hardest booties to make are for Corgis and Great Danes. There's just something about the shape of their foot, with Corgis it's from where the foot to their ankle is, it's just such a short distance that it's really difficult to find a pair of boots that fit him properly.

After about ten years I just gave up looking. All that time I just made sure that whenever I took him out, I took him to a place that wouldn't be too uncomfortable for him to walk on. But he was really pretty. He looked like Lassie, with long hair. Such a beautiful dog. And he was always smiling, he had a beautiful disposition, he loved everybody.

Me: So this was all before you had any dogs that you have now?

Ken: Well, Brownie Boy lived to be sixteen. We got Pippin here about a year after we lost him, and not long before Timmy passed away.

Pippin we got from Puyallup and then it wasn't too long thereafter we bought another. I was down to two dogs again and someone approached me as to whether or not I wanted another Corgi. I said yeah, I'm used to three and I was down to two. A beautiful Cardigan dog, I took her.

Me: So that was Destiny, here?

Ken: That's Destiny. Yeah, she's a pain in the butt. She's come a long ways, really.

Me: How old is she?

Ken: Let's see, she was probably six or seven when I got her, that was two years ago. Oh, yeah, she's eight and Gracie's a year older than Destiny. Pippin just turned three, three and a half, he'll be four pretty soon.

Before I bought Pippin, I was going to get a Belgian Shepherd, a Malinois, because it's

like the next best thing to a German Shepherd except they don't have the problem with the

hips. So I contacted a breeder in Oregon but they never got back to me. So I said what the hell,

I'll just go get another Corgi. That's where Pippin came in.

I tell people they're just like German Shepherds with little legs, they're bred for the same thing, right?

Me: Yeah, haha, I guess so! Little compact Shepherds.

Ken: Yeah, they're the best-dispositioned dogs. If you read about them they'll say they're big dogs with small bodies and that's what they are, basically. So yeah, I didn't know anything at all about the breed, I'd had Dachshunds, I'd had mutts, been around Collies and German Shepherds as a boy growing up. But I think besides being a good dog, they're just super cute. And that's why they got so popular.

Me: Well, I mean, look at them, they just . . . they're designed to make people smile.

Ken: These dogs, you know, in the last decade in particular you see more and more of them because they've gotten popular. There's a reason for it, and it mostly affects the girls. I've been walking down the street with my dogs and I've seen these middle school girls go nuts over them. One day a girl collapsed to her knees and started crying.

Me: When she saw the Corgis?

Ken: Cuteness factor.

Realm of Swords

The forthcoming tale has as its hero

Pepper Underfoot,
a Blue Heeler (Australian Cattle Dog)
and German Shorthaired Pointer mix,
owned by Christopher.

"Sit for a picture!" I told Pepper.

She wasn't sure.

"Sit, girl," I said, holding my hand high.

Pepper looked up at my hand, and sat. I clucked softly to keep her attention. She watched me, her ears pricked in my direction.

Pepper has what they call "rose ears," the kind that stick up but fold outward near the top, in a batwing type of cuteness. The deep black coloring extends down from her left one to form an eye patch that covers her whole cheek. Along with her shiny nose, this sets off the lovely black that speckles her milky coat.

"Good sit, good sit," I said, hoping to keep her in that perfect pose while I snapped a couple of photos. The background wasn't quite right, so I squat-walked like a duck for a few steps to the side to get an angle that wouldn't show the power lines. There. Pepper with a couple of red cedars behind her, and a laden huckleberry bush. Perfect.

We'd gone a long way from her house and it was almost time to turn around, but both Pepper and I wanted to know a bit more about this trail. "We'll just go up the hill to that bend," I said. And a few minutes later, "Just that next turn, I want to see what's around it." We went about a quarter mile through the trees by this method, until the clock on my phone insisted. We really did have to head back.

That's when the rabbit appeared out of nowhere. A short way down a little side trail, he stood on his hind legs, sniffing in our direction. But this was no cottontail bunny. This was a big guy. Jackrabbit, maybe?

I hadn't noticed that trail before, but it led downhill so when the rabbit hopped a few yards along it and then turned to peer at us I decided to follow. "This trail's got to meet the road somewhere," I assured Pepper. She didn't mind. The rabbit had sparked her interest, too.

The trail grew awfully steep, and both Pepper and I struggled to get down, but then it leveled out. The woods were thicker here, the trees smaller and brushier. Vine maple and dogwood were brightly dressed in fall colors. Wow. They'd turned a little early. These were the first fall colors I'd seen this year.

Weaving through the shrubs, we saw dark salal, too, and Oregon grape. Golden splashes of goatsbeard grew like bunches of ragged feathers on the hillside. The farther we went, the more colorful our surroundings became. The rabbit never darted for the underbrush. He stayed on the trail, scampering a short way and then sniffing around. The colors continued to emerge. I'd never seen so much spectacular fall foliage! We drew closer to the rabbit and I got a good look at him. He wasn't a rabbit, he was a hare. He stared me straight in the eye and gave a funny little smile.

The hare pointed with the index finger of his front paw. I strained to see into the shadows where he indicated, as it took a moment to focus. There was a hole there. A large one, and the hare disappeared right down it. The opening looked quite big, and the drop wasn't so bad. More like a slope. A tunnel, actually, now that I noticed. I looked at Pepper. She returned my gaze with big, eager eyes. We followed the hare down the hole. I could barely see the white of his tail ahead of us.

Initially, as we went along, the hole smelled of damp earth. At first, puck lights along the tunnel walls illuminated our way, but after a while torches in brackets replaced these. My sense of direction became confused as the tunnel continued. Were we going down? Or up? East, or west? I really couldn't tell. Eventually it became clear that we were climbing steeply. We went on and on. I don't know how long we climbed because magic can surely mess with time.

Light in the tunnel ahead grew stronger. Soon we found the source of that brightness to be a round hole just above us, an exit through the tunnel ceiling. Pepper and I climbed up easily and popped out of a rabbit hole into an exquisite garden. The air tasted fresh and it smelled like sun-warmed blossoms.

A little man lay on his side not far from the hole, resting his head on one hand and breathing hard. He had changed from the hare form, all except the ears. Long ears grew from each side of his head, starting near the temples. I knew this fellow. His hair and beard were long and white, his face a dusky brown. His name was Aldrei.

I knew this place, also. I recognized my style of writing in every aspect of this reality. I had built this world. Aldrei is a character in a story I wrote. We were clearly in his realm. Here, humans transform into animals. Or is it the other way around? I never did decide about that.

As surprised as I was to meet a character who I had created, it wasn't Aldrei I stared at. I gave him a questioning glance, and pointed upwards. We stood in the shadow of a medieval castle. This was no ruin, but a full-sized and functioning medieval castle in medieval times. The odors of sewage and smoke, of incense, of baking, and of livestock all attested to that.

I looked at Pepper, still on my leash. My first thought, as a devoted dog-walker was, *Damn. We're going to be very late.* Pepper looked okay, though, she wasn't wide-eyed, or trembling, or anything like that. We had both remained calm. That seemed odd.

The garden was small, but fabulous. High brick walls sur-rounded it, so of the outside world only the castle towers above were in view. Smooth lawns curved through thickets of roses, bunches of hollyhocks and columbines. Trellises and arbors held all sorts of flowering vines, some against the brickwork, some standing free. The perfume from the flowers and their color in the soft sunlight dazzled me.

"Aldrei," I said, "it's you!"

The man smiled.

"I can't believe it!" I said. My voice wavered slightly. "And the Jerboa, too! Hello."

Aldrei's dear friend, the Jerboa, was a mouse-like creature who stood on two long hind legs and held tiny forelegs to a fuzzy chest. An enormously long tail was being used at the moment as a prop to help the Jerboa rest in an upright position. Only a bit more than half as tall as Aldrei, the Jerboa had long, rabbit-like ears nearly the size of his.

It was clear to the two friends that I would benefit from a moment to make sense of all this fantastic impossibility. They led me toward Aldrei's house, promising me some pink lemon-ade. That sounded like just the thing. I unhooked Pepper's leash—something I would never, ever, normally do with a client's dog—and she followed at my heel. As we passed a well, I went and laid my hands on the ancient stone rim. I peered down at the water inside. Aldrei smiled. I turned, and continued to walk with him.

We arrived at a tiny garden house, an open, trellised affair with a small belfry.

"This is beautiful!" I said. "You live here, Aldrei?"

"In a way, I do."

"He lives underneath it," the Jerboa explained. "The current owners of the property are terrified of Aldrei. He's not welcome in the castle. But the Lady never comes out to the garden anymore, and the gardener is friendly."

"Castle," I repeated. "Where are we? The flag bears an image of a blackbuck antelope. And the garden well—I know that old well. It's from the house of Anemone. But what's a castle doing on this spot? It's all wrong."

"To be true, it is," Aldrei said.

"All wrong," the Jerboa added.

Aldrei offered his hand to me, saying, "Come, sit down, we'll explain."

Leaning back on cushions in the shade on the warm day, a cool drink in hand, listening to fountains gurgle and birds sing, and talking with magical animals, I began to feel at home. Pepper lay at my feet, listening to us talk and licking a beef knuckle bone. It was fresh and raw, and she enjoyed it immensely.

'Why is there a castle?" I asked. "Are we at Anemone? Where's the palace? What happened?"

"We're seven centuries before your House of Anemone. This is Castle Blackbuck."

I shook my head. "It's impossible."

The Jerboa peered at me through iced lemonade. "Apparently not."

"But there is no concept of war in the book I wrote. I wrote about a world that had no castles. Or canons. Or knights. None of those things. Nothing like that."

"Yes," Aldrei said, and he giggled. "But you built a world, and the world contained humans."

"Not wars, though. Not battles. No need for castles."

The Jerboa explained, in a low and patient tone, "When you create a world, it's likely to take on a life of its own. You're weaving together possibilities which already exist. In a way, you're choosing a story, not creating one. You can't possibly think that you control the world you've written about!"

I had a thought. "Wait, if I'm in this story right now, then who's writing it?"

"You are, silly," the Jerboa said.

"What?"

Aldrei spoke in his amused and lighthearted manner, "Look, the problem, we all agree, is that war has come to the land. Warfare Is entertaining and all that, but it destroys the scenery. And once they get going, fighting seems to be all that people want to do. To put it simply, Harriet, we want you to write it out of the story again."

I drained my lemonade. "What?"

"You'll have to rewrite the narrative."

"How do I do that?"

"You are the author of our story. The world will change by your course and your actions. You'll live for a time here, but time won't have gone by when you return to your world."

This news made me squeal. "Great, I get bonus hours of my life! I've always wanted bonus hours!"

"Sort of," said the Jerboa. "Time will compress in a certain kind of way. As in any story. A lifetime can be lived between the pages of a book."

"Hmm. I'll take what I can get, I guess," I said. "So, what is my quest, then?"

"You must find the Crones With Pens," Aldrei said. "A witch will give you a magic pen. Take it, and go and find the Crones."

Aldrei and the Jerboa set me and Pepper up comfortably in the garden house. We had plenty to eat and all the time we wanted for strolling around the countryside. They supplied me with medieval clothing and a beautiful white gelding. I didn't question how they knew I could ride.

After several weeks of this terrifically fun and carefree life—really, it was better than the best years of childhood—I started to feel antsy to begin my quest. It was Pepper who got us an audience with the Duchess. Passing through the courtyard one pleasant day, Pepper and I were compelled, along with everyone else, to stop and stand to the side. Urial, Duchess of Buckhold made a rare appearance as she went out for a walk in her grounds. The veiled Duchess approached with her handmaidens and her physician, and a page pushed a crude wheelbarrow-like chair behind her in case she tired.

As she drew even with us, Pepper whimpered and this caught the Duchess's ear. The procession stopped. A courtier came and stood before us.

"The Duchess admires the beauty of your dog and wishes to know which type it is."

"She is a shepherd dog. Bred for herding cattle."

This answer was relayed to the Duchess. The man returned and said, "Her Grace, the Duchess Urial the Third invites you to tea at four o'clock. Appear before the upper courtyard gate. Bring the dog."

"Thank you!" I said with a curtsey. I later found out that the curtsey was not a part of the tradition in this culture.

With a freshly-bathed Pepper, I stood waiting at the designated time. My silk jacquard gown had hues of purplish-blue. A moss-green shawl covered my shoulders, clasped at my throat with a carved antler brooch. I'd managed to get my blonde hair up in some kind of bun, and I wore dangly earrings supplied by the Jerboa. I felt quite presentable, although, in retrospect, I'm not sure the Duchess noticed my appearance much at all. I was led indoors and up a staircase at the end of the great hall.

She sat in a lovely room, but the wooden window shutters were held closed with an iron bar. The only light came from the coals of a fire and a trio of candles on the mantel. There were several courtiers present, among them a haughty priest of high rank who hovered over the Duchess as if he owned her. His name was Pogue. I'd heard of him.

Duchess Urial's eyes were for Pepper. We had a brief chat, mostly about the dog. Pepper delighted the good lady, and it was apparent that few things did anymore. It was easy to see a black-buck antelope in the woman's face before me, although much of her head was covered with dark gauzy fabric. Although her human form had that beautiful narrow facial structure, the pallor of her complexion was ash-gray and her neck bluish-purple from a rash. She was not an elderly woman, but one could have imagined so. Some unknown concern caused her eyes to appear sunken and dark, listless.

In our audience with the Duchess, we also met the witch. Her name was Miyaw. In contrast to the monochrome and melancholy of Urial, the witch Miyaw adorned herself with a feast of color, from the point of her hat to her bell-tipped shoes. After the Duchess departed the salon, the smiling witch stayed and spoke with me privately, stroking Pepper's neck and rubbing her belly. Secretly a friend of Aldrei's, the witch Miyaw, who rarely left the castle keep, spoke in a soft voice.

She told me why it was that companies of knights and sol-

diers at arms kept departing from the castle. A southern prov-
ince had called for assistance from the Estate of Buckhold. The
monarch of a neighboring country had accused them of stealing
a religious relic and had begun an invasion.

"Of course," the witch Miyaw said, "it's a ridiculous thought,
and merely an excuse for war."

I sighed. "That invasion, then, is what the priest was talking
about. He seemed to support the idea of battle."

"Who, Pogue? Yes, that is sadly so."

"He has power over the Duchess?"

The witch Miyaw lowered her voice even more. "The Lady
has succumbed to his poison more deeply than what I or the
physician can cure. The man Pogue is from an honorable boar
family, but his life is nothing but extravagance."

"Aldrei told me that the door to his privy chamber is made of
silver and gold," I said.

"It's true. And although he is an oafish and ignorant man,
and certainly without love for any god, Pogue has the Duchess in
his power. I fear for her life because she believes all the darkness
he whispers to her. She believes that sunlight will harm her, but
can't see that it is her fear of sunshine that cripples her."

"Horrible."

"Yes, it is. But several true priests and I are trying to help.
In a few days we will perform an exorcism to drive away the
intruding thoughts and controlling forces. I hope that, as the
author of our story, you will join us."

"An exorcism? I don't know."

"It's only a session of prayer and intervention to try and help
someone."

And so I agreed to attend the ceremony.

"There is another matter we must discuss."

"Yes?"

"As Aldrei will have mentioned, I have something to give you." She unrolled a bundle and handed it to me with the contents on top. "The quill is from a goose who granted it as a boon. The inkwell, of blown glass, came from across the sea."

"How beautiful," I said, turning the inkpot over in my hand.

"The stopper is of red cedar, carved into an antelope figure, as you can see. But it is the ink inside that is precious."

Running my finger over some hardened dribbles, I asked, "Because the color is red?"

"Because of the ingredients. This is editor's ink. It's made of blood, sweat, and tears from generations of writers. Acacia gum was added to improve the texture."

Eeew, I thought. I withdrew my finger quickly. I didn't ask anything else. I accepted the small bundle graciously, as one does.

"You'll want to carry that with you," she said. "And before the next moon, go and seek the crones who dwell in the high hills. You must find the Crones With Pens and bring this quill to them. They are mighty and they will help you to see that the story is revised in order to bring peace again to our world."

The Duchess Urial had granted me permission to fish in her private mountain stream, so over the next few days, when I wasn't lingering over a meal with Aldrei and the Jerboa, I would ride out on the white horse with Pepper and pull big fat rainbows out of a silver pond high in the nearby hills. How much fun it was to live in this world of my own making!

Returning over the great oaken drawbridge one afternoon, we encountered a member of the royal family coming in the opposite direction. It was the Earl, eldest son of the Duchess. He rode a fine dappled palfrey, a horse not flustered by the flapping of the purple and yellow pennants carried by attendants who walked beside him. The iron of the Earl's short-sleeved hauberk glistened in the sunlight.

I followed the example of the merchants and peasants, slowing our pace and moving to the side. But a squire dressed in velvet shouted something at us and blew a bone whistle. The shrill sound made Pepper bark, and my white gelding reared and nearly threw me. I recovered my seat and told Pepper to hush. But Pepper kept barking and the squire's face was now swollen both from anger and whistling.

He shouted at me again, "I said, 'Dismount before the Earl!' What doltish hobgoblin ignores our command?"

I climbed down from the horse and held his reins near the bit. I tried to calm the horse and dog. The young Earl stood in his bejeweled stirrups and grasped the hilt of his sword.

Then he, himself, shouted at me, "You of the ghostly pink complexion! Who are you, that you ride astride but keep your seat as though you are a queen? You're no queen. Foreigner, your ignorance of the customs of our society offends me! Draw your sword and we shall determine who has the right to ride past." The Earl dismounted, and his squire led the dappled horse out of the way.

I dropped the reins of the white horse. Pepper picked them up in her teeth. This surprised me, but I was already resigned to surprises since I must be dreaming. I raised my hands, palms toward the Earl, and took a couple of steps backward, bumping into the horse. I bowed my head slightly, in order that my gaze did not seem like a stare.

"Your Grace," I said, "I apologize, for sadly I am ignorant. I am making every effort to familiarize myself with your customs. In no way did I intend to dishonor you or this beautiful land." But I couldn't resist adding, "I am Harriet, a harbinger of peace. The purview of your honor, great sir, shall eternally prevail, but soon the loss of daughters and sons, uncles and cousins on the gruesome and bloody battlefield will occur no more. The time of war is over."

The Earl squinted and rubbed his chin, and spent a moment considering me. Then he sighed, shoved his sword back down into its scabbard, and motioned for his palfrey. Once back in the saddle, he glanced down and said, "On your way, witch."

I did know better than to look at him or answer. I retrieved the reins from Pepper and we continued on our way as soon as the Earl and his entourage had departed. I looked down at Pepper and said, "I believe I'm going to be late for the exorcism. I wonder what sort of trouble I'll be in for that! And what should I wear?"

Aldrei met me near the garden and took Pepper away with him to care for her while I was occupied. A short time later, as arranged, I followed a page up endless stairs inside the castle keep. We stopped at the door of a bedchamber. Presumably, the bedroom of the Duchess.

When I entered I could see her lying in the bed, her wrists tied to the bedposts. The witch Miyaw welcomed me.

"I wasn't aware this was involuntary," I whispered. "Won't she be furious?" (*We'll be executed!* is what I was thinking.)

"She?" asked the witch Miyaw.

"She?" I repeated, confused.

"Oh, how funny!" she said. "Our subject is not the Duchess

Urial. There, prostrate on the bed, is the priest, Pogue. The man is most ponderous, several times the girth of the Duchess." She laughed.

"Oh," I said.

The witch Miyaw looked me in the eye. "If we are successful, I have no doubt Her Grace will regain her health."

I asked what she meant.

"The Pogue. His is a position of great power, but his mind is weak. He whispers only needless evil to the Duchess, and it is the source of those whispers that we must banish from him today."

"Is it greed? Is greed the reason he plagues her?" I asked.

"It is greed, yes, which motivates Pogue; but it is his self-absorption we must address today. His buffoonish vainglory holds him under the sway of foreign powers. You see, an evil and wily king works him as a puppet to do his bidding."

"Oh no."

"A neighboring lord who wishes our land ill."

"Awful," I said.

"This is dangerous work, to be sure. But our world is falling apart, and right here before you. We need you to change the narrative."

"I see," I whispered.

"This is why you will ride with the pen to the Crones. Aldrei has told me they are wise and will help you know how to write."

The musty room was lit only with the flame of a dozen candles, a few of which were held by the practitioners. There were seven people present, including the patient who lay gasping and cursing on the bed. Three were priests; two with beards and one in skirts. Besides the witch Miyaw and myself, there was a woman with ebony skin and lovely salt-and-pepper hair. She had a patch over her left eye.

A priest began the ceremony with a sing-song prayer, joined by the witch and the other clerics. They made several more prayers, asking for healing for the man and that his mind and heart be strong. Then they began to beseech the demonic thoughts to be gone.

"I cast you out, demon intrusion!" the female priest cried as she laid hands on Progue's sweaty scalp.

"Depart, ill influences! Leave this man, give him peace!" cried the witch Miyaw, shaking her cane and ringing a bell. She blew on the man's face. He reacted as if a bucketful of biting ants had been thrown at him.

A terrible, reverberating voice came from far down inside his breast, snarling, "You haven't the power to discharge me!"

The witch was taken aback, literally--violently thrown backward by the gale force of the voice. She recovered her feet and called out in blistering intonation, "I command you to depart!"

The three priests moved closer around Pogue's hapless form.

The voice came even louder, "By the poisonous fartings of your dying God, I am not to be trifled with!"

Stunned by this extreme profanity, all four of the exorcists fell silent for a moment. Then the woman with the eye patch came to the bedside. From her pocket she pulled a small piece of cheese, and she held it in front of Pogue's nose.

"Quiet," she said.

Pogue calmed enough to sniff at the cheese, then tried to eat it.

"Quiet," she repeated, and fed him the cheese.

Pogue's dark doughy cheeks began to tremble, and then he started to shake. He cried. A howl came up his throat.

The woman whispered, "We have no fear of you."

Holding her candle near his face, the witch Miyaw began to sing a single tone. Louder she sang, and it was a pure note, an awful note, in the pitch of F sharp. The priests began another prayer song.

Tears ran down from Pogue's eyes, and for a few seconds his face showed enlightenment and sorrow. But the evil voice came again, spitting further insults and disdain.

"Be gone, foul sickness!" a priest shouted.

For two long hours, the spiritual fight went on. There was a lot of prayer, some face-slapping and shouting into Pogue's ear. The raging voice inside him grew horribly loud, and then, without notice, it vanished.

"Never return!" the priests cried.

They cut the bonds that held the man's wrists, but he made no attempt to flee. He sat up and held himself, and rocked and cried, on a bed soaked with sweat and urine, while the priests muttered prayers. The other woman and the witch Miyaw doused him with incense smoke and light from their candles. For another hour they prayed over him, asking for integrity to strengthen his mind and love to fill his heart.

Then it was time to leave. The female priest would bathe the man, and another priest stayed to change the soiled linens. A bedmaid was called in to assist.

The witch Miyaw and I left the room together. As we walked along the corridor, I asked her, "Is that all it takes? Will that man be healed of his evil influences? Are they gone?"

"They are gone," she replied. "Whether they return before

he wakes in the morning, or if perhaps he can be strong in his mind—this choice is his alone. Go, now, and wash your face, and pray in whatever way you may."

"Goodnight," I said.

"Goodnight, Harriet—and remember," she added, "you were brought to this world because we need your help."

Two days later I was finally packing my saddlebags for the journey to find the Crones With Pens. Aldrei came and sat down on the garden house floor next to me.

"There's a letter for you," he said. He handed me a scroll of parchment.

"Thank you, Aldrei," I said, wondering who might possibly write to me. Then I asked, "Have you seen Pepper? I haven't been able to find her. I'll need to feed her before we leave."

Taking a bite of an apple from the basket on the table, Aldrei took his time chewing, then looked at me and winked. "Perhaps the letter will help you locate her," he said.

"Oh, Aldrei, how could it?" I asked this, but of course he knew something. I broke the seal on the scroll carefully. I wanted to preserve the wax symbol with the letter A just because I'd never opened a scroll before. The symbol broke in half anyway, but I slipped both pieces into the pocket under my skirt.

I unrolled the parchment to read:

Good Health, my most esteemed friend,

I humbly request that this message be delivered to you by our mutual companion, as I must make haste to the southern reaches. The matter at hand concerns a religious object that has incited the call to war in the south. Two evenings ago, I beheld said object in the bedchamber of a certain priest, and have since come into possession of it. To expedite my journey, I shall be riding your white nag, renowned for its great speed.

It is imperative that I return this relic before a great battle erupts in the Field of Erinaceus, where tensions are mounting. I implore you to take great care in safeguarding this message and to be vigilant in your actions.

Please accept my apologies for taking your horse. Aldrei says he has another for you, perhaps not quite so swift.

This salutation was put down by the hand of a hare most helpful.
—Pepper
P.S. Remember my spots. Grace be with you. Luck.

"Wait," I said, "That was Pepper in Pogue's chamber? Pepper the dog? Can she transform?"

"Of course she can," Aldrei said.

"Of course," I replied, my mind staggering and trying not to burst. "And she took my horse."

"Yes, she's off to save the world. Or, at least, to prevent a war. Don't worry, you can follow on Flopsy and maybe you'll be in time to help."

"Flopsy? But I'm supposed to go and find the Crones," I said.

"That will have to wait. Pepper needs you."

I agreed. "I can't let anything happen to Pepper. She's my responsibility! I'll leave right away."

This is how I ended up riding a one-eared mule on my journey south. (The other ear had been bitten off, I hate to think by what.) I had to make haste to catch up with the dog I was supposed to be walking. Aldrei had reassured me that while I honored my quest only minutes would pass in the world where I walk Pepper.

Flopsy stood almost seventeen hands high, a good-sized animal, a nice buckskin color with a dorsal stripe. A splendid mule, not a transforming creature, but one could see in his eyes that he was as wise as the hills. I loved him immediately. He enjoyed having his ear scratched. Aldrei rode double behind me, and the Jerboa balanced on Flopsy's broad hindquarters, with the help of his long, tufted tail. We took much of the trail at a trot, but the Jerboa seemed to enjoy the challenge of staying aboard.

Our way took us through wildflowers in bloom on the rolling foothills of high, jagged mountains which faced the ocean. The air was salty and sweet, the forest at times grew thick and old, and yet it often opened up into meadows or the sandy beaches of rivers and lakes. My companions never seemed to tire, and so when we rested it was for my benefit.

On the second day, while crossing some grassy farmland, we paused so that I could rest and Flopsy could drink from a stream. While dozing on my back in the sunshine, resting my saddle-sore body, I listened to the trickle of the water. A shout caused me to sit up and look around.

The trail we followed had expanded into a wagon road, and we had stopped to have our break below it on the streambank. Up on the road, a man was yelling at someone. I stood up to investigate. Aldrei and the Jerboa lingered near the creek, uninterested. But this man continued in his loud and disorderly manner. He was taunting a young woman. I felt it wasn't my business, yet he seemed dangerous. I made my way up to the road.

Stooping to pick up a rock, the man threw it, hard, at the hound dog that hovered near the woman's feet. He missed, but he reached for another.

"Hey!" I shouted.

He glanced my way, but went ahead and picked up the rock. He held it on his palm, working his hand up and down slightly as if he were weighing the stone.

With my presence, the barefoot woman seemed to gain some courage. She said, quietly, to the man, "My dog has done you no harm. Leave us alone."

This started the man shouting again, something about dogs and how disgusting they were, and how she should get that thing off the road. He shook his fist at the dog, but he didn't throw the rock. He looked like a local farmer, but where his malevolence came from I did not know.

I did the only thing I could think of. I went and stood next to the woman. Perhaps this was foolish, making myself a target in addition. But I went to her, and quietly talked with her as if we had business about something else. We paid little attention to the man, or to the dog. He shouted a few more times, but, luckily, that's all he did. Then he wandered off down the road in the direction my friends and I had come.

Wakwak and her hound accompanied us as far as her village, several miles up the road. It was a sweet dog she had, a non-transforming domestic breed, with long brown ears flapping in the breeze. Wakwak thanked me again and again as we said goodbye. Aldrei winked at me.

"What?" I asked him.

He said nothing more, but I think he waved at me with the tip of his left ear.

As we continued on our way we came to a great bridge over a river. It took a while to convince Flopsy that the bridge was sturdy and safe, but, once convinced, he walked over it with no complaints. A full river rushed beneath us, delivering its swirling waters eastward to the sea. From the far bank, the road turned to the southeast and we followed the edge of a woods. Some of the trees stood taller than I'd ever seen. The Jerboa told me we were now in the territory called Bowne and these giant sequoias grew in a coniferous forest which covered most of the land. It was to the south of Bowne that Pepper had gone.

I lost track of how many days we traveled through this beautiful, open forest; perhaps a week. Then one day we crested a large hill to see a broad plain below us. A river stretched across to our left and on a cliffy island in that river stood a castle. Looking west across the plain we saw that among the groves of birch lay the colorful tents of the invading army. A palisade had been erected around the encampment, with soil piled up against the fence on either side, creating an ugly scar on the land. It ringed the tents of the elite, disappearing into the trees. Smoke rose from a dozen fires within the fence and without it, and that smoke collected in a cloud above.

After we sat watching for quite some time, Aldrei told me to guide Flopsy straight downhill to a thicket of alders that nestled at the foot of a cliff. As we neared the trees, we could see a sheet of fabric spread between tree trunks as a shelter. My white horse was staked out and grazing on snips of rough grass. We'd caught up with Pepper!

Busy feeding her twig fire, Pepper stood up when she saw us approach. I knew Pepper well as a dog, but how amazing it felt to look at her in human form! Willowy and nimble-footed, her movement was more canine than human. Her eye color was the same, amber, but I could only see one eye because of the black patch she wore. Her face, heart-shaped, just like the Pepper I knew, peeked out from under a flawless wrap of her braids of black and white hair. Her skin was a rich, deep black, and just gorgeous.

"Welcome, friends," she said, and then she smiled at me.

"Pepper," I said softly, "How wonderful that I can speak with you!" And then my first thought was, "I hope I haven't done anything disrespectful to you."

She laughed and put her arm around my shoulder. "It's a different world here. If you tried to leash me right now, you'd be hurt in the attempt! But in our ordinary life, it is a matter of keeping me safe. I know that, and I don't mind it. I'm thankful to be loved and cared for in a world where I have no understanding of big noisy things."

Soon the four of us sat around Pepper's fire, drinking honeyed ale. I found out that Pepper loves broccoli, and, especially, scrambled eggs. She's afraid of spiders. She told me how much she adores her human in our world, and that she missed him very much. But we had a job to do here. An important job.

Pepper said that the following morning the armies of the neighboring territory would storm the castle. Their challenge had been dismissed. The Estate of Erinaceus insisted they knew nothing of the religious relic. They demanded the invaders return to their own land at once. They'd rattled their longbows and made a show of their armies, within the castle walls and also outside, as the forces of their fyrd were gathered along the river.

We sheltered with Pepper that night. The four of us together prepared a warming soup. I gulped mine between hunks of brown bread. I was hungry, but also scared, so the soup went down better than the dry bread. Bedded down on the ground at the edge of the thicket, I spent most of the night staring at the dazzling starry sky. I thought about the immensity of reality, all those worlds and universes. I thought about man's inhumanity to man. Sleep finally came, but not long before sunrise. We rose to the clear light of a pink dawn. The dew was surprisingly light.

That morning, as we watched the armies assemble on the plain, my sense of dread steadily increased. I felt helpless. First to line up were the spear-wielders, the fortuneless people used as a meat sacrifice on the front lines. Those armorless soldiers wouldn't be going home to their families. Behind them the sword-wielders began to assemble. Their chain mail and shields shone in the early light. There would also be archers and pole-arms soldiers, infantry and cavalry. Grand companies of knights readied themselves to strut like roosters.

Pepper stood, and brushed off the back of her skirts. She tossed the remainder of her barley tea into the fire. She looked at me. "Well," she said, "saddle up. Let's go."

She gave no explanation and made no mention of returning my horse. I looked at Aldrei and the Jerboa. Still seated, both of them nodded to me, while Aldrei gestured, "Go along, go along!"

Knowing full well that I was putting my life in the hands of a pair of tricksters, I swung myself up into Flopsy's saddle and followed Pepper's white horse into the grassy lowlands. I rode at her flank like a servant. The armies kept building, there were hundreds of warriors organized in grid patterns on the turf. Ravens swooped and made gurgling croaks overhead, like happy shoppers at a lobster tank. I did not want to ride out onto that field. My heart pounded, and I felt sweaty and sick. I thought of turning around. I thought many times of turning around.

Pepper sat tall in the saddle, with the reins in one hand and a long skinny pole in the other. She headed for a large boulder near the center of the plain. When we were halfway there, she stopped. Dismounting, she came to my side as I sat on Flopsy. She looked up at me, and then untied and unfurled a cloth from the upper part of the pole. It was a white flag. She handed it up for me to carry, and returned to her white courser.

We arrived at the great rock. I held the pole, resting it on a stirrup, while the wind displayed our message. We waited there, watching the gathering armies. A sickening sight it was, the multitude of sons and daughters before us, ready to die for glory and someone else's greed. So much humanity and livestock, heaviness and clanking, that I could feel the reverberation traveling up from the ground through Flopsy's legs.

After quite some time, a party of several knights rode forward from the offensive armies to inquire about our request for colloquy. Pepper let them know that she had the religious relic in her possession. She refused to show it. She wanted to speak with their leaders. "As you can see, we carry no arms," she said.

Two of the knights stayed in place to guard us, while the others returned to their ranks with our request. We waited once more. The knights remained where they were. Flopsy stood patiently all that time, but the white horse was restless and fought the bit, dancing in place every few minutes and blowing. Pepper scratched herself nervously, but controlled the animal with relative ease. I wondered how she had learned to ride so well.

At last the truce party could be seen making its way along the perimeter of the armies. A company of about thirty, some of them riders, banners held high, approached slowly in formation. As they drew closer, we could see that there was royalty among them.

At the same time, representatives of the Estate of Erinaceus approached from the direction of the castle. They had received a message from Pepper the previous day. Among their number were witnesses, representatives of other lands, each in traditional costume. Both groups arrived at the rock.

We were surprised to see that the Queen rode with the truce party of her invading army. Pepper and I dismounted and I bowed my head. I remained standing by Flopsy, holding the flag, but Pepper led the white horse forward to meet her. Pepper held her hands aloft, to show she came in peace. She knelt before the Queen and her priests and officials.

The Queen regarded Pepper. She reined her horse to the side to have a look from a different angle. She scowled. What displeased her remains a mystery. She leaned and spoke to one of her attendants.

"Death to her!" the man shouted.

Two knights aimed their crossbows. Our white flag flapped indignantly in the wind.

"Wait!" I screamed.

The white gelding reared his head and took three steps, placing himself between the bowmen and Pepper. Rising to her feet,

Pepper moved around the horse again to where the Queen could
see her. Again she knelt. In this moment of confusion, Pepper
had a chance.

"Your Highness," she called, "I beseech you, grant me a moment of your time. I bear a matter of import to show you."

The Queen, from her ivory saddle, looked down her nose
at Pepper. But she nodded. The man raised a hand to stay the
bows.

Removing her blue velvet apron, Pepper laid it on a flat-
topped stone near the face of the boulder. From her saddlebag
she produced a bundle wrapped in a shiny scarlet and violet
damask. The attention of everyone present was riveted on her
as she slowly unwrapped the sacred object. I couldn't quite see
what it was. An ancient bone? She laid it gently on its silken
wrapper on top of the velvet. The priests and officials strained to
see. Her Majesty continued to stare at Pepper.

Backing away from the stone, Pepper called out again to the
Queen and her accompaniment:

"Hark! Oh noble Majesty, here before thee stands the precious relic thou hast sought for many hours. I, Pepper
of the Real World, from afar I hail, sent by the Estate of
Buckhold, to relate to thee this tale.

Behold, thy treasure lies upon yonder stone, returned
to thee by Buckhold's court alone. And with it comes
a message, of most grave import, from the Duchess of
Buckhold, and all her royal court.

They offer thee their deepest apologies and regret, for
one of their own, a treacherous priest, did beset their
own court, and by deceit did he gain this holy relic, causing much sorrow and pain.

But now, with the return of this sacred prize, the Estate of Buckhold seeks to make amends and rise, to beg thy forgiveness, and offer their own, and to restore honor to thy royal throne.

So here before thee stands Pepper, humble and true, from the land of the Real, to thee she doth sue, for the forgiveness and mercy of thy great Majesty, and to restore peace and harmony to all of thy country."

Pepper knelt once again, and then retreated, leading the white horse back to where I waited. We gave one another quick glances. I continued to hold my breath. Four priests came forward to look at the object. One of them picked it up with her white linen gloves and examined it closely. After a few nods and whispers, they wrapped the relic again in the cloth and placed it in a bag. They returned to their Queen. Then without ceremony or even acknowledgment, the entire company turned and set off to rejoin their camp.

I wasn't quite sure what had just happened. Did this mean there would be no battle? We stood and watched them walk proudly away, the bunch of us. Eventually we returned with the Erinaceus to their castle. We were fed well in the great hall, toasted by many and honored by the Duke and Duchess.

Aldrei and the Jerboa sat waiting at the high table when we arrived. Yes, they assured me, the Queen would take her armies and go home. We ate an enormous amount of food and drank a great deal of mead. We laughed together and talked about food, fashion, and the absurdity of humankind.

"After all this, I have yet to begin my journey to find the Crones With Pens," I mentioned to my friends.

Aldrei's nose twitched. He brushed the remains of his meal aside, and with the Jerboa's help, and a great deal of huffing and puffing, he pulled a massive illuminated manuscript from his linen sack and set it on the table. A cluster of onlookers from nearby gathered around us. Aldrei invited Pepper and me to take a look at the wondrous book.

The cover was undecorated, but as we turned the leaves, Pepper and I exclaimed over each. Fabulous calligraphy surrounded the gilded illustrations. In brilliant colors, here was the story I knew so well, but apparently with a host of prequels and epilogues and afterwords. A fresh, woody smell of papyrus rose from the pages, combined with the muskiness of the colored inks. This great codex was penned in an alphabet I'd never seen.

"Observe the text in red," Aldrei said.

I ran my finger over the script, admiring the artfulness of the strokes. Most of the flawlessly executed cursive was in black ink, some in blue, some green, but I found a few scattered blocks of text created in a rich maroon.

"Those are the passages that you have changed by your actions," said the Jerboa.

This comment made my eyebrows draw together. "I changed them?"

"The two of you changed them," the Jerboa said.

"You carried the red pen with you on your journey," pointed out Aldrei.

The Jerboa continued, "Each time you found a firm but gentle resolution to unwanted behavior, the pen edited the book. This magic of serenity has revised the story."

Pepper and I looked again at the pages.

"See all those red marks," the Jerboa said. "Whole sections have replaced themselves."

"It's the little things, you know," added Aldrei.

"So, the manuscript is restored?" I pressed my palms against my heart as if I could prevent it from leaping too high. This meant everything to me.

Pepper gave me a wide and toothy grin. "And, Harriet, in your joy, reflect on this: Certainly your characters in the book must go on to create stories and worlds of their own. Think of it! Worlds within worlds. All influenced by the editing which we made possible."

"What a crazy thought!" I said. I shook my head. I was too full of food, and perhaps not full enough of wine, for this conversation. "I suppose fantasy is limitless. I like ordinary reality. It's tidier. More comfortable."

"You've helped a lot of people by coming here," the Jerboa said.

"Then—I don't need the Crones?"

"Thanks to Pepper and the impact of her actions, you were able to rewrite without their help," the Jerboa said.

Aldrei added in a lyrical voice, "Crones with pens exist in your own world also. Seek them out. They are writers with a good amount of life experience to draw upon."

To acknowledge Pepper's brave deed of great consequence, hundreds of people gathered on a sunny grassland hillside to the south of the plain. Families came from far and wide; the poorest of peasants, the wealthy merchants, and even members of the court were on hand. Laboring with their spades and pickaxes, these people carved a colossal outline of a white stallion into the green hilltop. It was a beautiful, graceful figure. They used crushed chalk to fill the deep trenches that formed the design. Even with so many hands working, it took weeks to finish. Then, to celebrate the chalk stallion and what it represented, a feast for all was held out on the fields below.

"One day," declared an orator at the celebration, "all our lives shall be forgotten." A small woman, she stood on a bench before a long wooden table strewn with food and masses of fragrant roses. She waved her staff toward the chalk stallion as she belted out her words: "And yet this white horse shall abide, a token of peace, amid the shifts of fate! Until all things of war be broken and gone, until humankind marks the empty honor and hollow glory found in the fields of war and folk be blessed with never the notion of battle, but always in hearts rest, basking in serenity and affection, for that is best!"

The joyful festivities lasted into the night, with torchlight and dancing, and people ate greasy food and drank tremendous amounts of cider and ale. The white gelding, although he wasn't a transforming creature, was a guest of honor, given carrots and apples and bran mash with molasses. Half-grown girls in woaden blue and yellow dresses twisted bunches of wildflowers into his braided mane and tail.

The pulse of the music quickened as the hours went by, and the dancers never seemed to tire. Smells of sweat and roasted corn hung in the evening air. The revelers grew comical and obnoxious, singing loudly and sloshing their ale, while tumblers performed among the crockery on the tables. Laughter came as thick as the smoke from the bonfires.

During a particular swell of exuberance, the crowd hoisted Pepper and me into the air while people cheered and showered us with rose blossoms from the table, petals showering down.

I didn't want the attention, and in my saturated state I made a languid effort to be free. I batted at the petals tickling my face, and found myself lying under a tree, a red cedar, in the light of mid-day and with Pepper the dog at my side.

I sat up and brushed away some dead leaves that had fluttered down onto my chest. Pepper sniffed me, her leash still around my wrist.

"Pepper!" I whispered, "Pepper, what just happened?"

Pepper ignored me, and stretched the leash to sniff a clump of grass. She peed. She rooted around after some other smell.

Oh. It wasn't real, the fact sank in. Did I fall? Did I hit my head? I dug in my pocket for a bag to clean up the mess Pepper was making. Along with the bag I happened to grab a piece of wax. Quickly, I reached in to find the other. I held the two halves of the disc together, reforming the letter "A". I think Pepper smiled.

I would like to extend my deepest gratitude to those who helped make this book a reality:
To my dear, patient, and eagle-eyed editor, Anita Holladay.
And once again, special thanks to Keziah Wesley for his beta help and especially his exceptional technical help and design. Thanks to him also for allowing me to include the story he wrote.
And a golden thank-you to my other chief beta reader, the wonderfully talented Sara Neal.

Regarding the history of the Country Charm Conservation Area in Arlington, Washington:
I wish to acknowledge Bill Blake as the driving force behind both the Country Charm Conservation Area and the Stormwater Wetlands Park, among other local projects. He is a dedicated conservationist and educator who has made a lasting impact on the community and on the health of the river and local area. I appreciate the time he gave me and the conversation as we walked the bluffside trail.
In addition, I wish to especially thank: Roger Graafstra, Stacey Graafstra, Amanda Jo Bagdazian, & Rita Ehli Meehan.
Also: Hank Breekveldt, Valerie Perrigoue, Laurie Landis
Many thanks also to: Norm Engell, Ken Anderson, Kim Fischer, Troy Burgess, Chad Duskin.
Thank you to all those who responded on the History of Arlington FB page.
And much gratitude to the kind fellow with the key.

I am indebted to the wonderful Stillaguamish Valley Pioneer Museum staff and volunteers, including especially:
Joann Gray, Sally Fingarson Lindberg (subject of the river story), Michele Heiderer, A. Loren Kraetz, Sue Walde, & to Shirley Prouty for her wonderful 100 Years of Arlington WA series of books.

Concerning the stories set in Port Townsend, Washington:
Thank you to
Jerry Bowman - NW Carriage Museum
Shilah Gould of the Port Townsend Public Library
The Jefferson County Historical Society

For assistance with the accuracy of the Maltese Figurine story, thanks to:
Christina Claassen & Jeff Jewell of the Whatcom Museum, Bellingham, Washington
Douglas Cole, retired pilot, of Bellingham
Suzanne, librarian, Bellingham Public Library
Justin Taylor with Public Works, Bellingham
Todd Plummer, Trainer, Longacres and Emerald Downs

My gratitude also to:
Seán Dwyer for improving the Spanish and French wording in Très Chic
Ken Anderson for agreeing to the interview. I so enjoy our delightful conversations.
Daniel, for the use of his lion.

And of course, to the additional beta readers who so kindly gave their time:
John Reinier, Franklin Vincenzi DVM, Zante Wesley, Johnny Wesley, Lesley Collins, Brandy Morgan-Davis, Lisa Personius, Kevin Wesley, Susan Jacobs, & Ann Reid

And The Arlington Fiction Writers
Betsy Diedrick, Lisa Personius, John Reinier, Brandy Morgan-Davis, Keziah Wesley, Franklin Vincenzi, Justin Moses, & Sara Neal

My eternal appreciation to my family and friends, who support me with patience, love, and enthusiasm.

Image Credits:
Title image of Pippa in Unexpected Turns and images for Of Man And Mountain are by Keziah Wesley. The photo of Ken Anderson is by Laura Anderson. The photo of the corgi group is by Debbie Larsen. The paper texture used for the two Victorian photo album pages is by João Vítor Duarte on Unsplash.

Finally, I thank the sweet dogs and cat featured in these stories for being my friends, and I'm grateful to their owners for allowing me to borrow them for walks.

Made in USA - Kendallville, IN
43530_9781734208436
12.12.2023 1330